HIS PERFECT PARTNER

BOOK YOUR PLACE ON OUR WEBSITE AND MAKE THE READING CONNECTION!

We've created a customized website just for our very special readers, where you can get the inside scoop on everything that's going on with Zebra, Pinnacle and Kensington books.

When you come online, you'll have the exciting opportunity to:

- View covers of upcoming books
- Read sample chapters
- Learn about our future publishing schedule (listed by publication month and author)
- Find out when your favorite authors will be visiting a city near you
- Search for and order backlist books from our online catalog
- Check out author bios and background information
- Send e-mail to your favorite authors
- Meet the Kensington staff online
- Join us in weekly chats with authors, readers and other guests
- Get writing guidelines
- AND MUCH MORE!

**Visit our website at
http://www.kensingtonbooks.com**

PARTNER

Priscilla
Oliveras

ZEBRA BOOKS
KENSINGTON PUBLISHING CORP.

http://www.kensingtonbooks.com

ZEBRA BOOKS are published by

Kensington Publishing Corp.
119 West 40th Street
New York, NY 10018

All Kensington titles, imprints, and distributed lines are available at special quantity discounts for bulk purchases for sales promotion, premiums, fund-raising, educational, or institutional use.

Special book excerpts or customized printings can also be created to fit specific needs. For details, write or phone the office of the Kensington Sales Manager: Attn.: Sales Department. Kensington Publishing Corp., 119 West 40th Street, New York, NY 10018. Phone: 1-800-221-2647.

Zebra and the Z logo Reg. U.S. Pat. & TM Off.

First Printing: October 2017
ISBN-13: 978-1-4201-4428-4
ISBN-10: 1-4201-4428-6

eISBN-13: 978-1-4201-4431-4
eISBN-10: 1-4201-4431-6

10 9 8 7 6 5 4 3 2 1

Printed in the United States of America

*This book, my debut novel, has been a long time coming.
It wouldn't be a reality without the family and friends who
have supported me and cheered me on over the years.
First, to my parents, who have always been and continue to
be a source of inspiration. Their love for each other
and their family rivals that of Rey and Marta in this story.
Te quiero mami y papi, siempre.
To my sister and brother, who like Tomás and Yaz
believe in familia primero, I thank you for the comfort
of knowing that, no matter the miles between us,
we're always there for each other.
To my writing community . . . my Seton Hill University
Writing Popular Fiction MFA family
(hugs to my Troublemakers) and my Romance Writers
of America family, especially the Wet Noodle Posse, Pixies,
Firebirds and Dragonflies, and all my RWA mentors
and friends . . . thank you for teaching me
so much about writing and myself.
To my fabulous agent, Rebecca Strauss, and my incompara-
ble editor, Martin Biro, thank you for believing in me
and being a big part of making my dream a reality.
To my Latino sisters and brothers, may our culture
be celebrated and valued, always.
And most importantly, to my three amazing
and brilliant daughters . . .
Wow, I finally did it! Together we have laughed, cried,
created amazing memories, and have the often-silly pictures
to prove it. You three are the **BIGGEST** blessings in my life.
I'll love you forever! XOXO*

Chapter One

The hottest guy to ever hit Oakton, Illinois, lingered outside her dance studio doorway, bringing Yazmine Fernandez to a stutter-step stop.

Seriously, the guy was like manna-from-heaven Latino *GQ*—from the top of his closely cropped jet-black hair, down his six-foot muscular frame, to the soles of his shiny wing-tip shoes.

Behind her, seven pairs of dancers scrambled to remember the next step in the preschool father-daughter Christmas dance. But Yazmine couldn't look away.

"Hey, a little help here?" One of the dads waved at her from the back row.

"Sorry." Yaz listened to the music for several beats, then fell back into step with their "I Saw Mommy Kissing Santa Claus" routine.

In the studio's mirror-lined wall she caught the stranger's flustered scowl. Even frowning, he still made her heart hop-skip in her chest.

Dios mío, she'd obviously neglected her social life for too long. Sure, her dance card had been pretty full with other obligations for nearly eighteen months now, but her lack of partner-dance practice shouldn't account for the heat prickling her insides. In her line of work, hunky guys were always on the cast list.

Then again, drop an attention-grabbing, well-built man into a room full of suburban soccer dads, and a woman's thoughts naturally wandered down a road better left untraveled.

Untraveled by her, anyway.

The newcomer's gaze skimmed across the people in her studio.

Yaz brightened her smile, but he turned away without even noticing her. Disappointed, and strangely self-conscious, she tugged at the bodice of her camisole leotard as she led the group into a jazz square.

The song's second verse transitioned to the chorus repetition, and Yaz wove through the front line to get a better look at the back row. "Left hand, Mr. Johnson—your other left."

The dad groaned, his daughter giggling at his exaggerated grimace.

"Don't worry, you'll get it." Yaz peeked over the child's shoulder to the studio doorway again.

The hunk glared down at his phone, flicking through something on the screen. His mouth thinned as he slid the cell into the pocket of his suit jacket. Yaz's stomach executed a jittery little sashay.

This guy had to be in the wrong place. No way she'd forget meeting him before at the dance studio.

Yaz dropped her gaze to his left ring finger. Bare.

Not that it should matter to her. She'd learned the hard way it was much better to look than to touch. Especially if a girl didn't want to get her fingers singed, or her heart flambéed.

Besides, as soon as Papi's oncologist gave him

the all-clear, she'd be on the first direct flight out of Chicago, headed back to New York and Broadway. Nothing would stand in her way this time.

The holiday song drew to a close. Fathers bowed. Daughters curtsied. GQ stepped into her studio.

Anticipation fluttered a million, spastic butterfly wings in her chest. He probably needed directions to another business close by.

Yaz hurried toward him. "Excuse me, do you need some help?"

Or, better yet, a no-strings-attached date for a night out in nearby Chicago?

"Papá!"

Maria Garcia jumped up from her seat on the floor along the back wall, running to fling her arms around the man's thighs. Everyone else in the class turned at the commotion.

Increíble. Apparently the hunk *did* belong here. To the usually subdued, adorable five-year-old who'd joined the class in mid-September.

At his daughter's screech of delight, the worried scowl vanished from the man's features. Relief and joy surged in. For a moment Yaz bought into his pleasure, savoring the smile that softened his chiseled face with boyish charm.

Then, with the stinging slap of a bitter Chicago wind, Yaz recalled the number of practices Maria's father had skipped over the past two months—the number of classes when the child had sat alone in the back and the number of times she'd had to partner with Mrs. Buckley, her grandmotherly nanny, because her father had failed to show up as promised. Again.

The attraction searing through Yaz's body cooled as

fast as if she'd dunked herself into an ice bath after a marathon day of rehearsal.

Bendito sea Dios, the prodigal father, more focused on his advertising career than his child, had finally arrived—tardy, of course. Blessed be God, indeed.

"You made it!" Surprise heightened Maria's high-pitched cry.

"I sure did, *chiquita.*" Mr. Garcia scooped up his daughter and spun her around, the picture of familial bliss.

Maria grinned with pleasure.

Still, Yaz couldn't stop remembering the hurt in the little girl's eyes over the past weeks because of her father's absences. Legs shaking, she strode to the corner table at the front of the room and jabbed the stop button on her iPod speakers. "Everyone, let's take a five-minute water break."

Mr. Garcia and Maria stepped to the side of the room so the other class members could head to the lobby area.

Anger over the weeks of disappointment he'd brought on his daughter pulsed a heavy, deep bass beat in Yaz's chest. She sucked in what was supposed to be a calming breath and counted to ten. Then twenty.

So much for her brief fantasy of a friendly night out with a hunky stranger. Her first since long before she'd left New York to come home. That definitely wasn't going to happen. Not with this man.

"M'ija, I'm sorry I'm late."

The trite words burned Tomás's lips with their insignificance. No matter how many times he apologized, he knew he'd never forget the dejection crumpling

Maria's shoulders when he'd finally spotted her sitting in the back of the room. Knowing he'd put the sadness there was like a swift punch to his gut.

He tried so damn hard to be a good father. Still, more and more often it felt like he was falling short.

"It's okay." Maria gave him a sad version of her normally sunny smile. "At least you made it for a little while this time."

This time.

Guilt latched onto him, sinking its claws into his shoulders. Talk about feeling like a loser single parent. Lately, his drive to be the best at work had him shortchanging his daughter. Sure, he'd landed a prize client today, but the extended negotiations had made him leave the office late, remorse riding shotgun on his mad dash out of the city.

"Come on, Papá." Maria linked their fingers together. "I want you to meet Ms. Yazmine. 'Member, I told you about her."

Ha, it was impossible to forget. All Maria talked about was her new dance instructor. Apparently the lady walked on water.

Maria pointed to a tall, slender woman standing at a corner table up front. The previously crowded room and his anxiety over not being able to find Maria when he'd first arrived had to be the only explanation for his not noticing the beautiful instructor earlier.

Now, there was no missing her.

Ms. Yazmine's black hair was pulled back in a sleek bun low on her nape. On someone else the style might have looked severe. On her, it accentuated her smooth forehead, high cheekbones, elegant neck, and sun-kissed olive skin. She wore a black, figure-hugging spaghetti-strap leotard with tights, and a short, filmy skirt fluttered over the thighs of her long, toned legs.

Hands clasped, feet set in a dance position he couldn't name, Ms. Yazmine had him picturing a different kind of position altogether. One not quite appropriate for their current surroundings.

Heat pooled low in his body. *Ay, ay, ay*, this woman could sell sand in a desert. She was an ad-man's dream.

Hell, any man's dream.

A guy could probably get used to having a woman like her dancing around in his life.

Tomás sucked in a surprised breath, wondering where *that* thought had come from.

"*Vente.*" Maria paired her command for him to come with a tug of his hand, dragging him across the floor. "Ms. Yazmine, I want you to meet my *papá*."

Tomás could have sworn he saw her flinch, but the instructor set her iPod down and slowly turned away from the desk. She gave him a stiff, yet polite, smile.

"My apologies for being late. It's nice to meet you." Tomás held out his hand, noting Ms. Yazmine's hesitation before she placed her cool hand in his.

"I'm glad you could finally join us, Mr. Garcia." She might appear delicate, but her grip was as firm as her voice. "I was beginning to wonder if you'd make it."

There was no missing the reproach. Clearly they were starting off on the wrong note.

"Longer than anticipated meetings, shifting schedules. Sometimes they can't be avoided, no matter how hard I try. But I'm here now, ready to give this a shot." He swung an arm out to encompass the room, tamping down his irritation at having to explain himself. After all, he *was* twenty minutes late.

Experience, and his *mamá*'s advice, reminded him

that he'd catch more flies with *leche quemada* than vinegar. Something she'd often said as she spread the sweet caramel confection on his morning toast.

"Maria and Mrs. Buckley have been trying to teach me at home, but I've been told you're the expert."

Yazmine arched a brow. Probably letting him know she wouldn't buy his compliment so easily. Strangely, he found that appealing.

"I appreciate the thought," she said. "My students make my job easy though. They work hard both in and out of class."

"Well, I've got a mean salsa. I can handle a merengue, or a Mexican polka, but ballet . . . ?" He shook his head with a grimace. "Not really one of my strong suits."

"I can probably help with that." The edges of her generous mouth curved up, smoothing the censure from her voice.

Aha! A crack in her prima donna shell.

"*Sí*, Papá can't really get the grapevine." Maria's dark brown curls bounced as she crisscrossed her feet to demonstrate the step. "But I said you could help him. 'Cuz you helped me. You're the bestest dancer in the whole world."

Yazmine knelt down to Maria's eye level, flashing her a genuine smile brimming with warmth. An uncomfortable pang rippled through him as he wondered what it would be like to have Yazmine smile at him in the same welcoming way.

He cut the thought off before it went any further, his sense of self-preservation sharpened in the years since his divorce.

"Thanks for your vote of confidence," Ms. Yazmine told Maria. "Even better, I love seeing you so excited about dancing." She tapped Maria's nose gently, eliciting a giggle Tomás hadn't heard often enough in the two months since he'd moved them out of Chicago and into the more family-friendly suburbs forty-five minutes northwest of the city.

Right now, he didn't quite know what to make of Yazmine Fernandez. Her engaging smile and lithe body captivated him. Her subtle reprimand rankled. But he'd kiss the ground she walked on if she helped his daughter shake off her recently acquired reticence. He missed Maria's spunkiness.

Nothing he'd tried, not an impromptu trip to the zoo or an afternoon picnic in Grant Park, had helped. She'd been outgoing and talkative in her old kindergarten class. Here in Oakton, she'd withdrawn and still wasn't quite comfortable with others.

"I'm gonna be a famous dancer just like you." Maria's brown eyes lit up like Christmas morning.

"Sounds like a good plan. Why don't you go grab a quick drink from the fountain while I chat with your *papá*?"

"Okay!" Maria skipped off and Yazmine rose with a grace she'd undoubtedly acquired from a million or so dance classes.

"You're great with her," Tomás said.

"She's a pleasure to have in class. All my students are."

Alluring *and* comfortable with kids.

Stepping closer to the desk, Yazmine picked up a white binder. "Actually, I've found that any problems I encounter teaching are few and far between." She flicked a quick glance his way. "And rarely involve the children themselves."

There it was again, the hint of admonition from her. It pricked his conscience, making him feel like a front-runner for Worst Father of the Year.

Damn. He tightened his jaw, uncertain whom he was annoyed with more. Her for making the assumption or himself for having to admit that she might have a point.

"I take it you see me as one of those problems."

"I don't mean it to sound that way." Yazmine's chest rose and fell on a sigh. "Maria really wants to perform this routine in the Christmas show. Honestly, I'd love for the two of you to share that experience. But if you check the attendance sheet, I'm not sure it's going to be possible."

Yazmine leaned toward him so he could peer at the open binder with her. The scent of violets wafted in the air, tickling his nose. Unable to resist, he dragged in a deep breath, filling his lungs with her tantalizing perfume.

"Even though this is a special performance, the Hanson Academy of Dance attendance policy still applies. If a dancer had this many absences in a class for another number, we'd pull him from the show." Yazmine tapped the page in front of them.

He followed her pink-tipped finger from his neatly printed name across the row of spaces that should have been checked off to indicate his attendance. The blank spaces were glaring proof of his parental shortcomings.

The violets enveloping him withered, choked by the remorse settling around him like a toxic mushroom cloud.

"I'm doing my best." The words were more of a muttered curse, pushed through his gritted teeth.

"Please, you don't have to defend yourself to me." Yazmine pressed the open binder to her chest, concern blanketing her face. "Maria's the one who needs to know that this is important to you."

He gave her a curt nod, not trusting his voice to betray his growing frustration. Maybe he wasn't doing such a class-act job at parenting, but with his nanny's help he'd learn. Get better. He and Maria would be fine. Failure was not an option.

"Look, I shouldn't have—" Yazmine broke off. Her lips pulled down with resignation. "I simply want you to be aware of the situation. That's all."

Tomás was tempted to walk away, but he kept his feet firmly planted. He hadn't run from anything in his entire life. Now was not the time to start. No way would a simple father-daughter dance or an appealing yet prickly instructor get the best of him. Maria depended on him.

"Why don't we see how it goes today, and then we'll take it from there," Yazmine offered as the students returned.

Maria skip-hopped into the room. With a sweet grin that instantly relaxed his shoulders, she waved him over to join her in the back line of dancers. The breath-stealing tightness in his chest instantly eased. At the same time, his resolve to do his best for her hardened like quick-drying cement.

"Deal."

Yazmine blinked at his brusque tone.

"Don't worry. I can do this," he assured her, softening his words with a smile. "I won't let my daughter, or you, down." He made a silly face at Maria and she giggled and, that easily, wrapped him around her finger a little tighter.

From the moment he'd held her tiny squirming

body in his arms, he'd vowed to do whatever it took to make his baby girl happy. Nothing would change that.

Tomás slipped off his suit jacket and tossed it over the barre. Then he pocketed his cufflinks and deftly rolled up the sleeves of his white dress shirt as he moved next to Maria. The opening strains of "I Saw Mommy Kissing Santa Claus" filled the studio once more.

"Here we go, everyone! Five, six, seven, eight." Yazmine clapped as she counted out the beats.

Beside him, Maria counted aloud as well, the same way they'd practiced at home. He tried following along, but with his thoughts lingering on the intriguing instructor, he fumbled the opening steps.

"*Ay*, Papá, the other way." Maria nudged him with her elbow when he nearly collided with the dad next to them.

"Yeah, I know," he grumbled.

Great. It probably looked like he'd never practiced at home at all. Maybe Ms. Yazmine hadn't noticed.

He peeked up at her to check.

Her lips quirked with the hint of a teasing smirk he should have found annoying rather than enticing, she exaggerated her steps for him to catch on.

Before long, Tomás understood why Maria was so enamored with her teacher. Why Maria brimmed with excitement when she spoke of her dance class.

Yazmine Fernandez was great at what she did, full of a vibrant, intoxicating energy. Whether calling out the next move with encouragement, or waving her left hand at a dad reaching out to twist his daughter toward him with the wrong arm, she showed absolutely no sign of impatience. Her pride and delight in her job were palpable forces.

He could relate to that.

In spite of the negative tone of their earlier conversation, her charisma and charm beckoned him like a front porch light welcoming a weary traveler too long on the road. Too long on his own.

His mind lost in the idea of Yazmine waiting at home for him, Tomás bumped into Maria, knocking her off balance.

"Oof! Not that foot, Papá."

"*¡Perdón!* Sorry, I got it." Damn, between his minimal practice and his mind's unwelcome meanderings, he was doing a spot-on impersonation of someone with two left feet.

Halfway through the dance his frustration level rose again when he and Maria were forced to stand off to the side because he didn't know the rest of the steps.

"You'll learn it, Papá," Maria assured him. "We'll keep practicing together."

Together.

The word spread warmth through him as if he'd taken a sip of prime Mexican tequila. It had been Maria and him, the two of them together, since the day Kristine had chosen an overseas promotion over their marriage and child. It hadn't been easy, but he would figure things out. Even if it meant learning ballet to make Maria happy.

The strains of the song drew to a close and the rest of the dancers applauded everyone's efforts.

"That's it for this week." Yazmine glided over to pause the music.

Sighs of relief along with a muttered, "Thank goodness" rippled through the crowd of fathers.

"You're all doing a great job." Sincerity colored Yazmine's words, shone in the reassuring expression she shared with her students. "Remember to practice over the Thanksgiving holiday next week. We'll see you the following Wednesday. Same time, same place, same go-get-'em attitudes from everyone. Right?"

Across the room she sent Tomás a telling glance. Message received. No more absences. No tardiness.

She didn't think too highly of him. While normally he'd shrug that off as none of his concern, for some inexplicable reason it really bugged him.

He should smooth things over—for Maria's sake. Ms. Yazmine *was* her favorite dance teacher after all.

While everyone else headed for the coatrack by the school's front door, Yazmine stayed near the desk, thumbing through her iPod display screen. She didn't appear to be in a hurry to leave. Perfect.

"Hey, *m'ija*," Tomás told Maria, "grab your coat and I'll be right there."

"Okay." Curls bouncing, Maria danced out of the studio.

Relief at seeing her acting more like her old self tempered his unease over the potentially uncomfortable conversation in store for him.

Yazmine gathered her belongings as he approached her, steeling himself to play nicely with the sexy taskmaster. She glanced up, her brow furrowing when she saw him. "Is there something you needed?"

Loaded question.

Somehow in the course of half a dance lesson this woman had his mind considering ideas he hadn't allowed himself in years.

"We didn't really start off on the right foot tonight. I wanted to apolo—"

"No, don't." She held up a hand, her mouth set in a firm, no-arguing-with-me line.

"Excuse me?"

"I'm the one who should apologize. It's not—" She broke off, rubbing a hand across the worry lines marking her forehead, then smoothing it over her already slick bun before releasing a heavy sigh. "I've had a lot going on today. I probably came on a little too strong with you earlier."

Sincere words, but spoken with a mouth quirked in the opposite direction of a smile. The kind of apology his *mamá* would have made him try again.

For some bizarre reason Yazmine's half-baked apology charmed him. Made him want to change the negative vibe arcing between them, without looking too closely at why he felt compelled to do so.

"Apology accepted. And appreciated." He flashed her a reassuring smile. The one he used to sweet-talk his staunchest opponents in the boardroom.

Her frown deepened. Man, she was a tough cookie.

He didn't move, didn't change his expression. Allowed his smile to work its magic.

Then, like a soldier reporting for duty, she straightened her shoulders and gave him the barest hint of a nod. "Okay, then. You held your own fairly well today in class, up to a point. I can get you ready in time for the Christmas recital, *if* you don't ditch any more of our practices."

There it was again, the hint of a challenge. As if she still questioned his ability to hold up his end of the bargain.

Crossing his arms, Tomás gave Yazmine the once-over, intrigued, if slightly exasperated, by her conflicting signals.

Stern disciplinarian ruling her studio.

Affable teacher who charmed his daughter.

Sexy siren luring him with a single glance.

Megawatt smile on a mouth that didn't mince words.

Why should it matter whether or not she liked him? He was long past caring what others thought. Long past high school where, as the "wetback" from the wrong side of town on scholarship at Deburg Prep, he'd felt desperate for acceptance.

Maria's sing-song voice carried in from the lobby.

That's why he was still here trying to charm Yazmine Fernandez. Maria's happiness made this matter.

"Look, we don't have to be friends. Hell, we can settle for acquaintances."

"Mr. Garcia, I think we—"

"I'm not finished."

Yazmine blinked at his interruption.

"Maria's the most important person in my life. From the way you handled the class tonight, I can see why she admires you. I'm doing the best I can right now. Yeah, I'm aggravated when it's not good enough. But I'll do anything for my daughter, even get up on a stage and make a fool of myself. As long as she's happy. That's what counts. I'm pretty certain that's one thing you and I can both agree on. Right?"

His words hung in the air, an olive branch if she chose to accept it.

After several tension-filled moments, he watched as Yazmine's shoulders visibly relaxed. The worry lines marring her beautiful face smoothed and the tightness around her mouth eased.

Tomás waited, uncertain whether he'd get another swipe of her sharp tongue or one of her infectious smiles, calling himself all kinds of crazy for wanting the latter.

* * *

Ay Dios mío. Yazmine's heart skipped. Tomás Garcia in protective Papa Bear mode, his impassioned words gruff with sincerity, presented quite a persuasive package.

Arms crossed, she eyed him, trying to gauge how much of what he said was true. How much was a good spin from a man who made his living convincing people to buy what he was selling.

She'd played the workaholic game before, gotten hurt and hurt others. It was a dangerous pastime.

"Honestly, it's nice to hear how much you care about your daughter," she said.

"I'm glad you approve."

She narrowed her gaze at him, not sure whether he was teasing or patronizing her. "Look, I enjoy having Maria in my class, and I do my best to be a good teacher."

"Like I said, based on today I'd say you're quite successful. My daughter certainly thinks you can do no wrong." Tomás hitched a broad shoulder in a half shrug. "How about we try this again. I can make a better first impression."

"There's no need. It's fine. I respect someone who's dedicated to his work."

Hands on his hips, Tomás's eyes flashed with skepticism. "I sense a 'but' you're leaving out."

Ay, the man was the epitome of hardheaded. When it came down to it, she could be too. "You really want to know?"

"I wouldn't ask if I didn't."

"Fine. *But*," she stressed the word, "you should

make sure it doesn't leave your loved ones feeling second-rate."

His jaw muscles tightened and Yaz swallowed back a curse. Great, she'd crossed the line. Yeah, he'd pushed, but he was also a student's parent. She should have remembered that and thought twice before challenging him.

"Maria's a wonderful addition to my class," Yaz continued, a pale attempt at making amends, but she had to try. "Granted, she's usually a lot more reserved than today, but she's coming along fine."

"She hasn't dealt with our move here as well as I'd hoped." Tomás turned to glance back toward the lobby. Yazmine followed the direction of his gaze and saw Maria sitting with another student on one of the sofas. "I'm beginning to wonder if the move was a mistake."

Tomás Garcia as the confident ad-man she could easily deal with. His concerned-father side strummed a softer chord within her. A chord she struggled to silence. "It's only been a few months since you arrived in Oakton. Change can be hard on a kid, no matter her age or the situation. Give it time."

"You speaking from experience?"

She shrugged off the question. No need to spill her guts to him. To anyone.

Tomás dipped his head in a slight nod. "Time. That's what Mrs. B keeps telling me."

"Listen to her. Your nanny's a wise woman."

His mouth curved up and his dimple made another sexy appearance. A spark of awareness sizzled low in her belly.

Dios mío, she should have walked away after she'd

pissed him off. She had no business feeling any sort of attraction to him. She had no room for distractions.

Scooping up her binder, Yaz eased around Tomás, heading for the door. He fell into step alongside her, brushing up against her. The hair on his forearm tickled her skin, sending pinpoints of awareness peppering up her arm.

Yaz took a deep, steadying breath only to find herself appreciating his musky scent. *Basta*, she chided herself. Enough already.

"So you think it's too soon for me to worry about her?" Tomás asked.

"Uh, yeah." Yaz tried to focus on his question rather than her unpredictable hormones. "I'll admit at first I figured Maria was simply a shy child. But every once in a while I'd see a flash of her spunk. Then, when I mentioned the Christmas show, her hand shot up to volunteer. It actually took me by surprise."

"You and me both," Tomás grumbled, his chuckle softening his dry tone. "I thought she was kidding when she told me."

His humble words and easygoing charm were at odds with the man Yaz had envisioned during the weeks of his no-show routine.

"This dance class stuff isn't really my forte," Tomás muttered.

"Don't worry about the recital. If you're serious about practicing, you'll catch on. You did a decent job today."

"But there's room for improvement?"

"Yeah."

He threw back his head and laughed, a rich sound that swirled around her, enticing her to join in.

"You don't pull any punches, do you?" he asked.

"I get the impression you can take it. Though, I guess, I probably overstepped my bounds earlier . . ."

"Man, that apology is killing you. Isn't it?" He moved quickly, stepping in front of her to block her path.

Keep walking, she warned herself, unnerved that he seemed to read her so easily. That didn't bode well for a girl with secrets she didn't want to share.

"You just can't bring yourself to say the words if you don't mean them, can you?" The note of respect in his voice intrigued her.

"No, not really."

"Good. I'd rather hear the truth than some candy-coated lie. I'm a big boy."

It was like a hand-delivered invitation, but she stopped herself, barely, from letting her gaze travel the length of him.

What she would give for this man's level of self-confidence. But she was great at pretending. "I take every aspect of dance seriously. Even the father-daughter Christmas routine."

"And it's important to Maria, so that makes it important to me. Maybe we have more in common than we realized."

His naughty grin widened and Yaz gulped. Between his cleft chin, hide-and-seek dimple, and smiling eyes, she could get in some serious trouble with this guy.

The truth was, after her farce of an engagement to Victor had ended, she knew her life had no room for personal relationships. She understood well the sacrifices needed for her to be successful in New York. Papi had given up his dreams of stardom for their family. She owed it to him to see his dream for her come true.

Her heart heavy with the fear of disappointing her loved ones, Yaz edged away from Tomás Garcia's distraction. "Like I said, as long as you keep practicing and make it to class, you'll catch on, Mr. Garcia."

"Tomás." He placed a hand on her arm to stop her. Heat surged through her at his touch. "My name is Tomás. *Encantado de conocerte.*"

Dios mío, he was pleased to meet her?

The man stood less than a foot away, close enough that she could see his five o'clock shadow. Tempting enough to make her wonder if she pressed a hand to his starched, white shirt, would she find his heart pounding as fast as hers?

Ay bendito, she was undeniably losing it.

"Well, uh, Tomás, we'll see you after the Thanksgiving break." That gave her plenty of time to get her head screwed back on straight.

"Oh, you will certainly see me after the holiday. You can count on it." He gave her a cheeky wink, then strode out of the studio.

Her knees wobbled. Those words coming from any other parent wouldn't have made her think twice. Coming from Tomás Garcia, they made her think about a lot more than what should have been a harmless dance class.

Chapter Two

With the cold winter wind nipping at her heels, Yaz stepped inside Center Stage, Oakton's local shop for "all your dance and costume needs." Her gaze strayed to the footwear display along the far-right wall. She tugged off her wool cap, unbuttoned her red peacoat, and let the flood of fond memories soothe her soul.

As if it were yesterday, and even though Mami had been gone since Yaz was in high school, Yaz saw her mother standing there. Her dark curls framing her gentle face. Her patience never wavering despite Yaz's excitement over buying her first pair of toe shoes. Mami and Papi had championed her every step of the way as she endeavored to take New York by storm.

Yaz closed her eyes, seeking a brief respite from what had become the weight of expectations wrapped in family pride and love.

The sound of footsteps drew her attention and she let the memories fade.

The black curtain behind the glass counter fluttered to the side and Mrs. Morgan came out from the stockroom carrying a large box.

"Yazmine! What a wonderful surprise!" The older woman plopped the box on the counter and opened her arms for a hug. "I missed you the last time you came by. How are you?"

Yaz hugged her best friend's mom, enjoying the warm welcome. "I'm fine, thanks. Are you busy?"

"Never too busy for you. Look—"

Mrs. Morgan pointed to the framed *Playbill* on the wall over the cash register, Yazmine's signature scrawled across the front in red Sharpie ink. "In a place of honor. I love showing it off to our customers!"

"That's, uh, great." Yaz struggled to breathe through the herculean knot of pressure squeezing her chest.

"And to think, I remember the days of you and my Cheryl sharing sleepovers. All that giggling as you girls danced around the house." Mrs. Morgan cupped Yaz's cheek, then gave it a gentle pat. "Once you hit high school and I saw your focus, I knew you'd make it. Reynaldo must be so proud of you. He and your mom were always your biggest fans."

"Papi's still my best cheerleader." And the main reason she had to get back to New York and shine. For him. Not to mention Mrs. Morgan and everyone else in Oakton who assumed her rightful place was on a Broadway stage.

"How's he doing?" Mrs. Morgan moved back behind the glass counter, her face creased with a mix of sympathy and hope. "Cheryl told me his cancer's in remission, right?"

"Yes, thank God." Yaz kissed her fingertips and pressed them up toward the sky. Remission had become one of her favorite words.

"Honestly, sweetie, I was shocked when I heard you

were setting aside your career to come back and take care of him, instead of one of your sisters."

Yeah, most people didn't understand how she could step away from the glitz and glamour of New York. They didn't know that the break had been for her as much as for Papi. No one did.

She still couldn't bring herself to admit her doubts out loud.

"It was the right thing to do." Yaz stared down at the decorative hair combs and tubes of stage makeup in the glass display case, unable to look Mrs. Morgan in the eye and say the half-truth. "With Rosa and Lilí still in college, I couldn't let them take a leave of absence. Besides—"

She blinked back the sting of tears, forcing a smile to hide the fear she'd been battling since the day they'd found out about the cancer. "I wouldn't trade these months with Papi for anything. Now that he's doing better, I'm spending more time at Hanson's getting myself audition-ready. It's all good."

Or it would be—she simply needed to keep repeating that mantra to herself.

"So you'll be leaving us again, headed off to bigger and better things?" Mrs. Morgan leaned over to grab a pen next to the register.

Yaz bit her lip, measuring her words. Sure, New York was bigger than Oakton. But better? That was still up for debate.

"Looks that way."

"I always knew you'd do it!" Mrs. Morgan pointed her pen at Yaz, her face beaming with glee. "Imagine, our very own Broadway superstar!"

Yazmine flinched.

Superstar or superflop. She wasn't sure which label fit.

Anxiety surged inside of her like a race-car driver revving his engine.

"Speaking of Cheryl . . ." Her desperation to steer the conversation away from her failures kicked her voice up an octave. "The last time I talked to her, she mentioned a job interview in town. Has she heard anything?"

"I'm surprised she hasn't texted you already," Mrs. Morgan teased. "I got off the phone with her a few minutes ago. My girl's moving back home!"

"No way!" Relief kicked her knees out from under her and Yaz sagged against the counter.

Dios mío, this was fabulous news! With Cheryl back, maybe she would finally be able to confide in someone. Yaz hadn't wanted to burden her sisters. They were stressed about Papi already, why worry them with her issues. Tears of relief stung her eyes and Yaz held up her hand for a high five, hoping Mrs. Morgan didn't notice her sappiness.

"Cheryl will start at Bright Minds the first week of December." Mrs. Morgan gave Yaz's hand a slap. "Now, as much as I love chatting with you, I doubt that's why you stopped by. What can I help you with?"

"I'm hoping you might have found the order sheet for the Christmas recital costumes. It wasn't in the box when I unpacked everything at Hanson's."

"Oh yes, I tacked it to the message board in the back. Why don't you look around and I'll go grab it?" Mrs. Morgan disappeared behind the black curtain.

Leaving her peacoat on the checkout counter, Yaz headed off to peruse the sale rack, still smiling over Cheryl's good news. After her stressful morning, it was nice to see things were starting to look up.

She slipped her cell phone out of her dance bag's

side pocket, checking to see if she'd gotten a text message from Papi.

Confirming that she hadn't missed the alert tone because he had yet to respond to her apology text, Yaz sighed and dropped her phone back into the woven bag. Arguing with Papi didn't happen often. When it did, she wound up feeling guilty, scared, and frustrated.

For several weeks now he'd looked pale and fatigued, but every time she asked about it, he gave her the brush-off. Today she'd finally confronted him. Rather than answer her, he'd left in a huff for his weekly domino tournament at the rec center, informing her he was fine, not to worry.

If only it were that easy for her.

Yaz shoved a bright pink leotard aside, taking her annoyance out on the garment. The hanger's wire hook screeched along the metal pole, grating on her nerves just like Papi's obstinate behavior.

Across the shop, the front door opened, ushering in a bitter gust of wind.

"*Mira*, Papá, they have tons of shoes! Look, over there!" Maria Garcia's high-pitched voice trilled with enthusiasm as she pulled her father into the store.

One glimpse of the enigmatic man who'd been in her thoughts far too much since last Wednesday sent Yazmine ducking to hide behind a multicolored cloud of tutus.

"Slow down, *m'ija*," Tomás cautioned his daughter.

Like a Peeping Tom, Yaz peeked around a flounce of blue tulle, taking in the sight of those broad shoulders. Gone was the Brooks Brothers navy pinstriped suit. Today he sported a dark leather jacket over an olive-green sweater that accented his tanned skin, with a pair of jeans that fit him snug in all the right places. His shiny wing-tip shoes had been replaced by a pair of well-worn hiking boots. The epitome of a rugged outdoorsman. Camping had always been more her little sister Lilí's forte, but spending a night in a tent with someone as yummy as Tomás Garcia made Yaz reconsider. A sleeping bag on the ground didn't sound half bad if it meant snuggling up with a guy like him.

A trill sounded and Tomás pulled his cell out of his back pocket. "Wait a minute, Maria. I have to . . ."

His voice trailed off as he tapped the screen. Maria wriggled out of a puffy winter coat, then plopped down onto the bench in the shoe area, apparently used to her father not finishing his sentences. Her pouty lips said she wasn't too happy about it though.

The image of cuddling with Tomás in a sleeping bag evaporated as quickly as steam from a pot of Papi's favorite *asopao* simmering on the stove.

During Wednesday's father-daughter practice, Tomás had bristled at her insinuation that he was neglecting his daughter. She hadn't meant to offend the guy, but the proof that he'd been letting Maria down was clearly evident in Yaz's attendance binder.

Across the store, Tomás's thumbs tapped away at the tiny keyboard on his phone. Yaz stayed hidden, interested in seeing how the shoe-shopping trip would play out. Based on the little she knew about Tomás Garcia—fanatical about his job, relying on his nanny for most of Maria's caregiving—she'd bet he was out of his depth in Center Stage.

A few moments passed before Tomás tucked his phone away and hunkered down next to Maria so they wound up eye to eye. "Okay, *chiquita*, what are we looking for? You're the expert here. I'm ready to learn from you."

Nice start. She'd give him that. Yaz craned her neck to listen more closely.

"Ms. Yazmine said we should buy Capezio, 'cuz they are the bestest ones."

"And Ms. Yazmine knows her stuff?"

"Oh Papá, she knows everything. She's supersmart!"

Maria's exaggerated endorsement brought a heated flush of embarrassment to Yaz's face. She'd spent the past few days flip-flopping between being irritated with Tomás for his workaholic habits and exasperated with herself for mooning over him and his hotness. Thinking about his easy smile, sexy wink, and bedroom eyes at odd times throughout her day.

And night.

Now here Maria was singing her praises. The best thing to do was sneak out of the store before either father or daughter noticed her.

A heartbeat after Yaz remembered her peacoat lying on the counter, Mrs. Morgan emerged from the back stockroom. "It took me a minute, but here's your invoice. Yazmine? Where'd you go?"

Hunched behind the mass of tutus, Yaz watched Mrs. Morgan scan the store. The older woman called her name again and Tomás rose from his haunches, curiosity drawing his brows together.

Darn, no way she could sneak out now.

She took a scaredy-cat step out from behind the tulle, sending Mrs. Morgan a hesitant finger wave. "Over here."

"Ms. Yazmine!" Maria squealed with joy, running over to wrap her tiny arms around Yaz's waist for a tight hug.

Mortification at being caught hiding quickly gave way to delight at Maria's warm greeting. Yaz bent to give the little girl a squeeze in return. "I see you're doing some shopping today. It'll feel better to dance when your shoes aren't pinching your toes anymore."

"I hadn't realized that was an issue."

Yazmine glanced up to find Tomás had moved closer, his expression guarded.

"Maria's mentioned it a few times over the past couple of weeks," she said. "I think Mrs. Buckley planned on buying her a new pair over the break."

"Mrs. B left early for the Thanksgiving holiday. But I've got it covered." Tomás's dark eyes assessed her, the teasing spark from their first meeting on Wednesday now subdued.

Good. She had no problem distancing herself from a moody workaholic. She'd done it once before.

"That's nice to hear." Yaz ducked her head to look down at Maria, still plastered to her legs. "And you're correct, Capezio is a great brand. I'm sure you'll find the right pair. I'll see you after the break, okay?"

Yaz tweaked one of Maria's lopsided pigtails and then headed toward the cash register.

"What a cutie," Mrs. Morgan whispered.

"Yeah, she is."

"I was talking about the dad." The older woman chuckled when Yaz gaped at her cheekiness. "Honey, I'm older, not dead. Don't tell me you hadn't noticed."

Far too much for her sanity, but no need to admit that. "There's only one page from the order?"

Mrs. Morgan gave her the age-old I-know-what-you're-up-to stare moms across the globe had mastered. "All business, are you?"

While she and Mrs. Morgan went over the inventory

sheet, Yaz couldn't help but watch Tomás and Maria out of the corner of her eye.

They'd pulled several boxes off the shelf, obviously uncertain what size Maria would need. Tomás's hands dwarfed a slipper and he struggled with sliding it onto Maria's foot. His large fingers fumbled with the tiny decorative laces, his expression endearingly serious as he concentrated on his task. Maria wiggled her body, trying to shove her foot into the ballet shoe. They laughed with each other, Tomás pausing to wipe his brow before tackling the problem with another pair.

Yaz forced herself to look away. The touching father-daughter scene scratched at a hearth-and-home itch she'd ignored out of necessity. Since as far back as high school, when she'd started missing family dinners because of dance practice, then fast forward to how crazy busy she'd been in New York, it had become glaringly clear to her that family life and her hectic dance schedule did not mix.

Tomás's cell phone trilled again. He dug it out of his back pocket, scowling at the display. "I'm sorry, *m'ija*, I really have to take this."

"Okay, but not long this time. You promised, 'member?" Worried hope pinched Maria's round features, a heartache-y plea in her voice.

"I'll try to be fast," Tomás answered. How many times had Maria heard that same piecrust promise? "I need to step outside for some privacy. But I'll be right in front of the window so we can see each other."

Maria bowed her head, flicking her fingers at the pale pink ballet shoe on her lap. "I guess."

Tomás grabbed his leather jacket and connected the call, stopping the computerized ringtone. "Hi, John, are you still having problems with the program?"

He pushed open the door. The brisk winter wind rushed in, Tomás rushed out.

Yaz meant to keep her distance. She really did.

Yes, she loved her students, but getting too attached would make leaving that much harder when the time came. Make her homesickness that much worse than before.

After several gut-wrenching seconds of watching Maria struggle to tie the tiny shoelaces herself, Yaz threw in the towel on her willpower.

"Hi, sweetie, want some help?" She slid onto the wooden bench beside Maria.

"*Gracias.* Papá's outside, but he's coming soon." Maria sent a plaintive look at the front window. "We're shopping, then having pizza for lunch."

"Sounds like fun. Let me see what you got there." The size Maria had chosen was too big, but Yaz made short work of selecting the correct pair and tightening them on Maria's feet.

"Are you buying a tutu?"

The random question had Yaz fumbling with the second tie. "Hm? Uh, no, why?"

"'Cuz you were looking at them before."

Looking at them, hiding behind them. Chagrin teased the corners of Yaz's mouth into a smile.

"I never had one. But I will someday. When I'm a real ballerina." Maria hopped off the bench to execute a slightly wobbly turn. She dipped into a plié, then, arms curved in front of her, she slid her feet into the various positions Yaz had taught their class.

"I think you're a real ballerina now. Come on, let's try one on."

Minutes later, she and Maria stood in front of a full-length mirror admiring the purple tutus they'd slipped over their jeans. Arms raised above their heads, elbows bent so their fingertips nearly touched, they stood on tiptoes while turning in circles.

"You look mahhhvelous." Yaz's teasing tone elicited the response she'd been hoping for when Maria giggled. Yaz grinned back, feeling relaxed and at peace for the first time in days.

"I have to agree."

Yazmine's knees buckled at Tomás's deep baritone. He stepped into the mirror's reflection, her stomach quivering at his cheeky smirk. *Ay, ay, ay*, the sexy playboy was back.

She dropped her hands to her sides, then quickly slipped off the tutu. "We were—"

"Playing dress-up!" Maria's squeal could have been heard across town. "Wanna join us, Papá?"

"*Sí*, I bet the red one would look great on you." Yaz laughed at his scandalized expression. "Didn't they show you the costumes for the recital? All the dads agreed to dress in drag."

Tomás's eyes widened to the size of huge gumballs, his tan face turning a putrid yellow. He visibly swallowed, at an obvious loss for words.

Yaz bit her lower lip, fighting against the grin threatening. When was the last time Mr. Sexy Workaholic had been this tongue-tied? She waited a few beats, enjoying his discomfort before she let him off the hook.

"Okaaay, I'm kidding."

He huffed out a breath. "Very not funny."

"I don't know. I kinda thought it was." Yaz wrinkled her nose playfully as he wagged a finger at her.

They shared a laugh. The richness of his husky tone warming her like a cup of *café con leche*.

The bell above the shop door jangled and together

they turned to see who entered. Yaz noticed Tomás wince moments before a red-haired woman with a tad too much makeup rushed toward him, unwrapping a thick, multicolored scarf from around her neck.

"Well, my goodness, fancy meetin' you here. Sugar, you are a hard man to track down. Whatever happened to us meetin' for drinks?" The woman's Southern drawl oozed charm. The manicured hand she hooked onto his forearm spoke of her interest in more than "drinks."

Tomás backed up a step to stand shoulder to shoulder with Yaz. A bland look replaced his easy grin from moments ago.

"Life's been pretty busy," he replied, his words stilted to Yaz's ear.

"Honey, life is never too busy for a bit of relaxation, is it?" The woman's red-nailed hand slid up his arm to caress his biceps.

Wow, this woman oozed sexual attraction like most people oozed sweat. Unfortunately for Trina Weston—according to the nametag advertising her realty business—while she appeared ready to jumpstart something with him, Tomás's rigid posture and uncomfortable gulp told Yaz he felt otherwise.

"Hi, sugar." Trina wiggled her fingers at Maria, who danced around them in her tutu. "You sure look cute."

"Thanks! Papá and me are shoe shopping, then we're having pizza for lunch."

Tomás shook his head at his daughter, but she was too busy having fun to notice. Trina obviously didn't either. "I was thinking of grabbing a bite to eat myself. Maybe I can join y'all?"

Dios, if Tomás's spine stiffened any more, it'd probably fuse in that position. You would have thought he'd be used to women throwing themselves at him. This couldn't be something new. Good-looking men filled every dance call in Yaz's profession, and even she hadn't been able to banish him from her thoughts all week.

He turned to Yaz, a good-God-save-me plea in his chocolate eyes.

Caught off guard, she didn't respond and Tomás tilted his head imperceptibly toward hers, his intense gaze practically screaming for help.

Yaz didn't know what made her do it. Maybe that crazy, impulsive family gene she'd often chided Lilí about. Or the fact that she had a hard time seeing someone going down for the count without throwing them a lifeline. More than likely, it was her attraction begging to spend more time with this trouble-inducing man.

Whatever the reason, the next thing she knew, she'd hooked her arm through Tomás's and stuck her other hand out toward the Realtor. "I'm sorry, I don't think we've met. I'm Yazmine. Trina, is it?"

The Realtor's questioning gaze moved quickly from Tomás to Yaz and back. "Yes, ma'am, it sure is. Nice to meet ya."

"Likewise. I hate to disappoint you, but I've already snagged a lunch invite from Tomás." The flash of earnest regret in Trina's eyes pricked Yaz's conscience. She understood the sting of rejection and didn't relish being a part of this woman's. "You're welcome to join us if you'd like."

Trina's smile faltered, but kudos to her, she rallied. "I wouldn't dream of intruding, but thank you. Maybe next time?" She pointed a finger at Tomás in a teasing reprimand. "Don't be a stranger, handsome, ya hear?" Hips shaking, she strolled away before he could respond.

Tomás let out a rush of breath the likes of which made a girl think he'd barely escaped death. He sagged against Yazmine's side, his solid weight comfortable, yet heat-inducing in ways she needed to ignore.

"Thanks," he mumbled. "I've been dodging her since she sold us the house. Trying to politely let her know I'm not interested, but . . ."

"She hasn't gotten the message."

He barked out a short laugh. "You think?"

Her ego tickled with the pleasure of sharing an inside joke with him.

"So what kind of pizza do you like?"

Yaz waved off his question, nervously easing away to put some distance between them. "I didn't really mean what I said."

"Hey, I may not be interested in sharing a meal with Trina, but that doesn't mean I want to lie to her either. Come on, I owe you anyway." He gave her a half smile of encouragement, his dimple flashing in his cheek. "Maria, wouldn't it be nice if Ms. Yazmine joined us for lunch?"

Was he really going to play that dirty?

Sure enough, Maria stopped dancing to grab Yaz's hand, lacing their fingers. "Ooh, *sí, sí*! Please, Ms. Yazmine. *¡Por favor!*"

Ay, she was sorely tempted. By him *and* his cute little bundle of energy. His borderline flirtatious teasing sparked a volt of energy inside her she thought had long been shorted out. Maria's excitement invigorated her, the child's tiny hand warm and comforting.

Still, she'd be a fool to get too close to this family.

To fulfill her dreams, and especially Papi's, she

couldn't get sidetracked again. It wasn't smart for her to spend any more time with a man who brought to mind the painful lessons of her past. Especially when she'd tried so hard to learn from, but not dwell on them.

Being near Tomás Garcia made her feel like she'd grabbed onto a live electrical wire. Exhilarating and hair-raising. And ultimately lethal.

"I'm sorry, sweetie." Yaz bent toward Maria rather than direct her words to Tomás, even if it was the coward's way out. "I don't think I should go. I've got to look over this inventory sheet with Mrs. Morgan."

"We don't mind waiting for you," Tomás said.

"I can't ask you to do that."

"You aren't. I'm offering. Maria and I can figure out her dance shoes, maybe pick out a new outfit while you finish."

"Yes!" Maria fist-pumped the air.

"I'm not so sure it's a good idea." No, she'd bet money it was a bad idea. For reasons she hadn't shared with anyone, not even her sisters.

"Come on." He hiked up a shoulder in a half shrug, his dark eyes willing her to say yes. "It's lunch at a noisy pizza parlor. What could it hurt?"

She nearly laughed out loud. If he only knew.

For a year and a half now, she'd been home, nursing her wounds and rebuilding the wall protecting her heart. She was wiser and stronger for the humbling experiences she'd left behind in New York. Or so she'd thought. Until him.

Both times she'd been in this man's presence her precarious tower of emotions teetered like a novice wearing her first pair of toe shoes. Spending more time with him was not a smart move.

No matter how badly she was tempted.

Yaz opened her mouth to refuse the invitation. What came out instead was a weak, "Okay."

Tomás flashed a triumphant grin. Maria whooped for joy and set off on another round of twirls around the shoe display.

Yaz slowly backed away toward the counter to finish her conversation with Mrs. Morgan. Excitement and dread whooshed through her in a frenzied whirlpool, sparking her pulse into a quickstep rhythm.

Dios mío, she'd actually done it—thrown common sense aside and given in to this insane desire to play with fire.

Chapter Three

Man, how quickly things could change. Last night, lying in bed in the dark, Tomás had merely *considered* asking Maria's intriguing dance instructor out for a drink. Repeatedly listing the pros and cons in his head.

And now, less than twenty-four hours later, he found himself seated in a red pleather booth across a faux wood Formica table from Yazmine, slightly shell-shocked by his impulsiveness.

He'd painstakingly squelched all impulsive acts since marrying Kristine while at a conference in Vegas six years ago, complete with an Elvis impersonator and a curvaceous showgirl as witnesses. He still shuddered at the memory. And his *mamá* would never let him live that one down.

Yazmine Fernandez had been on his mind since he'd first laid eyes on her Wednesday evening. The idea of asking her out had crossed his mind more than once or twice. So technically, their lunch together might only be considered *semi*-impulsive.

Back at the dance store, the last thing he'd wanted to

do was take a call from work, knowing it disappointed Maria. Some days, between his home and work responsibilities, he felt more like a circus clown bumbling a juggling act.

He'd peeked through the storefront window while talking to John, intrigued by Yazmine and Maria's interaction. When the sexy dance instructor had shimmied her hips into that purple tutu, his libido had taken notice. When she'd spun around the display area with Maria, eyes twinkling with laughter, he'd sworn he heard her velvety chuckle in his ear.

Later, when she'd understood he needed rescuing from his Realtor—without his even saying a word—he knew he had to give this a shot. Life was about grabbing your opportunities. Instinct told him not to let this one pass by.

"Welcome to Luigi's." A scrawny, pimply-faced teen approached their table, pad in hand. "How 'bout we start with your beverages?"

The idea of sharing a drink with Yazmine brought back thoughts of Wednesday evening. After Maria and Mrs. Buckley had gone to bed, Tomás had toasted the coup of landing the Byer's deal alone in his living room.

Sitting in the dark, his *mamá*'s words had mocked him. "*M'ijo*, you need to find a good woman. One who appreciates the man you are."

For the first time in years, he'd contemplated what it would be like to celebrate his successes with someone special. Was he ready to open that door? Or was it better, safer, to keep it chained and bolted shut?

Today, he'd quit ping-ponging between the two questions and taken the plunge. Instead of an awkward first date with Yazmine, why not lunch with him and Maria? Keep things casual.

"And for you, sir?" the teen asked, pencil ready. "Your drink?" he prodded when Tomás gave him a blank look.

"Uh, root beer, please."

"Great. Menus are behind the napkin holder. I'll be right back."

Their waiter hurried off, waving to a group of teens seated at another booth across the restaurant, then deftly sidestepping a rambunctious toddler scampering around the tables, a frazzled mom in his wake.

Luigi's might rank low in the romantic ambience department, but it scored high on the family-friendly scale. That made it the perfect spot for them.

"So what do you like on your pizza?" He reached for a laminated menu.

"No anchovies or mushrooms for me," Yazmine answered.

Maria wrinkled her nose. "Yuck!"

Dark heads tilted together, Yazmine and Maria chatted about their favorite toppings, sharing an elated grin when they discovered their shared preference for pepperoni and black olives.

Bit by bit his giggly little girl was coming out of her shell again, in large part thanks to the engaging woman seated beside her.

A sense of peace spread through him, soothing his bubbling anxiety over the lunch date. Being here felt good.

As if on cue, doubt reared its serpent-like head, a remnant of the devastation from his botched marriage.

Sure, Yazmine spent hours with children every weekday, but while she didn't seem to tire of it, he couldn't help but wonder if she was too good to be true.

Kristine had barely lasted six months dealing with the responsibility of a baby, even though they'd hired a nanny to handle most of the day-to-day care.

He'd known Kristine was independent and driven. That's what had attracted him to her in the first place. Unfortunately, he hadn't fully grasped the depth of her self-centeredness until Maria was born.

Lesson learned: Look before you leap over the Grand Canyon of relationships and marriage.

The waiter arrived, plunking their drinks on the table and jerking Tomás back to the present. The kid took their order, then hurried off again.

"Have you been at Hanson's Academy for long?" Tomás asked Yazmine.

She nodded as she squeezed a lemon in her water. "Well, kind of. I started teaching in high school. Moved away for a while. When I came back home a little less than two years ago, I took a position again."

He tried imagining a younger, less mature version of the vibrant woman in front of him. No doubt she'd been just as arresting. "So you've always been a talented dancer."

"I like to think so." She flashed him a sassy grin that soothed his lingering unease.

"Since you were going over costume orders at the store, I take it you do more than teach classes."

"Mrs. Hanson started having health problems about six months ago. I took over the scheduling, placing students in the right level of classes and managing our special events. The extra responsibility's been challenging, but fun." Her eyes sparked when she talked about her work, luring him in with her enthusiasm, reminding him of the thrill of seeing her in action last Wednesday.

He pulled his straw wrapper off, relieved by the ease of their conversation. "Sounds like you've taken on a full-time job."

"Not really. Mrs. Hanson still plays a big role. Besides, working there allows me time to practice my dance skills when I'm not taking care of my father. He's been ill for a while."

"Papá, can I have some money to play a song?" Maria pointed to the jukebox near the front door behind him.

"Sure, *m'ija.*" He dug his wallet out of his back pocket. "If it gets cold by the door, come back for your jacket. Want me to help you?"

"*No, gracias.* I can do it."

He kept an eye on her as she slid out of the booth and headed to the front of the pizza parlor, her pigtails bouncing with each step.

"*Es preciosa.*" A gentle smile curved Yazmine's full lips, crinkling the edges of her eyes as she watched Maria.

"Thanks. I think she's pretty precious, too."

Yazmine chuckled, the warm sound vibrating through him. His body hummed like a swarm of locusts waking after years of hibernation.

"So let's see what I know so far. You're a beautiful woman who's obviously talented. Smart, if you're running the studio." He ticked off each item on a finger. "Caretaker for your father."

She ducked her head, her ponytail swooping down to drape across her shoulder. "And you're a smooth talker."

The blush creeping up her neck into her cheeks made her even more appealing. His body tightened with need.

Nearby someone's cell phone rang, the tone ominous. A warning sign.

She was reeling him in way too easily, his body giving in to primal urges he'd subdued of necessity in recent years. Caution advised him to slow things down. If not, he risked getting caught up in the moment, potentially doing something he'd regret.

"Enough about me." Yazmine spoke into the charged silence filling their table. "What's your story?"

"I'm an open book." He gave her what he hoped would pass for a lazy shrug. "What would you like to know?"

"Really?" She crossed her arms over the Chicago Cubs team logo on the front of her gray sweatshirt. The directness of her stare reminded him of the stern disciplinarian she'd been at the studio. "Okay then, what's with the workaholic rep you have around the studio?"

He choked on a sip of soda, quickly grabbing for a napkin to wipe his mouth. "Excuse me?"

"Oh, the mommy network is alive and thriving at Hanson's. They've certainly been chattering about you. I hate to tell you this, but now that you've made an appearance"—the edges of her mouth curved up in a rueful smile—"I'm sure the phone lines and text messages have been burning up the airwaves."

Great, as if that's what he wanted to be, the main topic of discussion around the studio lobby water cooler. "Thanks for the heads-up."

"No problem." Her gaze sharpened and she leveled him with another one of her I-mean-business stares. "But you're dodging my question. Does the reputation fit the man?"

He chuckled, more so to cover his discomfort over

a question that hit too close to home. Unfortunately, the determined jut of her jaw told him she wouldn't let him off the hook.

"I don't know that I'd necessarily label myself a workaholic," he hedged.

Twisting to the side, he propped an elbow along the back of the booth. Out of the corner of his eye he watched Maria, while at the same time trying to gauge Yazmine's mood.

The edge in her voice warned him that more than he knew rode on his answer. It reminded him of their uncomfortable conversation about his absences in dance class. Yet, her earnest gaze made him feel like this meant something more personal to her.

"How many hours a week do you usually work?" Yazmine pressed.

"Roughly, sixty." Sometimes more, depending on the account.

"Which probably means more."

He schooled his features, hiding his surprise at her insight. "When you're fighting to get to the top there are always sacrifices."

"Believe me, I know."

Interesting response.

Tomás eased back against the booth's pleather-cushioned seat and pushed up his sweater sleeves, enjoying their conversational volley. "Are you speaking from personal experience?"

"Ha, nice try. We're talking about you now. Not me. Climbing the corporate ladder doesn't leave you much time to spend with Maria, does it?" Regret laced her words, but her barb poked home.

Guilt flared within him, followed closely by the sting of annoyance. This was the second time since they'd met that Yazmine had called him out for something that really wasn't any of her business.

He sat up straight, ready to say as much, until his gaze met hers across the table. A tumultuous swirl of determination, sorrow, and guilt stared back at him. His annoyance at her rudeness drained away as easily as if he'd pulled the plug out of a bathtub.

It was like she somehow understood his daily struggle between work and family, even though she was a single, part-time dance instructor. It didn't make any sense.

Drawn by this strange connection to her, he answered Yazmine's question the only way he knew how—honestly. "Actually, no. I don't spend as much time with Maria as I'd like."

Yazmine started to respond, but he held up a finger to stop her. "Which is why my accounts are shifting and, after Thanksgiving, I'll be working from home two days a week."

Her mouth formed an enticing "oh" of surprise.

"Weren't expecting that, were you?"

She shook her head. "That'll be good for both of you."

"That's the plan." He waited a beat before throwing a challenge her way. "So, did I pass your test?"

Behind her dark eyes he could see her considering his question.

The jukebox switched from one Top Forty hit to another. Noise from the other patrons and staff buzzed in the air. After several seconds Yazmine's lashes fluttered down, momentarily breaking their eye contact.

"I guess I should apologize," she finally said.

"You guess?"

"Okaaaaay." She drew out the word with a droll smile

he found entirely too cute. "I apologize. The subject happens to be one of my hot buttons."

He laughed at her pouty-mouthed expression. Damn, she was almost as hardheaded as he was. "So I gathered. Maybe you should—"

"It's ready!" Maria skipped up to the table. Hot on her heels, their waiter followed, carrying a silver pizza pan.

"Here you go, one large half pepperoni and black olive, half pepperoni and mushroom."

"Mmmm! Smells yummy." Maria pinched off the strand of cheese dangling from the piece Tomás served her.

They filled their plates and ate in companionable silence for a while, but Tomás couldn't stop wondering what lay behind Yazmine's mini interrogation moments before. What might have caused the regret he sensed in her. Or what could have happened to bring out such a fierce reaction to his long work hours.

With Maria present he wouldn't pry. Instead, he listened to Maria and Yazmine chattering about the upcoming Christmas recital. His daughter's giggles formed a lyrical descant to Yazmine's throaty chuckles.

"My favorite TV show is *Dora*," Maria shared. "How 'bout you?"

That easily, Maria and Yazmine dove into a discussion about the things they liked more than pizza. She soaked up Yazmine's undivided attention, her animated face and gestures bringing a lightness to his chest.

A bittersweet pang ricocheted through him.

Why couldn't all of his and Maria's meals be like this—colored with laughter and sharing? Like his had been, growing up. Since their move out of the city, far too often he arrived home after her dinnertime, counting himself lucky to tuck her in before she fell asleep.

Sitting in Luigi's now, the casual atmosphere reminded him of boisterous family reunions back home with his parents, siblings, and a growing number of nieces and nephews. The love they all shared made him feel both blessed and lacking.

His failed marriage had convinced him that Maria was enough. He didn't need a woman in his life.

Being a single father might not be the norm in his culture, but in today's changing world it was more common. It might take some time, but he and Maria would be fine.

He took a sip of his drink, trying to wash down the lie.

Being here with Yazmine, the doubts he usually silenced had morphed into ear-piercing screeches. Making it harder to tune them out.

The restaurant door opened and instinctively he glanced up. A perfectly coifed Stepford-wife clone and a bleached-blond teenage girl in tight jeans and a designer-label winter jacket approached their table. The teen stopped close behind the woman, an uncomfortably pained grimace on her face.

"Ugh," Yazmine muttered under her breath. Tomás looked over in time to see her lip curl the slightest bit before she managed a forced smile. "Elaine, what brings you here?"

The Stepford clone gave a brisk nod in greeting, making a show of tugging her gloves off her hands, one finger at a time. "I saw you through the window and since I hadn't been able to speak with you at

Hanson's, I thought I'd take the opportunity to voice a concern I have regarding the Christmas show."

"We're in the middle of our meal, but I'd be glad to give you a call la—"

"This will only take a few moments." The woman lifted her chin, pretention wrapped around her like an Hermès scarf.

Intrigued, Tomás eyed the exchange.

To an outsider, Yazmine's demeanor and smile were polite, if not overly inviting. To anyone who had witnessed the power of her infectious grin first-hand, or seen it in his dreams the past several nights, the simmering irritation now lingering beneath the surface was obvious.

"Do you mind?" Yazmine directed the question to him.

Years ago he had lived to put snooty people like this woman, and all the other uptight Deburg Prep parents, in their place. Proving that he could succeed at their haughty school far better than many of their own children had empowered him. As a kid, it had blinded him with anger. As he'd matured, that anger had solidified into resolve. Now that he was older and wiser, women like this one only amused him.

"Doesn't bother me. As long as you're good," he replied.

A self-satisfied smirk curved the woman's bowed lips and she pressed on. "Lately Mrs. Hanson seems a bit . . . oh, how should I put this?" Her well-manicured hand fluttered through the air. "Scattered? Dare I say, unprofessional?"

Yazmine's mouth thinned. "Mrs. Hanson's attention has been on more important matters, specifically, her health. What exactly are you unhappy with, Elaine? Perhaps I can take care of it for you."

The teen slid Yaz an uncomfortable look over her mother's shoulder.

The mom arched a thin brow before launching into a complaint about some costume and a fitting. He understood "sequin" and "spandex," but got lost when "organza" and several other words were thrown in the mix.

However, the woman was on a roll, like a snowball heading downhill, ready to wreak havoc on whatever, or whomever, was in her path. He had to hand it to her, she could give a few Deburg Prep parents a run for their snobby money.

His admiration for Yazmine's cool-as-a-cucumber approach inched up a notch.

"Look, I can arrive early on Monday. The two of you come by and I'll re-measure Elizabeth myself. Does that work for you, Elizabeth?"

The teen nodded repeatedly.

"Great. I'm sure the costume company will help us rectify the situation. Now, if you'll excuse us, we'd like to finish our meal." Yazmine picked up her drink and took a sip, a clear signal the conversation was closed.

"Fine. We will see you on Monday before class." With a brisk jerk of her head, the woman departed, leaving a whiff of her no doubt Chanel No. 5 behind.

Her daughter mouthed a quick "I'm sorry" to Yazmine before hurrying off.

"She wasn't very friendly, was she, Papá?" Maria scrunched her face in disapproval.

"No, *m'ija*, she wasn't." He bowed his head in deference to Yaz. "Well handled. I see what you mean about most studio problems not involving the students."

"Funny how you remembered that." Yaz reached for her pizza, her lips curving in a grin.

"I'm smart that way. Seriously, it's impressive how well you're handling everything at Hanson's. Sounds like you have the know-how to run your own studio."

Yazmine stopped, her slice midway between her mouth and her plate. Surprise flashed in her eyes before her lids swept down. She swallowed, but didn't say anything.

"I'm full. Can I go dance, please?" Maria pointed to another little girl about her age, swaying side to side in front of the jukebox.

"Are you done?" Tomás picked up her plastic cup of milk, pleased to find it empty. "Good job. Okay, *m'ija*. Be careful to stay right there so you're not in anyone's way. And remember what I said about not getting cold from the door opening and closing."

"*Sí*, Papá."

Once Maria had left the table, Tomás continued the conversation. "From what you've said, you're practically keeping things running while Mrs. Hanson recovers from whatever she has going on. It's obvious you love your job, and you're good at it."

"It's not for me."

"How come?"

Yazmine set down her pizza slice, then reached for a paper napkin to carefully wipe the grease from her hands. A delay tactic if he'd ever seen one.

"Teaching at Hanson's is rewarding. But owning a studio?" She shook her head, her ponytail waving from side to side behind her. "That's not what I'm supposed to do."

Supposed to do. That sure sounded more like *expected to do.*

He started to ask about it, but his gaze zeroed in on a dollop of pizza sauce coloring the corner of her mouth. Right on the edge where her full lips met.

Temptation double-dog dared him to swipe it off with his finger.

Common sense made him settle for reaching across the table to gently dab at it with his napkin.

Yazmine sucked in a quick breath. But she didn't shy away.

"You, uh, had a little bit of sauce." His gaze wavered between her lips and her eyes. Damn, he had the crazy urge to lean closer and kiss her.

Yeah, crazy was right.

Slowly he eased back onto his seat, surprised—okay, more like confused—by his actions. Not to mention the ones he wasn't allowing himself to consider.

"Thank you," she murmured.

"Uh, sure."

He took a long pull of his soda, welcoming the trickle of cool liquid down his suddenly dry throat.

It took him a full minute to remember what they'd been talking about before he'd gotten distracted by her mouth. Hanson's, right. "So you're happy being a teacher? No plans to take over the place yourself someday?"

He caught the shake of her head before he turned around to check on Maria.

"Once we're certain my father's in remission and he's okay, I'm headed back to New York."

Tomás spun around so fast he nearly knocked over his soda with his elbow. "New York City?"

His sharp tone was probably the culprit behind the squinty-eyed perplexed expression on her face.

She nodded slowly.

"I wasn't—I didn't know you were thinking of moving."

"It's common knowledge at the studio. I'm sure Mrs. Buckley's heard."

The three pieces of pizza he'd eaten suddenly felt like huge Texas-sized boulders in Tomás's stomach. "I'm the workaholic, remember? I'm way out of the info loop."

"Right. Not even a tiny seedling in the mommy grapevine yet. But you will be," she joked, though he couldn't return her smile. Not when he felt like he'd missed a turn somewhere between meeting her Wednesday night and deciding to take a chance on getting to know her better today.

"I assumed Mrs. Buckley had shared my background with you, since I'm teaching Maria."

"Nope."

Mrs. Buckley had researched the area dance schools for him. He trusted her opinion and hadn't asked personal questions about Maria's instructor. He hadn't even been thinking personal thoughts about Yazmine, until recently. Big. Mistake. "Care to share the details?"

"Sure. It's old news around here." She shrugged lazily, like she hadn't just knocked the wind out of his newly opened sails. "I started dancing at Hanson's in elementary school and after graduation I headed to New York. I'd been a working dancer for over six years. Landed several off-Broadway shows, a few workshops. I was about to start another show when . . ."

Her voice trailed off. She frowned—at him or the memory. He wasn't sure which.

"When what?" he asked after several heavy seconds had ticked away. "Your dad?"

"Not at first."

"So . . ." He felt like a kid picking at a scab, knowing if he didn't stop he'd make it bleed. Yet he couldn't quit.

Yazmine fiddled with her straw wrapper, winding and unwinding the paper around her finger. Her eyes held a faraway, pensive look.

"You know how it goes. Promises made, but not kept. Someone looking out for himself. Apparently financing for the show was a problem, but only a select few were clued in. Then the lead dancer bailed, decided to hook up with someone financing a bigger production. It was a good career move for him."

She spoke matter-of-factly, yet the flecks of paper that had once been the straw wrapper now littered the table in front of her. "That old dog-eat-dog mentality. A reminder that this business can be harsh."

He wasn't quite sure if she was talking to him, or reminding herself.

"Nothing worthwhile is easy," he offered.

"Yeah." The word was said on a rush of air. Part scoff, part heart-heavy sigh. "Wise words."

"My father's. Drilled into me and my brother and sisters whenever we talked about giving up on something."

"Well, I don't plan on giving up. Too much rides on my success." Yazmine dropped the stump of the mangled straw wrapper on top of the pile of pieces. "But when I got the call about Papi . . . The show's demise, the lies I'd been told, the people who'd been hurt. None of it mattered."

Her voice trembled, a sign of some pain she kept well hidden. He recognized it. Had mastered the art of disguise himself.

"What happened to your father?" he asked.

"Lymphoma. Diagnosed almost two years ago."

Tomás winced. Damn, he couldn't imagine getting news like that about anyone in his family, much less his parents. "I'm so sorry."

"*Gracias.*" She flicked a red-painted fingernail at the olives dotting a half-eaten piece of pizza on her plate. "My mom's been gone for a while. She died in a car accident when I was in high school. So I came home to take care of him."

"You don't have any siblings?"

"I'm the oldest. My middle sister, Rosa, is a year and a half younger. She's working on her master's degree in library science, set to graduate in May. She has a job waiting for her here at our Catholic high school. My youngest sister, Lilí, is in her second year of undergrad. I wasn't about to let either of them mess up their scholarships."

"*Familia primero.*"

She glanced up, sending him a relieved smile he was happy to see. "*Sí*, family first. I guess your parents taught you the same motto?"

"One of many." He admired her devotion to her family. And now understood why the idea of someone putting work before loved ones was a hot button. "So you set aside your dream, to nurse your father back to health?"

"He needed me. Besides, I wasn't sure if I—there were things that didn't . . ." She waved off her own words. "I needed to be here."

She fiddled with the silverware, shooting him a smile probably meant to make him think everything was fine. Though she couldn't hide the slight tremor in her hand.

His ability to read people had always come in handy in the boardroom. Now he honed in on Yazmine's nonverbals, allowing her to "speak" to him with her movements and body language.

Gaze downcast, she dabbed a finger at the pool of water from the sweat off her glass. The way she pressed her lips together, as if considering her words, told him she'd wind up leaving some of them out. Probably important ones.

"It was time for me to return. Like I said, I needed to be here." She spoke so softly, he barely heard her.

Yazmine glanced up at Tomás. In the seconds before she looked back down, he caught a flicker of inner anguish, a hint of what he would have sworn looked like self-doubt. The idea floored him.

This woman ruled her studio. He'd seen her in action. She was great at sharing her joy with her students, didn't think twice about bandying shots back and forth with him. She held her own when confronted by a pushy mom. No way would he have thought she'd have even a sliver of doubt inside her.

"But, Papi's almost in the clear now," Yazmine continued. "I've regrouped. I'm ready to get back. Nothing's going to stop me this time."

She thumped the tabletop with her closed fist, emphasizing her last point. Her straight shoulders and steely-eyed expression spoke of determination. Still, he swore he caught a hint of unease underlying her war cry.

He'd never been much of a betting man before. If he were, he'd lay money down on the fact that whatever Yazmine had experienced in New York involved more than the normal show-business setbacks.

Much more.

Curiosity urged him to delve deeper. Common sense harped at him to back away. Any fledgling idea he'd held about asking her out on an "adult date" had to be squashed.

Despite whatever disappointments she harbored, Yazmine was bright-lights-and-big-city bound. He'd moved out of the city a few months ago. Searching for a slower pace, a more family atmosphere for Maria.

Something about Yazmine Fernandez pulled at him. Made him reconsider his single father status and count the number of years he'd been without a woman's touch. Despite that, he knew that any personal involvement with a career-focused woman would start him down a road he'd already traveled with Kristine, hitting every freaking pothole along the way.

Disappointment might taste bitter now. Heartache and disillusion would taste much worse later if he ignored the warning signs.

"Well, I may not know much about the dance industry, but from what I've seen and heard, you're good at what you do. I'm sure you'll head back to New York and find success."

"That's the plan."

Enough said.

The waiter appeared with their bill and Tomás reached out to take it.

"I can pay for my half," Yazmine said.

"No, this is our treat. We invited you."

On a whim that had come back to bite him in the butt.

Yazmine held on to the zipper of her black woven bag a moment longer, finally setting it down beside her when he shook his head and handed the waiter some cash. "Fine. But I owe you. Maybe we can do this again?"

Only if he were a glutton for punishment.

She was an interesting woman with a beautiful smile, amazing talent, and a dedication to her family he admired. She was tempting, but headed in the wrong direction for him.

"Thanks, probably not though." The words came out a little brusque and he rushed to soften them. "My schedule stays pretty full."

Scooping up the mess she'd made with the straw wrapper, she dropped the flecks of paper onto her plate. "Sure. The workaholic thing, I forgot."

"Any free time I have is devoted to Maria."

"As it should be." She spoke in the same cool tone she'd used with the Stepford wife earlier.

Even knowing anything between Yazmine and him was impossible, Tomás found himself regretting that his brush-off had her grouping him with the haughty mom.

"So, when are you heading back to New York?" The sooner she left, the sooner she'd stop being a distraction to him.

"When Papi's given the all-clear. Hopefully sometime after the New Year. I couldn't make it to his last appointment. And, it's kind of strange, he was pretty cryptic about what Dr. Lopez told him." She clasped her hands in front of her on the table, her white knuckles proof of her anxiety. "I'm having a hard time not worrying, actually."

He'd feel the same way if it were one of his parents.

Without thinking, Tomás reached out to cover her hands with his, offering comfort. Warmth immediately sparked through him, zapping his pulse.

He was wading into dangerous waters here. His attraction, like a strong current, pulled him relentlessly toward her.

Slowly he drew back, wanting to prolong the contact, knowing it'd be stupid to do so.

Yazmine cleared her throat and tucked a wisp of hair behind her ear. "My sisters and I'll dig any info we need out of him when they're home for Thanksgiving this week. As for New York, I've been working hard to stay in shape and I keep in touch with my agent. It's only a matter of time before I go back."

That sealed the deal. Soon they'd be living in two different states, with two distinctly different life goals.

When Kristine had moved out, he'd vowed never to put himself or Maria in a position to be rejected like that again.

He wasn't dumb enough to think he could protect Maria from everyone or everything forever. He could damn well try though.

If Yazmine had her sights set on the bright lights of Broadway, she wasn't the right woman for him.

His mind knew that. Now he just had to figure out a way to convince the rest of him.

Chapter Four

"Papi, you holding up okay?" Yazmine asked as they strolled down the neighborhood sidewalk late Sunday afternoon.

"I'm fine, *nena*. Stop badgering me."

Yaz bit back a frustrated sigh. "I'm not badgering, I'm—"

"*Por favor*, don't worry."

The disheartened note in her father's voice stopped her from pressing him. Instead, she looped her right arm through his left and leaned her head on his shoulder. His wool winter coat scratched her cheek, but she snuggled closer. "I don't mean to nag, but it's hard not to worry. *Te quiero,* Papi. "

He patted her hand with his. "I love you, too. Now let's enjoy the beautiful day. Before we know it, snow will fall and a walk to the park will not be as easy."

His labored breathing made her think the walk wasn't so easy for him now. Out of respect, she let the subject go, but her unease wasn't soothed. She wouldn't stop worrying until she went with him for his next doctor visit and she had solid answers. In three days Rosa and Lilí would be home for Thanksgiving. She and her sisters would get Papi to talk.

For now, Yaz simply enjoyed their stroll together along the leaf-strewn sidewalk. They passed brick-and-siding houses, their front porches and wide lawns adorned with pumpkins, pilgrims, and scarecrows. By this time next weekend the fall decorations would be replaced by poinsettias, Santas with reindeer, brightly colored lights, and nativity scenes. Soon snow would fall, blanketing her small town. Turning it into a winter wonderland.

She breathed in the crisp autumn air, welcoming its refreshing lift to her spirits, then waved back at a group of kids jumping into a pile of gold and red leaves. Their laughter carried on the sharp breeze, calling her to join in the fun.

Ay, how she loved the Thanksgiving and Christmas holidays. The cooking, the caroling. Families reuniting. Some of her fondest memories were of hours spent in the kitchen with Mami, Rosa, and Lilí, while Papi sat at the counter sneaking samples. Christmas morning wasn't the same without the mouthwatering aroma of a *pernil*, basted with scrumptious spices, slow-cooking in the oven. She'd learned that truth the hard way her first year in New York.

Barely scraping by financially, she couldn't afford time off her waitressing job, or the money to buy a pork roast for a Christmas dinner. On her own, far from her family, she'd never felt more alone in her life.

"Rosa will be here Tuesday, right?" Papi asked as they turned the corner onto Hamilton Drive.

Yaz nodded. "And Lilí's leaving Carbondale as soon as her last class finishes on Wednesday. They'll both be here in time to help put the turkey in the oven and start peeling the plantains for the *tostones*."

Ooh, she could already taste the fried green plantains.

Up ahead she caught sight of the rocket-ship slide on the outer edge of the city's park, their turnaround point to head home. The wind picked up, its cool bite hitting her full in the face and she ducked her head, hunching her shoulders in her peacoat.

"It will be good to have my girls together again. *Mis tres nenas.*" The sad, almost wistful note in Papi's voice as he talked about his three girls drew Yaz's concerned gaze. His normally cheerful face wore a brooding expression. His dark eyes brimmed with sadness.

Fear rose up in Yaz, chasing away her good spirits. Even when he'd first been diagnosed, Papi had remained upbeat. Lately though, something had changed. His usual excitement over Rosa and Lilí's upcoming visit had dimmed. He hadn't said anything about Los Paisanos having a practice session at the house, and the band always got together over the holidays.

Her chest tightened with anxiety as she thought back on his recent pallor and fatigue, his glum demeanor. Something had to be wrong.

"Did you and Pablo talk at the rec center about Los Paisanos coming over next weekend? I'm sure the girls would love to hear you sing again."

"No."

"How come?"

"We had other things to discuss."

Yaz grit her teeth, frustrated by his curt responses. Questions and fears she longed to voice clogged her throat. If she kept pushing, though, he'd only get exasperated like he had a few moments ago. Or yesterday when she'd pressed for details about his time at the rec center.

He usually returned relaxed and smiling, happy to share the latest news from Pablo or one of his other cronies. But yesterday he'd come home tired and pale. Sidestepping her questions, he'd asked about her day instead. Still smarting from Tomás's brush-off at the end of lunch, she hadn't wanted to share details either.

Ultimately, neither she nor Papi had wound up with much information about the other's day.

They reached the intersection and she trained her gaze on the town's park and outdoor sports complex across the street. Huge oak trees dotted the land, towering over the park to provide shade during the hot summer months. Today the trees stood like silent, barren sentinels in the crisp autumn air, stark limbs shooting up into the cloudless blue sky.

The light changed and Papi stepped off the sidewalk.

"Are you sure you want to cross?" she asked, afraid he'd get overtired if they stayed out too long. "Should we turn back and head home?"

He shook his head. "Not yet. Let's sit on a bench for a while and watch the children. Their energy keeps me young."

"You should come see some of my students in action. Their energy tires me out."

Papi chuckled. "Somehow, I don't think so. You're too strong for that."

Yaz laid her head on his shoulder again, buoyed by the return of his playful teasing. The rightness of the moment, of being here with him, calmed her. After her years alone in New York, she'd come to cherish time with her family. Since his health scare, she'd especially come to cherish every day with Papi.

Ay, she would miss walks like this when she left home again. It was one of many sacrifices she had to make for her profession, especially if she wanted to make her family and others in their small town proud.

Somehow she'd have to learn to cope with her homesickness. Grow a thicker skin to deal with the cutthroat mentality in the dance world. Prove to her cheating bastard of an ex that he was wrong. She *could* cut it in New York.

Because her dreams weren't the only ones at stake.

Papi's plans to pursue a music career had brought her parents to the Chicago area from their native Puerto Rico years ago. But when Mami developed complications during her pregnancy with Yaz, Papi found a more traditional job to pay the medical bills and provide for his growing family.

Countless times Yaz had thought about how successful Papi and Los Paisanos would have been if she hadn't come along so soon.

Papi may have given up his dream, but she'd never disappoint him by giving up on their dream for her.

"Do you remember when I used to practice dance while you and the guys rehearsed in the basement?" Yaz asked.

"*Ay*, those were the days, *ha nena*? I still love watching you dance, seeing you thrill the audience. It makes me proud."

Yaz clasped her hand with his. Her triumph as a Broadway performer was a gift she could give him. Small payment for all he'd set aside for her and her sisters.

"*Mira.*" Papi pointed to a dark-haired little girl wearing

a pink puffer coat over jeans and a pair of pink sneakers. "She reminds me of you girls at her age."

Yaz slowed her steps as she recognized the child.

Legs pumping, Maria Garcia ran toward the swing set amid shrieks of joy. Behind her, looking far too good in faded jeans, a scoop-necked black sweater peeking out from under his dark leather jacket, Tomás pretended to give chase, his mock evil laughter ringing in the cool wind.

Since his about-face and hasty retreat from Luigi's yesterday, the man had strayed far too often into Yaz's thoughts, despite her attempts to banish him. Along with her lingering attraction.

Her quickened pulse alerted her that she hadn't quite succeeded.

Maria reached the swings at about the same time Yaz and Papi reached the edge of the grass surrounding the play area.

"Hey, Ms. Yazmine!" Maria threw her swing aside, sending it flying in the air to loop over the top bar. "Papá, look who's here!"

Yaz grinned at Maria's exuberant greeting.

"How come you're here?" Maria asked, her breath coming in short gasps when she skidded to a stop in front of Yaz.

"I'm taking a walk with my dad. Papi, this is Maria Garcia, one of my special dancers at Hanson's. I think I mentioned we had lunch at Luigi's yesterday. Maria, this is my dad, Señor Fernandez."

While her father coaxed a shy smile out of Maria, Yaz looked up to find Tomás dragging his feet through the grass, apparently loath to move closer. The frown marring his handsome features said he wasn't pleased to see her.

The feeling was mutual. Well, mostly mutual.

"Hello," she said, aiming for cool and detached, though not quite sure she got there.

He responded with a brusque nod.

Like an idiot, she actually missed his playful banter, the flash of his sexy dimple.

"Reynaldo Fernandez, *encantado.*" Papi held out his hand to shake.

"Tomás Garcia. It's a pleasure to meet you, too. Your daughter is quite talented. My Maria enjoys her class."

Yaz drank in Tomás's praise, calling herself all kinds of a fool for enjoying it.

"*Gracias,* I think she is one of a kind myself." Papi pulled Yaz to his side in a one-armed hug. "She's always been my little star, *ha nena?*"

"Papi, *por favor,*" Yaz mumbled, embarrassed by his bragging. Though her certainty about her skills might waver from time to time, his remained constant.

"I'm sure you have much to be proud of."

Yaz frowned at Tomás's stiff-upper-lip tone.

Maria tugged lightly on Yazmine's coat sleeve, pulling her attention away from Tomás. "Will you push me on the swing?"

"Sur—"

"*M'ija,* don't bother her," Tomás cut in. "We don't want to intrude on their walk."

Irritation bubbled up in Yazmine's belly, pushing her to tell him where he could stick his overly polite façade. "Maria is never a bo—"

"That sounds like a good idea." Papi jumped into the conversation before Yazmine could voice her snappy comeback. "I need to sit on the bench and rest a few minutes. My stamina isn't what it used to be."

The fight in her instantly evaporated. "Are you feeling okay?"

"*Sí, sí*, don't worry. I only need a short rest." Papi patted her arm, probably sensing her concern. "Yazmine, why don't you push the little one for a while. Then she and Tomás can join us for dinner at our home?"

"Papi, I don't think—"

"We wouldn't want to—"

"Yeah!"

Maria's cry of approval superseded Tomás's and Yaz's denials.

"We have a big pot of *asopao*," Reynaldo said, bending down to Maria, an obvious ally in his plan. "If you don't help us eat it, we'll be stuck having leftover soup for days."

Maria's scrunched-up face let him know how little she enjoyed leftovers. "*Por favor*, Papá," she begged Tomás. "Can we go? Please, please."

Yaz held her breath, hoping he'd say no. Unable to quiet the silly voice in her head joining in Maria's pleas for him to say yes.

"*¡Por favor!*" Maria continued, her hands clasped in prayer in front of her. One firm glance from Tomás was enough to silence her.

"*Gracias*," he said to Papi. "I appreciate the offer, but I'm sure you didn't plan on surprise guests. Perhaps some other time."

His taut shoulders and grim expression told Yaz he'd rather there not *be* another time. She squelched a flare of disappointment.

From the beginning she'd known Tomás was a man to steer clear of. His fickleness only confirmed her opinion.

"I insist," Reynaldo pressed, straightening to his full

five-foot-eight height. Though he remained nearly half a foot shorter than Tomás, experience reminded Yaz that Papi was still a man to be reckoned with once he set his mind to something. "To thank you for treating my Yazmine to lunch yesterday while I played dominoes."

Yaz bit back a groan. Great, now she sounded like a charity case.

"Come on, Papá." Maria gave Tomás one of the best hang-dog expressions Yaz had seen in ages, all sad eyes and pouty lips. "Mrs. B is gone and you're gonna be stuck cooking for us."

Leaning toward Reynaldo, the girl lifted a hand to block one side of her mouth as she stage whispered, "And he's not very good at it."

Papi put his hands out, palms up, and laughed. "*Bueno*, there you go."

If there was ever a be-careful-what-you-wish-for moment, this was it. Earlier Yaz had grumbled about Papi's melancholy mood, wishing he'd perk up, get back to his old self. She loved hearing his booming laughter again, but there had to be another way to cheer him up other than inviting Tomás into her home.

"Papi, I'm not—" Yaz argued, only to have her words drowned out by Tomás.

"I really don't want to put you out . . ." Tomás trailed off as Reynaldo shook his head.

"*Por favor. No es molestia.* I would not offer if it was a bother. You will come for dinner. I even have a brand-new tin of *florecitas* to share."

"*Florecitas?*" Maria asked, her cute face lit with interest.

"*Sí*, little flower cookies from the Island. The perfect size for you."

Maria's eyes widened, her mouth forming a little "oh" of excitement.

"See," Papi said on a laugh. "We don't want to disappoint the little one, *no*? It's settled then."

After a quick wink for Maria, Papi ambled over to the bench near the merry-go-round.

Maria let out a whoop of joy and ran off to choose her swing.

Yaz stuffed her hands into her coat pockets and let out an exasperated huff.

A befuddled expression settled onto Tomás's face. "The man certainly knows how to win an argument, doesn't he? He'd be a killer in boardroom negotiations."

"No doubt." Yaz bobbed her head at Papi's wave when he sat down.

"He lived with a house full of women. He's survived PMS, boyfriend heartaches, and insanely high estrogen levels." Yaz lifted her shoulders in a resigned shrug. "I should have known you and I didn't stand a chance. Papi doesn't put his foot down too often. But when he does, he means it."

Tomás's deep chuckle snaked up her spine, wrapping around her chest to steal her breath. "I'll have to remember that next time."

She doubted there would be a next time. Though part of her hoped there would.

"Are you coming?" Maria called.

"Be patient." Tomás took a few steps toward the swing set, then paused to look over his shoulder at Yaz. "Are you up for this?"

Torn between following him or running for the hills, she hesitated.

Ultimately, Maria's ear-to-ear grin lulled Yaz out of indecision.

"Can I have an underdoggie? *Por favor*," Maria added at her father's raised brow.

Tomás grabbed Maria's seat with both hands to give her a big push, then he quickly stepped forward and ducked under her swing.

Maria squealed with delight.

"How about if I give you one, too?" Yaz asked, wanting to join in the child's fun.

"*¡Sí!*" Maria cried.

Yaz reached for the seat as it swung back toward her. Following Tomás's example, she ran under the chair, pushing it high into the air. She ducked to avoid getting whacked in the head and her foot sank awkwardly into the protective gravel scattered around the area. Her knee buckled, throwing her off balance, and she yelped in surprise.

"Whoa, *cuidado*." Tomás reached out to catch her before her face made close and personal contact with the ground. Instead, it made close and personal contact with his muscular chest.

She grabbed his biceps for support and suddenly falling was the last thing on her mind.

His muscles flexed under her grip. Awareness zapped her fingers, shooting straight to her core.

His words of caution moments ago took on a whole new meaning.

Ducking her head in embarrassment, she accidentally pressed her nose to the warmth of his neck. She inhaled, filling her lungs with his musky male scent, a hint of a woodsy aftershave adding a little extra kick. In a flash, she felt more woozy than if she'd downed a few Bacardi and Diet Cokes.

Ay, no dreams, no matter how vivid, did justice to the all-too-real potency of this man.

"Is your knee hurt?"

She felt his words vibrate along his neck, rumble through his chest, and into her.

That easily, she found herself falling again, this time for him.

Alarms shrilled in her head.

"Ms. Yazmine, you okay?" Maria's sweet, little-girl voice cushioned Yazmine's free fall into trouble.

Was she okay? Not really.

With Victor, at least she hadn't realized how big a mistake she was making. The man was an incredible dancer, but he'd turned out to be a wolf in sheep's clothing. Or nice dance wear, anyway.

With Tomás there was no getting around it. Falling for him was a big fat no. Capital N. Capital O. Capped off with an exclamation point!

New York. Success. Atoning for Papi's dashed dreams.

She repeated the words in her head, focusing on what they meant. Rather than on giving in to the tingling sensations being near Tomás brought to life inside her.

"I'm fine. Though for a second there I thought I'd be eating gravel for dinner," Yaz joked, hoping laughter would defuse the situation.

Regaining her footing, she straightened and looked up at Tomás.

Wrong move.

His face was only inches away from hers. Much too close.

"Uh, thank you." She cleared her throat, hoping Tomás didn't hear the damn-I-think-you're-hot rasp in her voice.

A light flared in his dark mahogany eyes, turning them to melted chocolate. For the briefest moment she swore she felt his arms tighten around her. Then he dropped his hands to his sides and stepped back. "You're welcome."

The remote, distant Tomás was back.

"*¿Estás bien, nena?*" Papi called out to her.

No, she was more like the opposite of *fine*. But she couldn't yell that back to Papi. Well-practiced at pretending, she pasted a reassuring smile on her face and waved off his question.

Tomás moved behind Maria to give her another push.

Yaz stayed in front of the swing set, maintaining her distance from him. She made silly faces at Maria, giving her the occasional nudge on her knees to keep her going.

She told herself to concentrate on her giggling student, not the child's temperamental father.

Unfortunately, that was like telling the tide not to come onto the shore. You could build that sandcastle all you wanted, but destruction was inevitable.

If she was smart, she'd keep reminding herself of that inevitability.

Chapter Five

Following Rey's directions, Tomás turned left into a subdivision nestled near the center of Oakton.

Tall oak and Bradford pear trees shaded wide lawns scattered with richly colored fall leaves. He cruised past an older couple strolling hand in hand along the sidewalk, then slowed down even more when he spotted some kids darting across several adjoining yards in a spirited game of tag.

The neighborhood was older, yet far from run-down. More like comfortable, inviting. Compared to his new neighborhood, where most of the trees were saplings recently planted by the builder, Yazmine's street had a homey, established feel to it, similar to his parents' back in McAllen.

Nostalgia strummed a wistful chord in his chest. The distance separating him from his family seemed greater now that he'd moved to the suburbs, away from the diversity of inner-city Chicago. Vacations and holiday trips to Texas didn't provide enough time together.

Of course, his parents always asking when he planned

on moving back didn't help. No matter how often he tried to explain, they still hadn't come to accept, much less understand, that his job and financial success were important to him. Both of which were more easily attainable in a city like Chicago.

The move to the suburbs provided the comfortable family lifestyle he wanted for Maria. Yet the city skyline looming in the distance reassured him that he'd also be able to provide financial security for her. Something he'd lacked as a child.

"Home, sweet home." Reynaldo pointed to a red-brick two-story house with gray shutters up ahead. "*Bienvenidos a mi casa.*"

In the back seat Maria craned her neck to see better. "Oooh, it's pretty."

Tomás pulled into the driveway, mumbling his thanks to Reynaldo for his welcome.

Frankly, he couldn't believe he'd gotten himself roped into another meal with Yazmine. Even after finding out about her career plans yesterday, he'd still spent the morning trying to hit the delete, rather than the play button, on the mental video of last night's vivid dreams.

All co-starring Yazmine.

Now he glanced at her in his rearview mirror. Mouth set in a grim line, she looked about as thrilled as he was by their forced dinner plans.

"Come inside. The soup should be ready." Reynaldo opened his car door and slid from the front passenger seat.

Tomás followed suit. No turning back now.

Maybe it'd help if he thought of this dinner as a fact-finding mission. An opportunity to confirm what he'd realized yesterday: As tempting as she might be,

Yazmine Fernandez was not a woman for him to mess with.

She had a one-way ticket aboard the next plane out of town burning a hole in her dance bag pocket.

He, on the other hand, had his sights set on planting roots in Oakton.

If there was one thing his failed marriage had taught him, it was that opposites do not attract. He'd do well to remember that.

His head finally in the right place, Tomás grasped Maria's hand to help her out of her booster seat. Together they followed Yazmine and Reynaldo up the cement walkway lined with orange and yellow chrysanthemums.

Reynaldo lifted his foot to take the single step up to the front porch and he swayed to his left. Tomás lunged forward to grab him, nudging shoulders with Yazmine when she did the same.

"*Estoy bien.* I'm fine," Reynaldo repeated, shrugging them both off. "I missed the step. That is all. No need to worry."

His last words were directed at Yazmine, a parental warning in his tone.

"Papi, maybe you should lie down." Anxiety puckered Yaz's brow.

"And not enjoy our company? *No*, I said I am fine. Now quit fussing."

The older man unlocked the door and stepped inside. Yazmine moved aside for Maria and Tomás to pass by, but he caught the flash of fear and frustration in her caramel eyes. Yesterday she'd mentioned her concern about Reynaldo's health. Hell, he'd feel the same way if Rey were his dad.

"We'll try to make this quick so he can rest," Tomás

said, stopping in the doorway to touch Yazmine's shoulder in a show of support.

Her gaze caught his.

Fire shot through him. Confusion sparked in her eyes in the seconds before she blinked and looked away.

"Thanks," she whispered. The vulnerability in her soft voice, the worried quaver in the single word ensnared him. His grip on her shoulder tightened.

He wanted to wrap his arms around her in comfort, offer his support. Only, he didn't trust himself to stop there. His attraction was still too fresh. Too raw. Too dangerous for where they were headed—nowhere.

"Excuse me, can I go in?" Maria squeezed in between them, knocking his arm off Yazmine's shoulder. And him out of his stupor.

Still, as he entered the open space of the family room, he flexed his fingers, certain Yazmine's heat had left an imprint on his palm.

She took their jackets without another word, turning to hang them on a wooden coatrack near the door. Tomás used the time to take in her family's home.

A pair of bongo drums bookended a dark-stained entertainment center to make unique fern stands that gave the room a cultural touch. Richly colored rugs dotted hardwood floors. However, it was the walls that drew his attention the most.

Family portraits and framed candid snapshots intermingled with paintings and prints of Puerto Rico's lush, tropical landscape. As the stairs ascended to the second floor, picture collages traveled up the length of the tan wall, maracas crisscrossed in pairs between them. The home's atmosphere spoke of family ties and a strong connection to their heritage.

It reminded him of his parents' house back in Texas. Filled with mementos that were testaments to their love for their culture and history. His mom would feel right at home here, like he immediately did.

"Make yourself comfortable." Yazmine motioned to the coffee-colored microfiber sofa and recliner squared off in front of the entertainment center.

Tomás peeked through the archway connecting the living room to a formal dining room. It flowed into the kitchen, where he caught sight of Reynaldo. The older gentleman stood at the kitchen counter removing the lid from a Crock-Pot. A puff of steam billowed forth, carrying the scent of simmering garlic and spices. Tomas's stomach rumbled, his mouth watering in anticipation of the authentic Puerto Rican meal.

"It smells delicious," he called to Reynaldo, then he turned back to Yazmine. "Since we moved out here, I miss being able to easily stop by Twenty-Sixth Street for a taste of home."

"You're in for a treat then," Yazmine said. "Papi's a great cook. My mom taught him well. You two go ahead and sit down while we get things ready." She brushed past him, leaving behind her subtle scent of violets.

Tomás glanced at Maria, bent over to peer at some photos on the end table. He should take advantage of the chance to peek into Yazmine's past. Confirm why they weren't compatible. Reynaldo shouldn't be waiting on any of them though. The older man needed his rest.

Instead of joining Maria near the couch, Tomás headed to the kitchen, where he found Yazmine shooing her father out of the way.

"Go sit down, Papi. You keep them company and I'll have dinner on the table in a few minutes."

"I can help," Tomás suggested.

"I'm a good helper, too. Mrs. B and my *papá* always say so," Maria chimed in from behind him.

"I'm sure you are." Yazmine's worried gaze strayed to her father's tired face.

Tomás took the hint. "Maria, why don't you ask Señor Fernandez to show you Yazmine's trophy case, the one he mentioned on the drive over?"

Maria's eyes lit up like he'd suggested they eat dessert before dinner.

Reynaldo chuckled at her enthusiasm. "*Vente, nena.* It's downstairs in the basement." He motioned for Maria to follow him and she hop-skipped out of the room behind Reynaldo's shuffling figure.

Suddenly, Tomás found himself alone with Yazmine. Something he'd thought about for a ridiculous amount of time.

"If only Maria could pass along some of her energy to my dad," Yazmine said with a sigh. "He could definitely use it."

"Couldn't we all."

"Yeah." She huffed out a short laugh. "I guess you're right."

"How's he doing?" Tomás stepped farther into the kitchen. "Has he said anything about his next doctor appointment?"

Arms folded across her chest, Yazmine leaned back against the counter, her bottom lip caught between her teeth. "No. Honestly, it scares me. I can tell he hasn't been feeling well."

Tomás opened his mouth to offer some words of advice, wanting to calm the shakiness in her voice. Erase the stark fear in her eyes.

She stopped him with a raised hand. "I'm sorry. You didn't come to hear my sob story again. We'll be fine. I'm venting, and I shouldn't be."

Turning away, she picked up a large wooden spoon and dipped it into the slow cooker.

She was right. She shouldn't confide in him. Worse, he shouldn't want her to.

Things would get messy—for him and Maria—if he didn't keep his distance.

Head bent, Yazmine continued stirring the soup. The mouthwatering aroma beckoned Tomás closer to peer over her shoulder. Reynaldo's invitation had mentioned stew, but this didn't smell like anything he'd eaten growing up.

"Not your regular beef and potato concoction, is it?"

"Even better. It's one of my mom's Puerto Rican specialties. *Asopao de gandules.* Pigeon pea soup."

"Smells delicious." Tomás took the spoon from her when she moved to put it down. He swirled it through the mixture, then turned in time to catch Yazmine reaching for some bowls high up in a cabinet.

Her ivory sweater crept up, treating him to a glimpse of her toned stomach above the edge of her low-rise jeans.

Now his mouth watered for a completely different reason.

His gaze traveled down the length of her legs and back up, past her elegant neck to the delicate curve of her jaw. Her dark, silky ponytail trailed over her shoulder, brushing across her breast.

Damn, if she wasn't the epitome of sexy and alluring.

He gulped, quickly turning back to stir the soup when Yazmine moved toward him, bowls in hand.

"Here." Yazmine tugged open a drawer to remove four soup spoons. She dipped one in the pot, then held it toward him with an open palm below it. "*Pruébalo.*"

He didn't think twice, his stomach urging him to follow her suggestion to taste the delicious-smelling food.

His mouth closed over the spoon, his eyes drifting shut on the burst of flavor.

"Mmmmm." He moaned his approval, and was answered by the soft sound of Yazmine sucking in a quick breath.

His eyes shot open.

She stood in front of him, one hand holding the spoon, the other cupped below his chin. He licked his lips, savoring the flavors on his tongue. Unable to resist thinking about savoring her.

The intimacy of the situation crackled around them. Strong, electric. Dangerous.

Yazmine eased back.

He swallowed slowly. Wanting more. Wondering about more. Like, would she taste as good?

Probably better. He'd lay money on it.

"What do you think?" she asked, her voice a husky rasp.

He thought he might be in trouble. Fat chance of him admitting that out loud. "I think you need to share your recipe with Mrs. B."

"Maybe I will." She dropped the used spoon in the sink with a clatter, then grabbed another one from the drawer. "If you're good."

"Depends on your definition of good." The double entendre slipped out before he could stop it.

She flashed him an impish grin. "You're incorrigible, *sabes?*"

"Yeah, I know." Not to mention a little insane.

She laughed and he found it too easy to join her. Too easy to fall into the trap of going with what felt good, instead of what was right.

Damn, he could get in a lot of trouble here.

His strategy of using this visit to stifle his attraction was in danger of failing. Miserably.

"Maybe we should get dinner on the table." He winced at the unintentional abruptness of his words.

Yazmine's smile faltered.

He softened his tone as an apology. "I meant, it's getting late. Your father's tired."

Not to mention, he wasn't making any headway in creating distance between them. On the contrary, he felt far too comfortable joking and flirting with her in the privacy of her kitchen.

Yazmine stared at him in silence. He sensed her measuring her words, measuring him.

When she finally spoke, it was with the cool demeanor she'd first greeted him with on Wednesday.

"There's juice and milk in the refrigerator. Why don't you make yourself useful and grab the drinks while I serve up the *asopao?*"

Great, he'd annoyed her again. Guilt gnawed at him, but he steeled himself against it.

Better to be on her bad side than on the receiving end of another inviting grin. Her smiles led him to forget about important things—like lines in the sand that should be left uncrossed.

* * *

"So you and your group actually recorded an album?" Tomás asked her father with surprise.

"*Sí*, at a studio in Chicago. We sold copies at our performances."

Pride for Papi swelled up in Yaz. She leaned back in one of the recliners in the library corner of the basement—Rosa's corner—listening to his and Tomás's conversation.

As soon as Tomás had asked about one of the black-and-white photographs of Papi and the other two men in Los Paisanos, she'd known the conversation would be anything but short.

If there was one thing Papi loved almost as much as his family, it was his music. His passion flowed in his words and the sparkle in his eyes.

Even though Yaz had spent the better part of the past two hours peeking at her watch, anxious for Tomás and Maria to leave, she didn't wish for that anymore. She couldn't. Not when she saw the joy in Papi's face as he spoke about his band and the gigs they'd played back in the day.

It was the same expression he wore when he talked about what he called her "unquestionable success" on the stages of New York. It was what pushed her to succeed.

"What kind of music?" Tomás asked.

"*Romanticismo*. The old standards, as they say here. Romantic ballads that have helped men woo their women for generations. It's how I won over my Marta, Yaz's *mamá*."

Tomás and her dad grinned at each other like two

buddies swapping locker room stories. Yaz rolled her eyes at the machismo.

"*Ay, pués.* It's mostly *mis compadres*, they know how to set the tempo of a party."

That was her father. Proud, yet modest.

"Well, nothing, Papi. It's not just your buddies," Yaz called out.

Side by side in front of the keyboard, flipping through pictures from different venues Los Paisanos had played over the years, Tomás and Reynaldo looked over their shoulders at her. One man older, shorter, tired, but handsome in her eyes; the other far too sexy for his own good.

Or hers, anyway.

"The group wouldn't have been the same without you and you know it," Yaz continued. "Who booked the festival gig that brought you here from Puerto Rico? And who finagled that first recording opportunity? Los Paisanos were a wonderful team, with you leading the way as much as the others. And you still are."

Tomás drew back in surprise. "So the group still plays?"

"Are you kidding me?" Yaz laughed, recalling the inside joke she'd heard throughout her childhood. "Even their wives couldn't keep them apart."

"*No, pero el cáncer si lo hizo.*" Papi's grim words instantly dulled their buoyant mood. He stepped away from the keyboard, haphazardly strumming his fingers along the strings of a nearby guitar.

"No it didn't. Papi, don't think like that. You'll be back, stronger than ever." Regret nipped at her conscience for bringing up the subject. "So you took some time off to regain your strength. Next summer you'll be serenading the crowds at Chicago's annual Puerto Rican festival again. Maybe we'll even get Rosa out there to dance, huh?"

"*Esa nena?*" Papi's laugh turned into a cough and he put a hand to his chest. "That girl never joins in. I told her she'd *have* to dance with me on her wedding day."

Yaz watched his gaze stray to Maria, his expression wistful.

Maria stood at the ballet barre Papi had installed when Yaz was little. Over the years she'd spent countless hours practicing, stretching, and honing her technique there. Oftentimes while she'd danced, Los Paisanos rehearsed and Rosa sat in a recliner reading. Mami's footsteps would sound overhead as she whipped up something tasty in the kitchen. And Lilí, the energetic tomboy, basically ran around getting into everything. Their house had been loud, full of laughter, love, and music. Always music.

"Here, let me show you how." Reynaldo shuffled over to stand next to Maria at the barre. Their reflection in the mirror-lined wall let loose a swarm of memories, stealing Yaz's breath.

How many times had Papi joined her there, teasing her with his clownish attempt at a plié? She'd looked forward to moments like this, watching him joke around with his granddaughter. Her little girl.

Only that would never happen. Not as long as she kept pursuing a career that wasn't conducive to family life and raising children. Not as long as she strove to succeed, for herself as well as him.

Years ago Papi had been forced to choose between his dreams of being in the spotlight with Los Paisanos and his responsibility to his growing family. She should have known better than to think she could have both.

Sometimes she wished her life had taken a different route. One without the pressure of living up to others' expectations. One where she felt comfortable with who and where she was.

She hoped a time would come when she could stop pretending she knew what she wanted. When she could honestly feel fully confident in her own shoes. Whatever they might be—ballet, jazz, sandals, or stilettos.

"Reynaldo is good with her."

Yaz started at Tomás's hushed observation coming from close by. Craning her neck, she looked up to find him looming over her recliner.

His genuine admiration for Papi weakened her resolve to remain aloof. No way could she *not* be attracted to a man who thought her father was as incredible as she did.

"Papi's had plenty of practice dealing with girls. But through everything, he's always been good with us."

Tomás hunkered down next to her chair.

Yaz sucked in a shallow breath, pressing back against her seat cushion. Up this close, she noticed the ring of black encircling the mahogany color of his iris. Practically felt the scruff of his five o'clock shadow. Couldn't help but breathe in his woodsy cologne.

"A guy could learn a lot from someone like your dad." Tomás smiled, his straight white teeth a contrast to his tanned skin. "He's been successful as a father and in his music career."

Guilt soured Yaz's stomach. She wasn't entirely convinced Papi would agree with Tomás's assessment.

Sometimes, when doubt took hold of her thoughts, she wondered what would have happened if she hadn't come along so soon. If Mami's pregnancy hadn't been so difficult. If Papi hadn't canceled the Los Paisanos road trip and started working for the US Postal Service. Instead of hitting the road and marketing their music, Los Paisanos wound up playing for local events and private parties. The men settled down to regular nine-to-five jobs, raising their children and families together. Creating memories of a different kind.

There were times she wondered if he thought about what might have been—if not for her.

That's why she was determined to let him live his glory days on stage vicariously through her. Any doubts she harbored about surviving in the callous dance world had to be silenced.

"Mami used to say the Island made special men. With my Papi being one of the best."

"He'd have to be to raise three daughters on his own. If your sisters are anything like you, I'd say he did his job well."

Yaz heard the smile in Tomás's voice and she glanced over in time to catch his dimple's wink.

A lightning bolt of attraction zapped through her.

She tried to shake it off, reminding herself to keep things light. "An evening of Papi's war stories, flipping through a few embarrassing family pictures, and you're an expert on me and my sisters, huh?"

Tomás's broad shoulders lifted and fell in a casual shrug. "I call it like I see it. With a mom as beautiful as yours, and a dad as vested in you, no wonder you're knocking it out of the park."

Heat rose to her face at his compliment.

In the dim coziness of the basement, with one of

Los Paisanos's CDs softly serenading them, she found herself in danger of falling for Tomás. Hard.

For the first time in weeks, her father was acting like his old self. For the first time in ages, she found herself totally relaxed. Thanks to this tantalizing man and his adorable daughter.

"Actually, you're right, my sisters are incredible women. But even they aren't as good as I am." She laughed out loud at Tomás's snort of surprise.

"I see Reynaldo's modesty didn't get passed down to you."

"Rosa inherited my share. She's the quiet one. Our kindhearted, wise little bookworm."

"And Lilí?"

"The wild one. Finally showing vague signs of responsibility." Yaz scooted over to let Tomás crook his elbow on her armrest. "She's an undergrad sophomore, majoring in Women's Studies."

"*¿De veras?*" Tomás slowly drew out the words.

"Yeah, truth. Why the surprise?" Sensing his genuine interest, Yaz angled closer. It was fun introducing him to her family.

"More like, admiration. I mean, wow! A spirited dancer, a quiet sage, and a spunky people person. I don't know how your father managed after your mom passed. There are days I'm overwhelmed with one and I have Mrs. B to help."

Tomás's honesty humbled her.

Yaz ducked her head, wondering if she'd misjudged him. The first day they'd met, she'd grouped him in with her ex—both self-centered workaholics. But the more time she spent with Tomás, the more she witnessed his interaction with Maria, the more she second-guessed her first impression.

Her gaze strayed to Papi and Maria. They faced each other, one hand on the barre, as they slowly bent in a deep plié.

"I used to do this with Yazmine when she was little," Papi said. "It is how I kept in such good shape." He patted his well-fed belly.

Maria covered her mouth with her free hand and dissolved into giggles.

"You should go join them," Yaz urged Tomás. "She'll get a kick out of it."

He sent her a dubious glance.

"I'm serious. Look at her."

Maria's tiny shoulders shook with laughter at Papi's silliness.

"As much as I hate to admit it"—Tomás tugged on Yaz's ponytail and rose from his haunches—"you may be right."

"Was there ever any doubt?"

He raised a hand to point two fingers at his eyes, then back at her in the age-old "I'm watching you" sign. With a sexy quirk of his mouth, he sidled away.

Shivers of awareness shimmied her shoulders as she watched him. She'd warned herself at the dance store yesterday that she was playing with fire.

This man was good. Just not good for her.

Leaning back against the recliner cushion, Yaz closed her eyes and took a deep, cleansing breath. Desperate to soothe the wistful ache in her chest. She knew what she had to do, and what type of sacrifices it required.

Suddenly Maria let out a surprised yelp.

"I got you!"

Yaz's eyes snapped opened at Tomás's exclamation.

When she saw his arms around Papi, carefully helping him to the keyboard bench, she sprang out of her chair. "¿*Qué pasa?*"

"Nothing's going on," Papi answered. "I stepped awkwardly and twisted my ankle, *eso es todo.*"

"Are you sure that's all? You look pale."

Maria laid a hand on his knee. "Are you okay, Señor Fernandez?"

He gave her a reassuring pat. "*Sí, nena.* I'm okay."

Papi slowly reached into his back pocket for his handkerchief, blotting his face with a shaky hand. The fear that had haunted Yaz through the previous weeks rose out of the shadows once again.

"It's getting late. We should be heading home." Tomás's deep voice broke the tremulous silence. "Yazmine, will you please help Maria with her jacket upstairs? Rey can rest a minute while I convince him to sell me a Los Paisanos CD."

Yaz's gaze moved from her father's pallid face, to Maria's scared expression, to Tomás's strong figure.

He must have sensed her hesitation because Tomás jerked his head toward the basement stairs.

"Here, give me a hug goodnight." Papi opened his arms for Maria. "You will have to come see me again, soon."

"*Gracias.* I had fun dancing with you." Maria gave Papi a hug, then stepped back and slipped her tiny hand into Yazmine's. Together they turned toward the stairs.

"We'll be right behind you, Yaz, no worries," Tomás assured her.

It was the first time he'd used her nickname, as if

they were friends. Yaz nodded, finding herself once again grateful for his presence.

Once they reached the foyer, she forced herself to concentrate on zipping up Maria's jacket. Worrying about Papi had become second nature to her—maybe she was reading more into the situation than it warranted.

Everything was fine with him. It had to be.

Tomás slid a bar stool closer to where Reynaldo sat on the keyboard bench. "Forgive me for asking, but are you sure you only twisted your ankle?"

Rey hadn't stumbled so much as wilted. Like someone had flipped a circuit breaker, knocking out all his energy.

The older man nodded, but didn't say anything else, despite Tomás's intense scrutiny.

Tomás bit back a frustrated sigh; he'd hoped Rey would confide in him. Tonight, getting to know Yaz's father had reminded him of how much he missed spending time with his own dad. The two older men shared a deep devotion to their family and culture, not to mention a strong work ethic.

Several quiet beats passed before Tomás recognized another similarity—pride. The Achilles' heel of many Latino men, himself included. It would take an act of God to get them to admit a weakness.

Wise enough to know when to push and when to ease off, Tomás relented. Still, the creed *familia primero* flashed through his mind.

Family first. The saying he'd heard since his childhood, handed down from generation to generation. In the Latino community, family included close friends and neighbors. Like Yaz and Reynaldo had become tonight.

Tomás pulled out his wallet to hand Rey his business card. "Here, hang on to this. If there's anything you need, doesn't matter what it is, you let me know, okay?"

"*Gracias. Te lo agradezco.*"

Tomás shrugged off the thanks and appreciation. "I mean it. Anything at all."

Rey stared down at the card, answering with a slow nod.

"If you're up for it, I say we get moving before Yaz comes looking for us. She's not one to back down, is she?" Tomás put a hand under Reynaldo's elbow to help him up.

"I see you are getting to know her well. That stubborn streak she has comes from my Marta." Rey groaned as he stood up. "You have to be patient with her. That's all."

As they climbed the stairs, Tomás admitted he'd need something other than patience when it came to Yaz. More like, the self-discipline to resist her charms, especially if Rey asked for his help. For his and Maria's sake, he couldn't afford to make a wrong move.

At the top of the stairs they found Yaz and Maria peering at a group of framed photographs. When he drew closer, Tomás realized it was a collection of *Playbill*s and photographs from Yaz's New York productions.

His gaze caught on a candid photo of Yaz with a well-known actress. Both wore figure-hugging cocktail dresses and heels. They stood at a theatre entrance, arms around each other's waist, faces lit by their bright smiles. A crowd of fans swarmed behind them, pens held out for autographs, cameras ready for candid shots.

Here it was, barely two feet from the front door, proof of his and Yaz's unsuitability. The irony sucker-punched him.

The photo collage was a reality check to keep him from making the same mistake he'd made with Kristine. To stop him from heading off on another attraction-fueled drive with a woman more interested in racing on a fast track headed in the opposite direction.

He waved good-bye to Yaz and Rey amid Maria's cry of "See you soon," wondering how the hell he'd gotten himself into this mess.

After getting to know Rey and making a commitment that he could be relied upon if needed, staying away from Yazmine, not thinking about her, might prove next to impossible.

Chapter Six

"Did you and Cheryl have fun shopping today?" Rosa asked.

Yaz looked up to find her sister setting the last of the dirty dinner dishes next to the sink for her to wash.

"Black Friday at the mall was a madhouse." Yaz finished rinsing a glass and put it on the drain board. "The best part was sitting in Starbucks catching up. I'm excited Cheryl's moving back. Though I hate that breaking up with her boyfriend is why she decided to come home."

"*Que pena*," Rosa murmured.

"Yeah, it is a shame," Yaz answered. "But good for her for moving on if he can't recognize how great she is."

"I hear you, and I'm all happy you two had some girl time, but what I *really* wanna know is . . ." Lilí sidled over, her eyebrows waggling with mischief. "Who's this Tomás Garcia guy Papi keeps talking about?"

Yaz cringed, nearly dropping the soapy glass she held. *Ay Dios mío*, she wanted her sisters poking around about Tomás as much as she wanted the bright lights of Broadway to darken.

"He's nobody." Her pulse skipped at the lie. "His daughter's a student at Hanson's. Papi and I ran into them at the park the other day."

"Since when do you invite students and their stud-muffin dads over for dinner?" Lilí playfully bumped hips with her before swiveling to put away a stack of dried salad plates.

"It was Papi's idea." Yaz pointedly ignored the "stud-muffin" comment. No need to add fuel to Lilí's nosy fire. Her sister had been itching to pair Yaz up with someone new since the whole Victor debacle had blown up. "Believe me, I wouldn't have invited the man over if it was up to me."

"Oh really?" Rosa asked, the words sounding more like the "aha!" of a private eye discovering a closely guarded secret. Though really, in her soft blue turtleneck sweater, loose-fitting gray slacks, and low-heeled black Steve Madden boots, Rosa looked more like Nancy Drew than Sherlock Holmes.

"Don't go reading anything into it," Yaz answered. "Tomás Garcia is a moody workaholic with a cute five-year-old daughter in need of mothering. Not exactly my cup of *café con leche*."

"'Methinks the lady doth protest too much.'" Rosa's crossed arms and speculative narrowed gaze had tremblings of unease tickling the back of Yazmine's neck.

"*Por favor*, I am not a heroine in one of your Shakespeare tragedies, waiting for you to character analyze me."

"Touchy, touchy." Lilí swatted Yaz's butt with the dish towel, then plopped down on a wooden chair at the kitchen table. She propped her booted foot on her seat, her bent knee poking out of a hole in her ripped jeans. "I sorta think I'm with Rosa on this one."

Yaz glared at her younger sister. Traitor.

"I know, hang a banner from the rafters." Lilí spread her hands through the air in front of her, emphasizing her point. "Rosa and Lilí actually agree on something. *Imposible.* Ouch!" She rubbed her arm from Rosa's pinch. "Hey, you're supposed to be on my side, remember? She's about to crack."

"Crack schmack. There's no story here." Yaz dropped a handful of clean silverware into the drain board with a clatter. "Quit jabbering and finish your job."

"I don't knooow," Lilí sing-songed, her spiked pixie haircut and Cheshire cat–grin highlighting her impish personality. "Inviting a babe over for dinner isn't like you. Dance has always come first. Well, except for jerky Victor—but we won't go there." She waved a hand as if shooing a pesky fly. "So who's the hottie and how serious are you?"

Yaz pulled the drain plug in the sink. The gurgle of water being sucked down the pipe made her wish she could pull the plug on this conversation as easily.

Leave it to Papi to stir things up with her sisters. Over the past two days, every time she'd tried to broach the subject of his health, he'd counter by saying something about his new "good" friend Tomás.

"Earth to Yazmine." Rosa waved an arm in the air, drawing Yaz's attention. "What's on your mind?"

"Or better yet, who? Come on, girl." Lilí slapped her hands together, then rubbed them briskly, warming up to her pestering. "I'm in between guys at the moment, so throw me a bone. *Por favor, chica,* cough up the details. I want 'em all, especially the raunchy ones."

Leaning back against the sink, Yaz wagged a finger

at her little sister. "You are too sassy for your own good, girl."

Lilí's grin widened.

"Knock it off." Rosa scowled at Lilí, then turned to Yaz, her expression earnest. "Seriously, it's good to see you showing some interest in dating again."

"I'm not."

"Ever since you broke off your engagement to Victor and came home," Rosa continued, ignoring Yaz's objections, "you've been . . . I don't know, different. You barely talk about what happened."

"There's nothing to tell." Or that she cared to admit.

Rosa frowned, her concern evident in the pinch of her lips.

Yaz knew her sister meant well. Rosa always thought about making others happy. Doing her best to make sure all was right in the world.

That wasn't always possible though. Not in Yazmine's world anyway.

Her heart raced, guilt and disillusion pounding a bongo drum beat in her chest at her sisters' persistence.

No way she'd confess that, after finding Victor in bed with one of their show's producers, followed by his spiteful but well-placed taunts, so much of what she believed about herself stood in question.

Between their studies and Papi's health scare, her sisters had enough on their plates already.

She had to figure out a way to get over her hang-ups on her own. When she went back to the city, she'd only have herself to rely on anyway.

"Are you sure you're okay?" Rosa pressed.

The kindness in her sister's brown eyes, that keen maternal instinct so like their mom's, had Yaz nearly giving in to the overwhelming urge to lean on Rosa for support.

Yaz wouldn't though. She was the oldest, and Rosa had been the caregiver for far too long after their mother's death. Now it was Yaz's time to be the strong one.

Frustrated with herself, she snatched up the dish sponge and started wiping off the counters. It didn't hurt that doing so also helped her avoid Rosa's intuitive gaze. Her sister was going to make a damn fine high school librarian when she graduated in May. She'd be someone the kids could rely on for advice and guidance. Someone who was always there. Unlike Yaz.

"Yazmine—"

"Victor and I are over. And that's a good thing," she interrupted Rosa. His last barb about her not having what it took to succeed may have knocked her knees out from under her, but at least the scumbag was gone from her life. "Now I can concentrate on my career when I head back. That's all I need."

Out of the corner of her eye she caught Rosa slowly shaking her head, her sister's face pinched with disappointment. "I still say you're holding out on us."

Even Lilí, normally too busy moving at a mile a minute to notice the details around her, eyed Yaz with an appraising look. Apparently college was helping her baby sister grow up. Take things more seriously. Too bad she had to start with Yazmine's troubles.

"*Están locas*," Yaz muttered, irritation pushing her tone toward sulky.

"We're not crazy," Rosa countered. "Even before Victor showed his true colors, you didn't seem happy. Not to me anyway. That's why I didn't push to be the one who came home to care for Papi."

"And give up your scholarship?" Yaz snared the

kitchen towel off of Lilí's shoulder, drying her hands and joining them at the table. "I don't think so."

"And who made you the decision maker for all of us?"

"Excuse me?" Yaz blinked in surprise at Rosa's impassioned tone.

"I'm the one who kept the house running after Mami died." Rosa pressed a hand to her chest. "Lilí was too young and you were too busy with dance."

"I know." Yaz shared a nod of agreement with Lilí, confused by the flush in Rosa's cheeks, the pain darkening her sister's eyes. "You took on a lot back then. Maybe too much."

"I didn't mind because it's what I'm good at, making sure everyone's taken care of. That's why I should have been here when Papi needed someone. Not you."

Stark vulnerability flashed across Rosa's features before she tucked her chin, dropping her gaze to her clasped hands. Her shoulder-length, wavy, black hair slid forward to brush her cheek, shielding her expression from view.

Yaz shot Lilí a what's-going-on-here look.

Lilí shrugged, answering with her own wide-eyed, beats-me expression.

Several seconds of tense silence ticked by and Yaz was still at a loss for what to do or say.

Finally, Rosa heaved a deep sigh. She stabbed a hand through her hair, combing it out of her face. "I'm sorry. I shouldn't have said anything."

"Yes, you should. If something's bothering you, tell me."

"Never mind. If being here with Papi helps you deal with whatever happened in New York, whatever you're *not* sharing, then you needed to come home. Only—" Rosa reached across the table to grasp Yazmine's and Lilí's hands. "You three are all I have. I need you to be okay."

Rosa's mouth trembled, tears glistening in her dark eyes.

Yaz blinked several times, trying to clear her own blurring vision. Fighting the lump shoving its way up her throat to choke her.

Dios, how she wanted to confide in her sisters. Admit that she wasn't sure of anything anymore. That part of her was afraid maybe Victor was right and she didn't have what it took to make it in New York.

Shame kept her from saying the words out loud.

"I agree," Lilí chimed in. "You haven't really been yourself. And if you ask me, it's all because of that *sinvergüenza* Victor. N-n-no!" She held up a palm to stop Rosa's reprimand at her curse. "You know it's true. He had *no* shame. I say, good riddance to the jackass."

Lilí skewered Yaz with a surprisingly authoritative stare. One Yaz had often used to keep her younger sister in line over the years. Damn that girl for turning the tables on her now.

"*Pero nena*, that doesn't mean you crawl into a cave and let him win," Lilí continued. "For nearly two years now your life has revolved around taking care of Papi and teaching at Hanson's. When was the last time you had any fun, girl? More importantly, when was the last time you had any sex?"

"Lilí!" Rosa said on a shocked gasp.

"Oh, please, don't be such a prude." Lilí scowled at their middle sister. "Yaz needs to jump back on the horse and get that jerk out of her system. This Tomás guy sounds like he might work. It's not healthy for a woman to ignore those needs. Even if she's taking care of them herself."

"*¡Ay Dios mío!*" Rosa groaned, rolling her eyes.

Yaz laughed. Leave it to Lilí to cut the tension in the room with something outrageous. "I won't dignify that question with an answer."

"*Gracias*," Rosa muttered.

"Yeah, right, let's not offend your delicate sensibilities." Lilí's grumbled complaint set off the typical round of verbal sparring.

"Why are you always so uptight?" she complained.

"Why can't you behave more responsibly?" Rosa countered.

"Hey, hey, hey!" Yaz raised her voice to get their attention.

These same questions had been bandied back and forth between her sisters for years, but they didn't have time for squabbling now. "You two'll have to argue later. There are more important things we need to discuss. Something's going on with Papi. And you two have to help me get him to talk.

"Papi, don't be mad at us," Yaz pleaded. She laid a plate with scrambled eggs and toast in front of him early Monday morning, then eased down next to him, hoping to make him see reason.

"*Sí.*" Rosa nodded from her seat across the dining room table. "We're worried about you, that's all."

"You do not have to be," he assured them. "And I am not mad. Certainly, I did not appreciate you ganging up on me before Lilí left yesterday. And I do not want you missing class today, Rosa. You will leave right after breakfast."

"I will."

"Good. Now I will admit, Dr. Lopez told me I should talk with you girls. So did Tomás."

"Dr. Lopez is right," Rosa said. "Papi, you can't keep—"

"Wait, did you say Tomás?" Yaz broke in, surprised his name had even come up. "What does he have to do with this?"

"He asked me when we spoke on the phone the other day. Like I said, he is a smart one, that boy. I enjoyed his company, didn't you?"

Papi picked up his fork and took a bite of his eggs.

Yazmine's gaze connected with Rosa's, her thoughts immediately jumping back to the conversation with her sisters Friday evening. Lilí's "get back on that horse" speech taunted her.

"He called the day after Thanksgiving to see how I was doing," Papi said when he finished swallowing. "Like I say, *es un hombre bueno*. You should meet him, Rosa."

"I'm sure he is a good man," Rosa said, ignoring Yaz's shake of her head. "If you like him, I bet I will, too."

Yaz scowled at her sister. Brown-noser.

"He and the little one should have returned yesterday," Papi continued. "Maybe they can come again this weekend. Invite them when they are at Hanson's for Maria's lessons, okay, Yazmine?"

Great, so now it seemed like Tomás was Papi's new buddy. Soon he'd be hanging out with all the other *compadres*.

Her stomach clenched at the idea. Tomás was too much of a distraction. Too much of a reminder of what she couldn't have if she followed Papi's dreams to New York.

"It's nice that he called you, *pero . . .*"

"But what? Is there a problem?"

Yaz swallowed an exasperated groan. "Yes, Papi, there is. Now stop trying to change the subject. The girls and I are worried about the tests you said Dr. Lopez plans to run. What exactly is going on?"

A lump of fear and unshed tears lodged in her throat. She turned to Rosa, hoping for some backup. Lilí had left for Southern Illinois University the day before only because it was a five-hour drive and she had an eight a.m. class this morning, but she'd gotten in her car begging them to get straight answers from Papi. All he'd admitted so far was that Dr. Lopez had some concerns so they were running more tests.

"Look, it could be nothing, right? As soon as we get the results, we'll ask Dr. Lopez what treatment he recommends." Rosa tucked her hair behind her ears, her earnest gaze and matter-of-fact tone as usual calming Yaz's unease. "We're going to beat it. For good this time."

"*No, nena.*" Papi wiped his mouth with a napkin, then reached for his mango juice. "I am done fighting."

"What?"

"Papi, no!" Yaz's cry of alarm mixed with Rosa's.

They exchanged a panicked glance.

"The chemotherapy, the sickness, the fatigue. If the cancer is back, I cannot go through that again. I will not put you girls through it either. It is not worth it."

The finality in his tone filled Yaz's entire body with dread.

"*Por favor*, don't do this." She grasped Papi's forearm,

desperate to hold on to him as long as she could. "I won't let you give up."

"None of us will," Rosa added.

Yaz was certain the stark fear on her sister's face mirrored her own.

"I am not giving up," Papi answered matter-of-factly. He glanced from Rosa to her, his stern expression meant to silence their argument. Like when they'd been moody adolescents complaining about a decision he'd made that they didn't agree with. They hadn't won those arguments either. "I choose to enjoy the time I have left in peace. That is all."

"*Pero*—"

"But nothing." Papi cut off her argument, his tone firm, unyielding. "I told you girls yesterday, this is my decision. I am not going to put my body through that again. *No vale la pena.*"

"Of course it's worth it," Yaz argued. "How can you say that? You can't give up. It's like, like you're choosing to leave us." Tears rasped in her voice, threatening to spill down her cheeks.

Angry—with herself for not being able to reach him, with her father for rolling over—Yaz pushed back her chair to stand.

Papi grabbed her wrist to stop her. Despite the fatigue he constantly battled, his grip remained strong.

"*Ay, nena*, do not be like this. I am not 'choosing' to leave you. I love you girls. You have been my salvation since your *mamá* died." Rosa hiccuped on a sob and Papi turned to her. "*Por favor, entiéndanme*—I need you to understand me. I am tired of fighting the way the doctors fight."

Yazmine's heart ached at the exhaustion slumping his proud shoulders. The despair weighing down Rosa's features. No man should be forced to make a decision like his. No daughter should have to stand by and watch him suffer.

"Papi," Yaz pleaded, falling to her knees at his feet. Desperate for him to stay strong.

Without him . . . *Ay*, she couldn't even begin to think about it.

Papi gave her the strength to follow the path he had paved for her. When thoughts of not being good enough plagued her, his guidance and belief in her talents lifted her up. Gave her wings to soar.

Without him she didn't know who she was, where she fit in.

The pain of loss consumed every part of her until it was all she could see, feel, taste. Anguish stole the fight from her and she laid her head in his lap with a muffled sob.

"*Ay, nena.*" Papi combed a hand gently through her hair, then he nudged her chin for her to look up at him. He stared into her eyes, gifting her with the love in his heart. "Your life has been on hold for too long because of me."

"There isn't any other place I'd rather be. You need me. Together we can beat this." She stared back, willing him to agree with her, choosing to do all he could to beat this insidious disease.

Instead, he offered her a gentle smile. The patient, loving expression he'd blessed her with countless times throughout her life smoothed the lines of his handsome face. "We can celebrate the life I have left. We will all be together again in two and a half weeks for the Christmas holiday. Dr. Lopez will have more information by then. *Si Dios quiere—*"

"I don't care what God wants." Yaz sat back on her haunches with a huff.

Rosa flinched, her hand moving in a quick sign of the cross.

"Don't say that," Papi admonished. "What would your *mamá* think? We taught you better than that. Now, whatever happens, I want to spend my time enjoying *mis chancletas.*"

She shared a bittersweet smile with him at the Puerto Rican nickname for girls whose fathers only had daughters. "We're not your 'little sandals' anymore, Papi."

"I know. You're all grown up. With opinions of your own."

Yaz wrinkled her nose at his disgruntled tone.

"Lilí is doing well in school. I pray she may finally find the path that will make her happy." Papi nodded slowly, turning his attention to Rosa. "And you, next fall you will finally take your place at Queen of Peace Academy. Yazmine—" He cupped her cheek. "You have stalled your career for too long. I am afraid you are not happy, *nena.*"

"Me?" Her pulse skipped with anxiety.

She tried so hard to keep her insecurities hidden. The last thing she wanted was to put more stress on her father. He needed his strength to beat this cancer.

"You don't have to worry about me. I'm New York bound." That'd been her signature remark since before Cheryl and her other high school friends had started their college searches. Before her insecurities had taken root. Before Victor's harsh rebukes had seared her with doubts. "I'll take the town by storm, just like we've always planned. Success, for both of us."

"I have had my success—your mother, you girls.

Playing with Los Paisanos." Papi took hold of her shoulders. "Nursing me through another chemotherapy treatment that does not work will not help you find your place."

"Right now, it's here with you. Help—"

The house phone rang, cutting off her argument. Rosa glanced at her watch. "It's probably Lilí in between classes. I don't know why she's not calling my cell."

"You girls and your henpecking." Papi bit into his toast with a grimace.

"But you love us anyway." Yaz gave his knee a love pat and stood. "And don't think we won't keep trying to change your mind. Or ask Dr. Lopez to talk some sense into you."

He muttered something under his breath as she reached for the cordless receiver hanging on the kitchen wall. "Hello?"

"Yazmine?"

Yaz paused under the arch connecting the kitchen to the dining room. Her thoughts were so tuned in to the argument with Papi it took her a moment to place the voice. "Tomás?"

"I hope I didn't catch you at a bad time. I'm dealing with a little emergency at the moment."

"Is everything okay with Maria?"

"No, no, Maria's fine. Sorry, I didn't mean to alarm you."

Yaz heard a car honking through the phone line before Tomás spoke again.

"It's Mrs. Buckley. Her daughter is pregnant and they had to rush her to the hospital in Seattle. I'm trying to get Mrs. B on the next flight out, but I have a huge potential client coming in this afternoon and the nanny service can't send someone over until tomorrow."

Yazmine's heart stalled. She knew Tomás's next words before he uttered them.

"Would you be able to pick Maria up from school and keep an eye on her for a little while this afternoon? I know it's an imposition. But you're my last hope."

Yaz cleared her throat, aware of her father's and Rosa's speculative gaze. "You only need someone to watch Maria today?"

"The agency said they'd get back to me about a replacement by the close of business. I know you're busy. If I had any other alternative . . ."

"Is something wrong, *nena*?" Papi asked.

"It's Tomás," she said, quickly explaining the situation.

"Go, do not worry about me," Papi said when she finished.

"I can stay until tomorrow," Rosa offered.

"*No*, you will not miss your classes. Already you should be starting your drive back to Champagne. I am okay," Papi assured them. "A friend needs help, so we help. *¿Verdad?*"

Of course, he was right.

So what if that friend pushed her buttons. Especially ones she'd deliberately put on pause after Victor. She'd be fine.

Closing her eyes, Yaz plunged ahead. "Okay. I can stay with Maria."

Tomás's sigh of relief gave her a measure of peace that she'd made the right decision. "Great. I owe you. Mrs. B is beside herself with worry about leaving Maria, but her own daughter has to come first right now. I'm on my way home to pick up Mrs. B so I can drive her to the airport."

"What's your address and I'll be right over."

Tomás rattled off directions to his house, then hung up.

As the line went dead, Yaz prayed she hadn't made another mistake.

"So you will go help Tomás and Maria," Papi said, once Yaz replaced the phone on its charger. "It is good that he called you."

Yaz wasn't so sure about that, but she didn't have time for second-guessing.

She gave Papi a quick kiss on the cheek, warning him their conversation wasn't over. Rosa opened her arms for a fierce hug.

"I'll be in touch," Yaz whispered in her sister's ear. "You drive safely."

Moments later she was in her car, heading toward Tomás's house, mind boggled by how she kept getting tangled up with him.

Over the Thanksgiving break she'd tried her damnedest to keep the handsome father out of her thoughts. Not an easy feat when faced with Papi's praise for his new "buddy" and her sisters' pointed questions about the guy.

So much for keeping her distance outside of the dance studio. Instead, she had foolishly asked the lion for detailed directions leading straight to his den.

Chapter Seven

Tomás eased his BMW into his garage, feeling like he'd gone ten rounds with Muhammad Ali instead of a slightly pudgy, aging yet sharp-witted CEO. He rolled his shoulders, easing away their tension.

What he needed was a little quiet time with Maria followed by something he could easily nuke in the microwave for dinner. Add a glass of wine and maybe he'd finally be able to relax.

First, he needed to iron out the babysitting details with Yaz. The thought of that stressful conversation made the knot of tension in his neck tighten all over again.

He'd called Yaz as soon as the agency had let him know they couldn't get someone full-time out here for a few more days. Thankfully she'd agreed to fill in.

Now, his feet dragging, he opened the garage door and stepped into the dimly lit kitchen. Silence greeted him.

"*¿Hola?*"

He glanced at the neon numbers on the stove's glossy black display panel: 8:45. Damn, fifteen minutes past Maria's bedtime. He'd counted on her still being up. Especially with her knack of bargaining for more time, asking for one more book.

Unless . . .

With her favorite dance instructor on nanny duty, no doubt Maria was on her best behavior.

Leaving his wool coat and briefcase on the kitchen island, Tomás strode through the formal dining room, then skirted the navy leather couch in the family room, loosening his tie along the way.

"Hello?" he called out again.

"Yay, Papá's home!" Maria's high-pitched voice rang out from the back of the house.

He grinned, catching a whiff of her bubblegum-scented soap when he passed the hall bath.

As he neared the end of the hall he heard their chatter, a different sound from the usual one that greeted him at the end of the day. Mrs. B's wheezing laugh didn't call to him like Yazmine's husky chuckle. He pictured Yaz's enticing grin and his gut tightened.

Pausing outside Maria's door, he peeked around the corner into her little girl sanctuary.

Fresh from a bath, wearing her Little Mermaid pajama dress, Maria nestled comfortably under her Pepto-pink princess comforter. Her dark curls were the perfect halo for her angelic face.

That quickly, the stress of the day melted off him like butter on a hot tortilla.

This is why he worked so hard. Why he stopped at nothing to be the best at his agency, landing the long-shot deals that brought in the big bucks. Anything to afford him the opportunity to come home to his precious little girl and find her happy and healthy. Unburdened by financial strain, and the stigma of its brand.

"*Buenas noches, señoritas.*" He eased into the room, grinning like a fool at Maria's whoop of joy.

"Oooh, you're in time for another story!" she squealed, clapping her hands with glee.

"Did Mrs. B get off okay?" Yaz looked up at him from where she knelt on the floor in front of a corner bookshelf. Barefoot, dressed in skinny jeans and a red form-fitting sweater, her hair falling in a satiny, black sheath to the center of her back, she looked comfortable, at home. Inviting.

His blood instantly heated.

He nodded mutely in answer to her question, not trusting his voice.

"Good." Two books in hand, Yaz padded over to sit on the edge of the bed. She finger-combed Maria's hair out of her eyes, and his child looked up at her with an adoring expression.

Tomás relaxed against the doorjamb. It felt so natural, watching the two of them together, as if Yaz reading a bedtime story with Maria was an everyday occurrence.

Only it wasn't. And with her resolve to move back to New York City it never could be.

He flinched at the reminder.

Don't get too used to this.

Across the room, Yaz tilted her head as she brushed her hair off her shoulder, exposing the length of her elegant neck. A primal urge to taste her olive skin, feel her pulse on his lips, nearly knocked him to his knees. He pressed his shoulder against the door frame, determined not to move.

"Any news on Mrs. B's daughter?" Yaz asked.

"Uh, not yet. I haven't gotten an update."

He tugged his tie off and unbuttoned his top button, itching to move closer to the bed, to her.

"How come she didn't called us, like we do when we get home from Abuela's?" Maria fluffed her blankets, scooting over to make more room for Yaz next to her.

"She did, on my cell phone. But she was hurrying to get to the hospital, *m'ija*," he said. "Now, how about you? Did you have a good day with Ms. Yazmine?"

Maria bobbed her head with enthusiasm, setting her black curls bouncing. Her eyes lit up as she began regaling him with the story of an afternoon split between baking cookies at Yaz's house and practicing at the dance studio.

"And then Señor Fernandez said I made the bestest chocolate chip cookies he ever tasted! I told him he had to try Mrs. B's when she gets back."

Maria continued jabbering away, and for the first time all day he felt a measure of relief. As far as she was concerned, nothing earth-shattering had happened. Mrs. Buckley had simply left for a trip and Yaz had stepped into their nanny's shoes. No big deal.

"*Vente*, Papá, read with us." Maria gave her bed a pat.

His gaze strayed from Maria to Yaz, perched on the right side of his daughter's bed, Dr. Seuss's *One Fish, Two Fish, Red Fish, Blue Fish* in her lap.

The two olive-skinned, dark-haired beauties looked like mother and daughter, snuggling in a warm bed, enjoying quality time together. A bedtime story. Nightly prayers. Shared hugs. A cocoon of family love.

His *mamá*'s usual nagging for him to find a wife to warm his bed and help raise Maria mocked him.

All he had to do was join them and the picture would be complete.

Complete, but a lie. Their situation was temporary. Yaz was here as a favor. Nothing more. He couldn't afford to let himself forget that.

"Come on," Maria repeated.

Self-preservation kept his shoulder glued to the doorjamb. "That's okay. Three's too crowded. It's almost time for Ms. Yazmine to head home anyway."

He forced a smile, trying to soften what had inadvertently come out sounding more like a dismissal. Probably because his mom's words kept goading him. Torn between accepting his daughter's innocent invitation and maintaining his distance from the one woman who threatened to scale his defenses, he'd come across like an ass.

Yaz stared at him for a moment, questions flashing from her dark eyes. Then her smile faded, a curtain of reserve draping across her face.

"You know what, *mamita*?" Yaz brushed a hand over Maria's curls again, and then rose from the bed. "Your dad has been waiting all day for his special time with you. I'm going to let you two snuggle before bed."

"Will you be here in the morning?" Anxiety touched the edges of Maria words.

"Um, I think so." The glance Yaz sent Tomás let him know she harbored some doubt. "But I'm always only a phone call away. Remember I put my cell number on the fridge, okay?"

Maria nodded solemnly, no sign of her enthusiasm from moments ago.

"*Buenas noches*. Sleep tight." Yaz pressed a kiss to Maria's forehead.

Tomás angled his body, making room for her to pass when she reached him. It wasn't enough. Yaz's arm brushed against his chest as she walked by. Fire flashed through him.

"Excuse me," she murmured.

The touch of disappointment in her voice pricked his conscience. He hadn't meant to hurt her feelings, merely protect himself and his daughter.

"Yaz, wait."

She paused several steps away from him, but she didn't turn around.

"I didn't mean to upset you."

"She's been asking about you since dinner. Tuck her in. I'll wait in the kitchen so we can talk."

She continued down the hall without waiting for his response—her shoulders stiff, her steps purposeful. Still, he couldn't help noticing the seductive sway of her hips.

Tomás bit back a frustrated sigh.

What was it about this woman that continuously knocked him off kilter? Erasing whatever good sense he'd managed to acquire over the years.

Hell, he'd been lauded for his people skills, praised for his ability to sweet-talk the toughest of clients. Yet with Yaz, he couldn't seem to stop sticking his foot in his mouth.

She had pitched in today without any qualms. The right way to thank her did not include making her feel uncomfortable.

He moved to go after her, intent on apologizing again.

"You ready, Papá?"

Maria's call stopped him.

This is where he should be. With her. Not following a woman who tempted him without even trying.

"For you, *princesa*, always." He stepped across the tiara-shaped throw rug in the center of her room. "What are we reading tonight?"

The bed dipped as he sat down and Maria leaned over to rest her head on his chest.

Tomás closed his eyes, letting the day's stress seep out of him.

Right now, with his daughter safely cuddled in his arms, her bubblegum-scented shampoo floating up to him, he could almost pretend that everything was right in his world.

He hugged Maria tighter. Time with her never failed to recharge his battery, soothe his soul. More importantly, it kept him focused on his priorities as he reached for the life he wanted for them.

So his family portrait wasn't necessarily the one he'd envisioned years ago. Maybe the sexy temptress waiting for him out front belonged on a different canvas. None of that should matter. He couldn't allow it to.

Alone in the kitchen, Yaz refilled her glass with cold water from the refrigerator dispenser. The stream of liquid flowing into her cup was the only sound in the dimly lit room, making the thoughts clamoring for attention in her head obscenely loud.

Fifteen minutes ago she'd been content, happy even, sitting alongside Maria, surrounded by her pink frilly bedsheets. Then Tomás had shown up, his tie loosened, his hair mussed after a hectic day. His face tired, but his grin still electric.

Suddenly she'd been swamped by a contrast of emotions.

Desire, for this man who, despite his workaholic reputation, seemed to truly care about his kid.

Peace, at the idea that she could really belong in his home, caring for his precious child.

Fear, that for her, a life like this was impossible.

Her head and her heart had gotten caught up in the undertow of feelings, unsure which way was up and which was down. Or which emotion she could trust, if any.

Ultimately, she'd seen the discomfort in Tomás's eyes when Maria had asked him to join them and reality had barged in to crash her pajama party.

She had no business playing house with Tomás and his daughter. She knew better.

The sound of Tomás's shoes on the hardwood floor signaled his approach.

Yaz stayed near the fridge on the far side of the kitchen, leaving the island as a barrier between her and the doorway. Reminding her of the distance she needed to keep from Tomás.

For all their sakes.

"Did you get her settled down?" she asked when he entered.

"Out like a light."

"She reminds me of Lilí at her age. A ball of energy always on the go."

Tomás chuckled, the deep rasp brushing against her keenly tuned nerve-endings. "Yeah, she keeps me on my toes."

Their hushed tones lent an air of intimacy to their conversation. One she tried to ignore.

"I appreciate you being here tonight," he said, opening a cabinet and reaching for a glass. "Sorry for being so late. It happens from time to time, and my meeting couldn't be rescheduled."

"Not a problem. I knew what I was getting into when I agreed to help. Did you hear back from the nanny agency about a fill-in?"

"It's a little dicey."

Tomás dragged a stool out with his foot and sat down with a sigh. Moonlight filtered in through the window above the sink, casting shadows throughout the room and leaving his figure in sharp relief. "They have a variety of nannies who can take turns for the next few days, but they don't want to commit a full-time fill-in until I know when Mrs. B will be back. Problem is, I really don't want Maria dealing with a revolving door of new people."

Yaz leaned back against the fridge, considering their options. Knowing what she wanted to offer, afraid to say the words.

She took a deep breath, then stepped off the cliff. "Why don't I watch Maria until we know what's up with Mrs. B?"

"I don't know . . ." Tomás speared a hand through his hair, leaving it more mussed than before. "It might be more than a few days."

"I don't mind."

"I know today threw off your regular schedule."

"It's okay. We made it work."

For some reason Yaz didn't want to delve into, it felt vitally important that he allow her to do this. That he have the confidence in her to trust her with Maria.

Tomás rose from his stool and stepped toward her. "It's a lot to ask. I owe you already."

"You do. So say yes."

"You want me to pay you back by asking you to keep disrupting your life to care for my daughter?"

"*Sí.*"

He stopped less than a foot away from her.

Yaz gazed up at him, straining to read his expression in the darkness. That crazy side of her, the one she silenced more often than not, cried out for him to keep moving. Come closer.

The quiet of night. The intimate atmosphere. The dappled moonlight filtering through the window casting muted shadows around them. It all created the perfect romantic setting for him to lean down, brush his lips across—

"Excuse me." He raised a hand out to her.

"Hmmm?"

He wiggled his cup in her direction.

¡Ay Dios mío, que idiota! She scurried aside, giving him access to the fridge behind her.

"Sorry!" She laughed, the sound nervous to her ears, as she rounded the kitchen island, putting distance between them once more. "Today was a little out of the norm, but Maria handled it well."

"She didn't give you any trouble?"

"Are you kidding?" Yaz waved off his question, glad he hadn't noticed her momentary slip into dreamland. "Maria's an angel."

"But she's a five-year-old angel. She has her moments."

"We all do."

Tomás filled his glass from the water dispenser in the door, then took a healthy drink before setting his glass back on the island countertop. "Speaking of moments. Back in Maria's room, I didn't mean to upset you."

"Forget about it."

The last thing she wanted was to explain why or how his words had hurt.

It was her own dumb fault for wanting what she couldn't have. "If you're agreeable to me watching Maria until you hear back from Mrs. B, we should go over our schedules. I might have to move a couple things around at Hanson's, but I'll do my best to keep Maria's normal routine."

"Are you sure? I don't want to take advantage of you."

Oh, the ways in which she wouldn't mind him taking advantage of her. She just couldn't go there.

"I'm positive."

Tomás grinned. His dimple shot her a teasing wink and she found herself free-falling for his charm all over again.

"Okay then, let's do this."

Nervous excitement fluttered in her belly.

"Mind if I make myself a sandwich while we talk?" Tomás tugged on the fridge door. "I haven't eaten anything since a Danish at my desk around ten this morning."

"Actually, I saved you a plate from dinner. It's in the microwave. Unless you don't like roast with potatoes and carrots and a side of mac n' cheese." She pointed past his shoulder into the open refrigerator. "There's a bowl of salad on the top shelf."

"If I like?" Tomás blew out a breath, giving her an are-you-crazy glance over his shoulder. "You're a god-send. With Mrs. B gone, I figured I'd have to fend for myself. Thanks."

Moments later Tomás motioned for her to join him at the kitchen island.

While he devoured his dinner, they went over his work hours and Yazmine's commitments at Hanson's. With Maria in kindergarten from eight to twelve Monday through Friday, Yaz would still have her mornings free for her own dance training or to take Papi to any appointments. Afternoons and evenings they could split between their houses and the dance studio when Yaz taught lessons or Maria had class.

"It'll be a bit of a juggle. But I'm game if you are. I'm sure Maria will be thrilled." Tomás set down his fork and used a napkin to wipe his mouth. "With me working from home on Tuesdays and Thursdays, that'll help. We might be okay. Thanks to you."

"Quit saying that."

"I'm serious," he said. "I know Maria would be uncomfortable if I had a parade of strangers rotating in and out. With my mom taking care of my sisters' kids, there's no one else I can call. Like I said earlier today, you're a godsend."

"So, for tomorrow," she said, uncomfortable being the subject of his gratitude. She wasn't this man's savior. No matter how much that crazy little voice in her head cheered at the idea. "Since tomorrow is Tuesday, you'll drop off Maria at school, and I'll pick her up at noon. Same thing Thursday. Right?"

"Right."

"Seems like we've covered everything then. It's been a hectic day. I'll get out of your hair so you can relax."

She rose from her seat at the same time he did, plate in hand. They sidestepped around each other—him moving to the sink, she to the counter where she'd left her purse—and her hip accidentally bumped his.

Heat sizzled through her, leaving a trail of smoldering sparks.

"Dinner was delicious," he said. "But you don't have to cook for us like Mrs. B did. I can grab takeout on my way home."

Yaz huffed out a breath, irked that he didn't seem to be affected by their close proximity.

"Don't be silly. Papi and I cook every night, what's a little more? I'll see what Maria likes and as long as you're not picky, we'll be fine."

She slid her purse strap over her shoulder, but Tomás grasped her hand and she froze in surprise.

"I know you have a lot to deal with. The recital, your concerns about Reynaldo's health. I'm sorry to add to it."

"You're not. Honestly, this gives me something to focus on other than Papi's refusal to have more treatment."

"So-o-o . . ." Tomás drew out the word as if trying to decide how to proceed. His thumb caressed the back of her hand and her stomach tightened with need. "Reynaldo talked to you about his health?"

Once again, dread circled over her like a hungry vulture. "The girls and I spoke with him yesterday before Lilí left. Rosa stayed till this morning so we could try and talk some sense into him. Right now we're waiting for more tests."

"I'm sorry you're going through this." His voice deepened with regret and he squeezed her hand. "It's got to be difficult."

She nodded dumbly, unable to do much more while his thumb played havoc with her sanity. A soft brush to the right. A warm caress to the left.

A simple gesture that had her tingling with pleasure and anticipation.

"Will you let me know when you hear anything?"

"Um, sure." She needed to pull her hand from his. Stop the foolishness. Only, she couldn't bring herself to break their connection. Not yet. "Thanks for checking on Papi while you were out of town. It meant a lot to him."

"I was worried." Tomás lifted his broad shoulders in an easy shrug. "He reminds me of my dad—you know, good solid man, devoted to his family, hardheaded at times."

"Yeah, that's him." They shared a smile, the thread of their mutual love for their parents tying them together.

"Are you sure you're okay?" he asked, the concern in his gravelly voice another gentle caress to her stressed soul.

The sting of tears burned her eyes. Tears of frustration that Papi's cancer might still be a threat. Tears over her desire for dreams she couldn't have. Tears for those dreams she wasn't sure she wanted any longer. Yaz closed her eyes against the harsh reality of it all.

"Maybe this isn't such a good idea after all," Tomás whispered. "*Es mucho.*"

Yaz shook her head, confused about so many things, but somehow certain that helping his family would help her, too. "No, it's not too much. In fact, it's a great idea. Seriously. Papi enjoys spending time with Maria. It'll help keep my mind off things I can't control and alleviate some of your stress. I'll be all right. I can handle it. I'm a big girl."

"A big girl with big goals. I remember. But *you*

remember, if there's anything I can do to help, only say the word. I mean it."

He tugged her hand and she suddenly found herself in his embrace. Her breath hitched in her chest, every nerve-ending in her entire body going haywire.

His strong arms wrapped around her and it felt oh so natural to rest her head on his shoulder, encircle his waist with her arms. Revel in the thrill of his firm body against hers.

For a second she swore he pressed a kiss to her head. Then he pulled back and she figured it must have been wishful thinking on her part.

"I mean it," he said, "anything at all, understood?"

Again, she nodded mutely.

He released her and Yaz grabbed onto her purse strap with both hands to keep from reaching out to him. The urge to lean on the support and strength he offered overwhelmed her, nearly sucking away all rational thought.

She couldn't give in to it. Couldn't allow herself to.

"I'll, uh, see you tomorrow," she whispered, backing out of the kitchen.

"Let me walk you out," Tomás offered.

"No need. I know the way."

In a lust-induced haze she made a beeline toward the foyer. Toward Papi and, ultimately, toward the future he wanted for her in New York.

Still, she couldn't help but wonder what it'd be like if instead she was headed back to the master bedroom with Tomás. If they were crawling into his bed together.

Dios, she knew it would feel *so* good.

Right up to the moment when it ended.

Which it inevitably would when she left.

Yaz pulled the front door closed behind her with a

decisive click. She leaned back against it, taking a deep breath of the frigid, early December air. These fruitless schoolgirl fantasies had to stop.

Tomorrow she'd do well to remember her place in his family dynamic and the promise she'd made to Papi a long time ago.

Chapter Eight

Tomás approached the Fernandez's front door, biting back a tired sigh. Eight thirty on a Friday was way too late to be getting home.

He dragged a hand through his hair, dropping it down to rub the ever-present kink in his neck. Everyone in his office stood on notice: The Linton Jewelry account was a must-win.

He truly believed no one else could put together a better proposal than he could. Still, he had promised Yaz he'd do his best not to pull such late hours. This was a horrible way to end her first week as Maria's temporary nanny.

The cold winter wind kicked up and he burrowed deeper into his wool coat, stiffly raising his arm to knock.

Moments later Maria called out, "Who is it?"

The sound of her high-pitched voice relaxed his shoulders. "The big bad wolf, freezing in this cold weather!"

The door swung open and Reynaldo stood on the other side, Maria peeking out from behind him.

"Papá! You're home! Come look what Señor Fernandez is sharing with me."

Before Tomás could answer, Maria spun on her stockinged feet and ran back into the family room.

Rey waved him in. "Come inside, *m'ijo*. We're letting the heat out."

Tomás followed the older man, stopping to hook his jacket and scarf on the wooden coatrack. "My apologies for being so late. I hope I haven't inconvenienced you."

"*No, no, está bien.* Yazmine had a private lesson with one of her older students. Something about rehearsing for a college audition." Rey ushered him into the family room. "Maria and I have been fine. Right, *nena?*"

"*Sí. Mira*, Papá. Look what we have."

Maria knelt by the wooden coffee table in front of the couch where a bounty of pictures and show *Playbill*s were spread out. An empty plastic bin lay on the hardwood floor next to the table.

Tomás moved closer.

"It's all stuff about Ms. Yazmine," Maria explained. "From her dance shows and parties. Doesn't she look beautiful?"

"Sit down while I heat up your dinner. Maria can show you what we have been digging through." Rey motioned at the couch as he crossed the dining room into the kitchen.

"You don't have to do that," Tomás called after him.

"Yazmine left a plate for you. *No es ningún problema.*"

The microwave's beeping and his past experience with Rey's stubbornness let Tomás know it wouldn't do any good to argue that he could serve himself.

"Here she's playing dress-up at a party." Maria held

out a picture of Yazmine wearing an old-timey cigarette-girl costume. A short black skirt hit her mid-thigh, revealing a pair of sexy legs in fishnet stockings. Stiletto heels highlighted her shapely calves and a bustier accentuated her tiny waist and eye-catching cleavage. A box filled with movie theater candy hung from a strap around her neck to complete the outfit.

Man, if she came knocking on *his* door for Halloween, candy would be the last thing on his mind.

"And here she's at dance class with her friends."

Maria ate one of the little flower cookies Rey must have put in a small bowl for her, then handed Tomás another picture. This one had been taken in a room much like the ones at Hanson's Academy of Dance, only these students were all adults. Their sculpted dancer figures sported the usual leotards, tights, filmy skirts, and some type of jazz shoe he'd seen the older girls wearing at Hanson's. Still, it was Yaz who grabbed his attention.

Her engaging smile and the light in her caramel eyes inevitably called to him, invited him closer, overshadowed everyone else in the photo. The saucy curve of her lips hinted at her quick wit and fun-loving attitude. The one that made her students love her, and drew him to her.

Or maybe it was the way she didn't pull any punches. Or the flare of heat her touch ignited inside him. Like it had last night in his kitchen.

Whatever the hell had possessed him to hug her? One minute he'd been comforting her. The next he was grabbing her like a besotted teen.

What he couldn't deny was that when she was

around, good or bad, for the first time in a long while he felt alive.

"Here you are." Reynaldo strode into the room carrying a TV tray with a plate of food and a glass of tea.

"*Gracias.*" Tomás took the proffered tray, his mouth watering when he got a whiff of the spaghetti and meatballs. "Did the three of you spend the evening reminiscing?"

"*Ay* no, Yazmine hasn't wanted to look at those pictures in a while. Ever since she got home, really. I took them out to show the little one after Yazmine left for her lesson. It kept Maria busy, while I rested on the couch."

The older man slowly eased himself down into the nearby recliner, his body sinking into the cushions on a heavy sigh. Fatigue weighed down Rey's features, carving deep grooves on either side of his mouth.

"How about this, Papá?"

Tomás glanced at the photo Maria handed him. In this one Yaz wore a dark red strapless cocktail dress. The glittery material skimmed her trim figure, accentuating enough to put a man's imagination in overdrive.

He tore his gaze from Yaz to the man beside her, his arm wrapped around her waist. One of Yaz's hands was pressed to the guy's broad chest, her head leaning against his shoulder. They seemed close, comfortable with each other. Yaz's smile shone in her eyes, her happiness evident in her broad grin.

The man had more of a football player's than a dancer's physique—wide shoulders, muscular arms, well over six foot. Whoever this guy was—friend, lover?— Yazmine looked pleased to be with him.

"Doesn't she look pretty?" Maria asked.

"Let me see, *nena*." Rey held his hand out for the picture.

She slid the photo across the table to him.

"That's Yaz and Jeremy. Nice young man, very smart. His family is from Chicago, but he works with a computer company in New York."

Tomás refused to voice his question about this mystery man. Or allow himself to care. Instead he concentrated on a topic that should be more important to him than Yaz's love life. "How are you doing, Rey? Have you spoken with your doctor this week?"

Rey grimaced. "We did the tests. I should know more when all my girls are home for the holidays."

"I'll be praying for good news."

"Me too." Rey's chest rose and fell on a heavy sigh that spoke volumes about his concern. "It is a comfort knowing that if my Yazmine needs anything, she can count on you. Right, *h'ijo*?"

The question hit with bulls-eye accuracy, forcing Tomás to face a reality he hadn't wanted to deal with. Now that their lives were so intertwined, there was no way he could keep his distance from Yaz. He'd have to stay on his guard to avoid getting hurt.

"Of course. Anything Yazmine or your other girls need, I'm there."

"*Te lo agradezco.*" Rey leaned back and set his chair to rock with his feet as he repeated, "I really appreciate it."

His appetite gone, Tomás rose to take his half-eaten plate of food to the kitchen.

It seemed like he took one step away from Yaz and

temptation, only to be reeled back in by the crappy situations life kept throwing at them.

Dios, don't let his promise to Rey come back to haunt him.

Her cell phone displayed 9:47 p.m. by the time Yazmine slid into her car in Hanson's parking lot. She waved good-bye to Suzie, waited for the teen to drive away, then tapped the icon to access her voice mail.

Her breath hitched when Tomás's rich baritone spoke in her ear, apologizing for being so late tonight. His tone was dull, tired. Slightly discouraged even.

None of those were something she recalled hearing in his voice over the past week that she'd been caring for Maria. Maybe the afternoon team meeting he'd mentioned this morning hadn't gone well.

Before she thought twice about it, she hit "call back." Seconds later he picked up.

"Yaz?"

"The one and only."

Even his chuckle sounded weary.

"I got your voice mail. Long day?"

"Exceedingly. Finished with your lesson?"

"Yeah, I'm headed home now." She anchored the phone against her shoulder to buckle her seat belt. "Papi's probably sleeping, so I thought I'd check in with you, make sure everything was okay when you picked up Maria."

"She was fine. Thanks for dinner. Sorry again for running late."

"No worries." Through the phone she heard the sound of liquid being poured.

"I was getting ready to have a glass of wine to cap off the evening," Tomás said. "Care to join me?"

About to turn her key in the ignition, Yaz paused.

That was a loaded question.

All week she'd done a decent job of keeping her thoughts about him on a platonic level, which hadn't been easy after their touchy-feely moment in the kitchen that first night. It probably wasn't a good idea to push her luck by saying yes.

"You still there?" Tomás asked.

"Oh, sorry, I'm getting settled in my car. Are you drinking white or red?"

"Picky, picky."

More like biding her time. He had no idea how tempted she was to bag all her good intentions and say yes.

"Come over."

"It's a little late, don't you think?" Lame argument.

"Please, it's not even ten," he shot back, his tone daring her. "Besides, it'll give us a chance to evaluate how the week went."

Okay, that put a new twist on the invitation. This was shoptalk. Babysitting, work, nothing personal. She could handle that.

"I'll be there in ten. And if you have a Riesling, I'll take a glass."

The sound of his rich laughter brought a smile of pleasure to her face. She disconnected the call, then put her car in gear.

Chapter Nine

Within minutes Yaz pulled up in front of Tomás's house. The porch light welcomed her, but other than a faint glow through the living room window, the rest of the house remained dark. A shiver trembled across her shoulders at the clandestine feel.

Common sense let out one last war cry, clamoring for her to call Tomás back with some excuse to cancel.

Her less sane side prevailed.

Head ducked down against the cold, wishing she hadn't forgotten her earmuffs at home or that she'd grabbed a thicker scarf, she scurried up the front walk. One deep breath later and she was rapping lightly on his front door.

"Your Riesling, *señorita*," he greeted, holding out a wineglass for her.

"Ooh, you're good. But let me in first." She brushed past him into the entryway so he could close the door behind her. "It's freezing out there."

"They're calling for snow over the next few days. Thankfully it's warm and toasty in here. Come in."

She hung her peacoat in the hall closet, deciding to

keep her scarf on until she warmed up, then followed him to the family room where a fire blazed, lending heat and an air of intimacy.

Two new throws draped the back of the navy leather sofa and loveseat, and a bottle of wine nestled in an ice bucket on the coffee table. Jazz music trilled in the background, adding to the room's cozy atmosphere.

If Tomás hadn't made it clear he wasn't interested over lunch at Luigi's, not to mention his repeated use of the word "friend" during the past week, she might have wondered at his motives. Frankly, the only thing she probably had to worry about was her own imagination going wild.

"Have a seat." Tomás set her wineglass on the coffee table and sank into one corner of the couch.

Yaz followed suit, choosing the opposite end. Making herself comfortable, she pulled a throw over her legs before reaching for her drink. "Were you having Riesling already, or did you open a bottle for my benefit?"

"Wouldn't you like to know?" His dimple winked at her with his grin.

Dios mío, there was no way he could be any more handsome.

She cautioned herself to keep her focus. Babysitting, work schedule. Mundane topics. "So, how was your day?"

"Man . . ." Tomás rubbed the back of his neck, his face pained. "I can't tell you how much I appreciate your help. This is about the worst time in my career for me to have this kind of distraction from work."

Yaz took a sip of her drink, feeling the heat as the sweet liquid warmed its way down her throat.

The firelight flickered, sending undulating waves of light and darkness over him in a sensual dance. He'd swapped his business suit for a pair of faded jeans and a tan-colored sweater. With his stockinged feet propped up on the coffee table, he looked comfy, sexy. Dangerous.

"I had every intention of leaving the office at a decent hour," he said.

"Uh-huh. I'm sure."

"No, seriously. This isn't workaholic denial talking. We had a meeting about a potential account that's pretty big and it ran way later than any of us anticipated."

Starting to feel warm, Yaz untied her scarf and laid it over the back of the sofa. This was the first time all week they'd had time to talk about more than Maria's care. She settled into the cushions, enjoying the chance to hear him share about his work.

"If we can land the Linton account it would be a real coup for our agency."

She sat up in surprise. "As in, *the* Linton Jewelry?"

A corner of his mouth curved up at her obvious awe. "Yep. *The* Linton Jewelry."

"I gotta say, now I'm impressed. From here to New York, everyone's heard of Linton's."

"And my plan is to grow it coast to coast. That's why this proposal has to be brilliant. Classy. Timeless. Every word that comes to mind when you think of Linton Jewelry, only bigger. Bolder. And at the same time, more memorable." His passion for his job came to life in the animation on his face, the determination glinting in his dark eyes. "This account will put our agency on the map. I'm talking, huge!"

In his exuberance, he sloshed wine out of his glass.

She chuckled at his "oops!"—liking the fact that he could laugh at himself along with her.

"I get a little excited when it comes to my job." He wiped at the spill on his tan cable-knit sweater with a napkin.

She nearly suggested he take the sweater off, rinse out the wine before it set. But that suggestion seemed too . . . well, suggestive.

No way was she opening that Pandora's box.

"There are two other agencies in the mix," Tomás continued, thankfully unaware of the side trip her train of thought had taken. "But I *will* win this account."

She didn't doubt it in the least.

"Linton and love, with you for a lifetime." Yaz murmured the words, drawn into his advertising world by his charisma's pull.

"Not too bad." He toasted her with his glass. "You got any more?"

She grinned. "I can see why you're so good at your job. Your excitement's catching."

"I think the same thing about you in class. You're pretty amazing."

Her cheeks heated, and it had nothing to do with the fire blazing in front of them. More like, the one crackling inside her at his praise.

"*Pues*, not everyone can be as good as us, right?" she teased.

He threw back his head and laughed, a deep throaty bellow that rumbled through her, reaching deep recesses she'd convinced herself to ignore.

"You are too much, you know that?" he said.

"I'll take that as a compliment."

Tomás chuckled. He shifted his feet off the coffee table to crook a knee on the sofa cushion between them. "It's not often I get to discuss work like this at home. Usually it's Barbies and Disney Channel with

Maria. I try to give Mrs. B her privacy in the evenings. This is nice."

Yeah, it was.

"That's what friends are for, right?"

She threw the word out there for both of their benefit. Damn if she couldn't completely keep the wistfulness out of her voice.

She took another sip, her gaze meeting his. A log crackled and split, shooting sparks into the air behind the grate. The jazz music in the background swelled to a crescendo, before drowsily reaching its end.

The word "friends" hung between them, daring either of them to deny it.

She wanted to. Oh, how she wanted to.

She knew better though. New York beckoned— even if there were times she wondered whether or not it was the right place for her.

Tomás leaned over to pick up the wine bottle, breaking their unspoken connection. He tilted the bottle toward her. "More?"

"Half a glass. I still have to drive home." Plus, she needed to keep her wits about her.

He refilled their glasses and they settled into an easy silence until the next song started.

"Ooh, one of my favorites," Tomás said as Etta James's sultry voice crooned "At Last."

Before Yaz realized his intent, he put down his glass, rose from the couch and held his hand out to her. "Will you give me a dance, Ms. Yazmine?"

She hesitated, certain that saying yes, as badly as she wanted to, wasn't a smart move.

"C'mon."

The teasing glint in his eyes paired with his dimple's wink was too much for her to resist.

She placed her hand in his. The warmth from his palm and the inviting grin on his handsome face were another one-two punch to her flagging determination to keep things between them platonic.

He led them to the area in front of the fireplace and she moved into his arms easily, as if it was where she was supposed to be. For this moment, she'd allow herself the treat.

Still holding on to her hand, Tomás slid his other arm around her waist, firmly guiding her body closer until her chest pressed against his. Yaz tipped her chin to rest it on his shoulder, her temple pressed against the side of his face as he swayed them to the music.

They moved in a slow circle and she closed her eyes, giving in to the pleasure of being in his arms. His musky, earthy scent mingling with the smell of burnt wood in the crackling fire created a heady incense that made her woozier than the wine.

"I haven't done this in ages," Tomás said softly.

"What?"

"Dance."

"Are you kidding? You danced in class on Wednesday," she answered, enjoying the rumble of his laughter and the way it shook his muscular chest against hers.

He spun them in another slow circle, then she yelped in surprise when he leaned her over his arm for a deep dip, holding her in place so she had to squeeze his shoulder and hand for balance.

"Somehow, this isn't quite the same," he said, his voice gruff.

His eyes flared, his face a silhouette of angles in the firelight.

Dios mío, was he going to kiss her?

Did she want him to?

Who was she kidding? Of course she did.

Before she could figure out what to do if he leaned in for a kiss, Tomás pulled her up to stand, deftly moving them back into the song's tempo again. As if he wasn't affected by the electricity humming between them.

Her legs shaking, Yaz followed his lead.

Then he started humming softly in her ear, the slightly off-key tune endearing. It was as if his voice, his strength, his . . . everything hypnotized her. Made her forget reality.

Fear born from self-preservation choked the breath from her. She could not fall for this man. It would derail all her plans. All Papi's plans for her.

Thankfully the poignant song drew to a close and Yaz took a step back. Her mind grasped for something to help get them, get herself, back on track as "friends." Panicked, she blurted out the first thing she thought of.

"I don't mean to pry, and you can tell me to butt out if you want, but I was wondering about Maria's mother. You haven't mentioned her."

Tomás's mouth thinned. He dropped his arms from around her, turning his head to stare intently into the fire.

Yaz held her breath, uncertain if she had overstepped her bounds.

After several tense moments, he moved to sit back down on the sofa.

Gingerly she followed suit.

The question had been traipsing in and out of her mind since earlier this week when she'd noticed that all the photos in the house were of Tomás's family or Mrs. Buckley. Maria had taken great pride in "introducing" Yaz to her family via each and every picture. During the tour the little girl had made a vague comment about her mom going away, but hadn't elaborated.

"I wondered when you'd get around to asking," Tomás finally said. "Most people jump right in, whether it's appropriate or not."

He shifted on the cushions, crooking his elbow along the back of the leather sofa. "Kristine and I met right after I moved to Chicago. Our agencies teamed up for several accounts. It was a bit of a whirlwind between the two of us. Fast and furious, you might say. The marriage was a spur-of-the-moment decision when we were in Vegas for a conference."

Yaz swallowed a gasp of surprise at his admission. He didn't strike her as the impetuous type.

"About eight months in she got pregnant, unplanned. Turns out neither of us really knew what we were getting into. Or with whom. I guess you could say we both went in with blinders on. And the pregnancy ripped those off pretty quickly. That's when we realized I wanted a career and a family, Kristine only wanted the career."

Yaz watched Tomás in the flickering firelight, the half shadows making the angles of his stoic expression more harsh. His words and tone were impassive, as if he shared the details of someone else's story, not his own life-changing divorce.

"Kristine grew up an only child with a mom more interested in her own wants and needs. They weren't close. Barely even spoke during the holidays. She never mentioned her dad, and her grandparents had passed when she was younger. It's ironic really. Kristine used to rail about her mom's selfishness. But when it came down to it, Kristine was exactly the same."

He traced the lip of his wineglass with a finger, his

gaze lost in his story. "We hired Mrs. B right before Maria was born, because Kristine wanted to go back to work as soon as possible. It didn't matter. Kristine lasted about six months of motherhood before deciding she'd had enough."

He paused, his jaw tightening. Yaz couldn't tell if it was a sign of his lingering hurt or leftover anger. Or both.

She didn't ask. Instead she let him get the whole sordid story out, sorry she'd even brought it up. Sure, her curiosity about his ex might be satisfied, but she hadn't meant to dampen his mood.

"Her company opened an office in London and she jumped at the opportunity to get away," Tomás continued. "Made it clear in no uncertain terms that her job meant more than we did. The divorce was simple and quick. She willingly signed away all parental rights. As far as the courts are concerned, I'm Maria's only parent."

Tomás took a hefty gulp of his wine, punctuating the end of his tale.

Yaz sensed his buried pain, saw it in the hollowness of his dark eyes. A kindred pain burned in her chest. She'd experienced rejection's vicious bite, too. Still smarted from it.

"Relationships can really suck, huh?" she muttered.

Tomás huffed out a harsh breath, but didn't say anything as he refilled his glass with the last of the wine bottle.

"I can't imagine a mother leaving her child behind, especially one as precious as Maria," she murmured.

He jiggled his glass in a small circle, intently watching the liquid spin, edging close to the rim, but not quite enough to spill over.

"Kristine wasn't—still isn't, I guess—wired to have a family. The only contact I've had from her since the divorce was a 'desist' response to an email I sent with a picture of Maria on her first birthday."

"Wow." The word slipped out before Yaz could stop it. The idea of not even wanting a picture of your daughter was completely mind-boggling.

"Yeah, that surprised me, too." Tomás nodded slowly, staring down at his glass. "But deep down I knew the truth. Staying with Maria and me would have held Kristine back. Eventually she would have resented us. My mistake for jumping into something too quickly, without enough forethought. One of my rare impulsive moves. But I can tell you one thing—"

He looked up at Yaz, his determined gaze piercing her in the dim lighting. "I won't make that mistake again."

Her mind ran through everything she'd learned about his ex and she kept coming back to one question. What kind of idiot walked away from her own child, not to mention a man as dedicated to his family as Tomás?

Sure, Yaz was walking away from the idea of having a family, but it wasn't the same as abandoning one she already had.

"So, you're sticking with single parenting, or have you thought about marrying again?" she asked, surprised at the stab of disappointment the thought gave her.

He shrugged. "We're holding our own. It's not always easy. But I *do* know, I won't get involved with another woman without first being positive she's a good match for me. And especially for Maria."

"That's difficult to judge right off the bat. Even

when you think you do know someone, who's to say they won't blindside you at some point anyway?"

"Well, I plan on making sure she's the right type."

"*Right type?*" The fire popped, as if echoing Yaz's bewilderment.

"Yep. Mrs. B and my mom have been hounding me to find a mom for Maria, but before I start dating anyone, I need to make sure she wants the same things I do. I'm not taking any chances again."

"News flash!" She tilted her glass toward him, emphasizing her point. "It's not always that easy."

Tomás pshawed at her comment. "I've planned every career move I've made, from high school to college to now, and it's worked so far. I didn't do that with Kristine. I jumped first and thought later. Like I said, won't make the same mistake."

"But you're not talking about a career move," she countered, pulling her knees up onto the couch and angling more toward him. "I mean, what exactly makes a woman 'right'?"

"Someone who wants to be a loving parent to Maria, and any other children we have together. Someone who's a partner, not a corporate climber with a career-before-family mentality."

"Um, excuse me? Hello, Mr. Workaholic." She gave him a wiggle-fingered wave.

"Hey now." He pushed her hand down, trapping it on the back of the sofa under his. "I'm working on that. Not counting tonight, I've been home at a decent hour all week. I even made it to dance rehearsal on Wednesday."

Yaz slid her hand out, enjoying the warmth of his too much for her own good. "I'll give you this week. Let's see how it continues."

"Slave driver."

She narrowed her eyes, but her glare turned into an eye roll at his grin. "Let me get this straight, you're looking for a woman with a strong mom instinct and no workaholic tendencies. Anything else?"

"Sense of humor. Dependable. Trustworthy." He slowly ticked off the items on his fingers. "A team player."

"As long as it's *your* team?"

"Mine and Maria's. We should all want to be on the *same* team."

"That doesn't sound very romantic." More like pragmatic. "What about love, attraction?"

"Love, as in the mushy, I-can't-get-you-out-of-my-head type?" Tomás scoffed. "Doesn't interest me. I tried that once. Lust fades. I'm more interested in finding a companion. Actually, until Mrs. B had to leave, I wasn't thinking about this at all. We were doing fine. But I've realized I can't rely on nannies to help me provide stability for Maria long-term. I need a partner."

"*Ay, que deprimente.*" If the wine bottle hadn't been empty, Yaz might have poured herself another glass.

"It's not depressing. It's called being realistic."

She wrinkled her nose in distaste. Sure, companionship might seem better than being alone, but what he was talking about felt hollow. Empty.

Tomás quirked a brow at her. "Don't tell me you're a hopeless romantic who believes in love and hearts and roses. I thought you were a diehard ladder-of-success climber."

His words held a ring of challenge, almost like he was egging her on, daring her to deny them. Then again, maybe it was her own insecurity, her own indecision and uncertainty, coloring her mindset.

Uncomfortable, Yaz tucked a loose strand of hair from her ponytail behind her ear. He was dancing too close to her darkest secret. A fear she had only hinted at with Cheryl the last time her friend had been home.

"I'm both," she finally answered. "While marriage and a family may not be in the cards for me, my parents were living proof that a good marriage is possible. Your idea sounds a little calculated. When love bites you, it bites you. Right or wrong, there's nothing you can do about it."

"You speaking from experience?"

She sucked in a sharp breath. Memories of Victor and his selfishness, of her naïveté in believing she could have it all, clamored to the surface.

Buying herself some time to answer, she drained the last of her wine.

"Want me to open another bottle?" Tomás offered.

"No, it's late." Leaning over, she set her glass on the coffee table. "I should get going."

"Funny . . ." Tomás narrowed his gaze, assessing her. "You had plenty of time when I was spilling my dirty secrets. I ask one question and suddenly 'it's late'?"

That was her cue to exit stage right.

"Speaking of secrets, if all you're looking for is a partner rather than a romantic connection, you might get lucky at Hanson's. Word's out about me helping with Maria, and a mom asked me about you after class the other night."

"You're kidding, right?"

"Nope." Yaz grinned at his scandalized expression. "Let me know if you want her number. She's a divorcée, two kids about seven and nine. Pretty nice lady from what I can tell. But I can ask around."

"No!" Tomás was up and off the sofa like a hot ember from the fire had popped out and landed on him.

Yaz laughed, enjoying his wide-eyed horror as she unfolded her legs and stood up. "Hey, I don't mind helping you out if you'd like."

She stepped toward the foyer, Tomás coming up behind her.

"*No gracias*, I don't need any more matchmaking. I've got Mrs. B and my mom riding my tail as it is. Which reminds me, I forgot to mention, Mrs. B called today."

"And?"

They stopped in front of the coat closet in the darkened entryway. Tomás snagged her jacket off a hanger, then held it up so she could slip her arms in the sleeves.

"Her daughter was put on full bed rest. Mrs. B has to stay until the baby arrives. Probably the end of December, maybe even the first week of January. I put in a call to the nanny service this afternoon. They're going to let me know about a replacement tomorrow."

Yaz froze, her right arm partially in her jacket sleeve, her body waging an internal skirmish. *Ay*, her head told her to do one thing. Her heart wanted something completely different.

She closed her eyes, agonizing between the two.

Por favor, this was a no-brainer. When would she get a chance like this again?

She spun around, pulling the jacket out of Tomás's

hands. "Tell them never mind. That you already have someone."

He drew back, his brows angling down in confusion. "Who?"

She met his gaze, begging him with her eyes to agree.

"No." He put up his hands, palms facing her. "You've got enough on your plate already."

"I can do this. It's three weeks, four tops."

She could see his indecision, practically watched his mind going through his options, thinking of every angle or alternative to ensure he selected the best one, like he apparently did with everything else. Even his love life, if you could call it that.

She wasn't ready to walk away from whatever they were doing here. Not yet. Tomás and Maria needed her. She wanted more time with them. Even if it could only be for a little while.

Yaz shrugged on her jacket, then grabbed his biceps with both hands. "Look, things went well this week, right?"

"Yes, but—"

"What's a few more then? I can do this." She stared up at him, willing him to see her sincerity. Willing him to have faith in her.

"What about your dad?" Tomás's frown deepened. "I don't want to stress him."

"Are you kidding? He'll be all for this. He loves having Maria around. It's good for both of us."

"Are you sure?"

"Positive."

She drew in a breath. Hoping. Praying. Needing him to say yes.

After a few heart-pounding seconds, Tomás nodded his agreement. Elation bubbled up inside her and she clapped her hands with glee, like Maria had when Papi suggested ice cream for dessert earlier.

Tomás's lips curved in a shadowy tease of his usual grin.

"You're an amazing woman, Yazmine Fernandez." His raspy whisper sent shivers of awareness tingling through her.

He reached out to tuck her hair back. His fingers lingered, brushing along the shell of her ear, before his hand slipped down to cup her cheek. The heat of his touch warmed her heart and she nearly let her eyes drift closed so she could better savor the sensation.

Nearly.

Instead, she summoned the cheesy grin and forced sauciness that had hid her inner turmoil for years. "Did you ever doubt it?"

He chuckled, his dimple peeking out at her.

"And now that I know about your Perfect Partner Plan—"

"My what?" His hand slid from her cheek as he drew back.

"—you'll really think I'm good when I hook you up with the right woman." The idea stung, but the second item he'd listed—someone who wasn't career focused—took her clean out of the running.

"Don't even think about it," Tomás warned, opening the front door.

"Thanks for the drink, Romeo. Don't forget to practice with Maria this weekend. I'll see you bright and early on Monday."

She threw him an impudent wink for good measure, then sauntered away.

Saturday morning, Tomás awoke tired and cranky from a restless night. He opened his eyes, squinting in disgust at the scrap of brightly colored material lying on the pillow next to his.

After Yaz had left the night before, he'd gone into the family room intending to clean up the remains of their wine fest and hit the sack. Instead, his gaze had honed in on her scarf draped across the back of the sofa.

The next thing he knew he was settling onto the cushions, Yaz's scarf in his hands. Her soft violet scent clung to the delicate material and he brought it to his nose, dragging in a deep breath. The silky scarf was more fashionable than winter worthy, but he'd relished the smoothness, imagining himself draping it around her neck, slowly tugging her in for a mind-numbing kiss.

The wine must have gone to his head. That was the only reason why he would have asked her to dance. Holding her in his arms had been a miscalculation. A sensory-overloading one. He'd come *this close* to kissing her, tasting the wine on her lips. Instead he'd spilled his guts about his past with Kristine. Yaz made it far too easy to relax in her company. Far too easy to let his guard down. He hadn't felt that way with a woman since . . . hell, probably never.

He had allowed himself a few minutes to ponder the possibilities, then made himself get up and tidy their mess. However, rather than leave the scarf in the kitchen to return it on Monday, he'd flung it over his shoulder and headed to his room. Then he'd changed and washed up for bed. Alone.

All the while, the scarf lay like a tease in a pool of reds, blues, purples, and gold on his black sheets.

Ultimately he'd fallen asleep with the damn thing next to him, his mind going over the what-ifs and what-couldn't-be's. Even in his dreams, her subtle scent had tantalized him.

Now, with the sun shining through his curtains signaling a new day, he rolled out of bed, annoyed with himself for mooning over something he couldn't, shouldn't desire. Feeling out of sorts, he strode to the master bath, leaving his bed unmade and the scarf untouched.

Moments later he stood in the kitchen sipping a cup of steaming coffee, his mind bouncing back and forth between a sexy, appealing Yazmine Fernandez and the Linton Jewelry campaign, the traitorous scarf once again in his hands.

He stared out the kitchen window at the backyard, marveling at the blanket of snow covering Maria's swing set, the wooden picnic table, and the shrubbery lining the perimeter of the fenced-in yard. Sunlight sparkled off the fresh snow as if shards of Linton diamonds had been sprinkled across the surface.

The perfect backdrop for the ad campaign? Maybe, if it featured Yazmine draped in colors to match the silky material she'd left behind. Diamonds glistening from her ears, around her elegant neck. Lips painted red, eyes shooting a come-hither glance beneath lowered lashes.

"*Buenos días*, Papá."

Tomás started at Maria's greeting. He turned to find her clambering up onto a stool at the island. Still dressed in her Disney princess footie pj's, her hair sleep-mussed, her cheek sporting a crease from her sheets, she brought a lightness in his chest.

"Good morning, *m'ija*. Did you sleep well?"

"*Sí*. Hey, watcha got there? It's pretty." Maria set an elbow on the island top and cupped her chin in her hand.

Tomás held the scarf up for her to see. The material dangled in front of him, the sun glinting off the gold threads.

"That looks like Ms. Yazmine's," she said.

"I think it is. I found it in the family room. She probably left it here by accident."

Yeah, because she'd been too busy teasing him about setting him up with a mom from the studio. The thought still made his gut clench with dread.

Maria frowned, a little line forming between her tiny brows. "Hmm, I thought she wored it last night. She showed me before her dance lesson. How'd it get here?"

Tomás bit back a chagrined smile. Figures, the one time he wished she wasn't paying attention, his child shows off her skills of observation.

"Oh yeah, she stopped by to tell you good night after her class, but you were already sleeping," he fibbed.

No need to admit his weakness—that when he'd heard her voice over the phone, the invitation to join him for a glass of wine flew from his lips before he thought better of it. The desire to see her, to spend more time in her company, had been too strong to resist.

"Can I try it on, please?" Maria tugged the end of the scarf. It slid through his fingers, reminding him of the silkiness of Yazmine's hair when he touched it.

Images of the heated dreams that had invaded his sleep paraded through his mind. All of them starring Yazmine wearing her flimsy scarf, and not much else. His blood pulsed, instantly flowing to places it shouldn't with his daughter around.

He forced his thoughts to more appropriate, safer avenues like work, or his and Maria's plans for the day.

Admittedly, he wasn't doing such a good job of thinking platonically when it came to Yazmine. At least he was aware of the problem. That was the important first step in keeping a leash on his attraction. He had the rest of the weekend to get a grip on things.

If not, come Monday, he'd be in trouble.

Chapter Ten

By the time Monday morning arrived, Tomás had come to a decision. Before he left for work, he'd find a way, a subtle way, to ask Yaz if she'd put him in touch with the mom from Hanson's who'd asked about him.

It was the only solution to keep him from going crazy.

He'd spent the entire weekend thinking about Yaz's damn scarf, barely stopping himself from asking Maria for it back so he could see if it still held Yaz's subtle violet scent. Even sitting at his desk, when his mind should have been on the Linton campaign, he'd found thoughts of her vying for his attention.

This insane infatuation had to stop.

It was all a sign, really. Without Mrs. B, his life was in turmoil, but he couldn't rely on the nanny forever. Mrs. B was getting older, and she'd made it clear that she wanted to spend more time with her own grand-children. Her family emergency was a glaring wake-up call, a warning that while he couldn't raise Maria alone, having a live-in nanny might not be the best solution.

The American dream he'd always envisioned for

himself featured a mom, a dad, and kids. It was time he took some action to create that ideal for his daughter.

Starting today.

Tomás leaned against the kitchen island nursing a cup of coffee, his mind turning over potential lead-ins to his question. Yaz sat on a stool across from him, going over the day's schedule while Maria finished her cereal.

Fresh-faced, dressed in black leggings and an "I love DANCE" sweatshirt, her long hair woven in an intricate braid, Yaz resembled one of the high school girls she taught at Hanson's. She grinned at one of Maria's knock-knock jokes, her laughter-filled gaze sliding to brush over him before going back to Maria.

Awareness heated his blood, sending it surging south. Damn, he felt like a randy teen again, his libido spiraling out of control around the hot girl on the dance team. Years later he still couldn't have her—for different reasons now.

"Oh, I almost forgot!" Maria hopped off her stool, eyes wide with concern. "I hafta get the book I borrowed from school! Be right back!"

She raced out of the kitchen, pigtails flying.

Now was his chance to ask.

Tomás cleared his throat before venturing in. "Between school, lunch, and her playdate, sounds like you two have a full day."

Yaz nodded, reaching for Maria's napkin to wipe up some milk splatters on the counter.

"By the way, if there are any notes from Maria's school I should see, feel free to leave them on my desk like you did last week. And if you don't mind, will you get me that phone number you mentioned Friday night and add it to the pile?"

Yaz's hand paused mid-swipe. Her slack-jawed look of shock was not the reaction he'd anticipated. "Janet Miller's? The mom from Hanson's who asked about you?"

Tomás gulped. Maybe this was a mistake. He plunked his coffee mug on the island, ready to follow Maria and think of something he'd forgotten in his bedroom.

Then he noticed the infamous scarf fashionably tied around Yaz's neck. Taunting him. His resolve to move forward hardened.

"It's time. Mrs. B's emergency, our talk the other night, it all got the wheels turning in my head."

Not to mention, being around Yaz stirred up a hornet's nest of thoughts and needs that swarmed around him, stingers ready to zoom in for the kill.

"Got your Perfect Partner Plan all figured out, huh?"

"I'm, uh, not actually calling it that."

"Tomato, tomahto." She picked up Maria's bowl and edged past him on her way to the sink, not once making eye contact. "I guess when you decide to move, you move quickly."

For a second he thought her smile seemed a little forced, but she bent to place the bowl in the dishwasher and Tomás couldn't see her face anymore. Maybe he was projecting his own misgivings onto her. Dating again meant taking a huge step in a direction he'd tried to convince himself for years was not for him.

Yaz closed the dishwasher, then leaned a hip against the counter, her usual morning cheer dulled. "I'll get the number from the studio and text it to you later."

"Great, I appreciate it."

Then why didn't he feel any sense of excitement?

Or his usual certainty when he set out on a course of action? Anything but this . . . emptiness.

"I'm ready!" Maria came bounding down the hallway, her purple and pink backpack slung over her shoulders.

So was he. Wading carefully into the dating pool, he'd be better able to provide for Maria.

Now that he had asked Yaz for the number, there was no turning back.

"Explain this to me again. With everything your dad's going through, you take on a temporary nanny gig? What gives?"

Cheryl motioned for Yaz to scoot over on the old floral couch in the back room at Center Stage.

What gives?

Dios mío, if that wasn't the million-dollar question.

With an hour until the shop opened at ten, she and Cheryl had the whole store to themselves. They had finished organizing boxes for inventory and had gravitated toward their favorite "girl talk" spot in high school.

The sofa material had faded and the cushions were now lumpy, but the smell of dance shoes, makeup, and packaging material set off a slide show of fond memories in Yaz's mind. Good or bad, Yaz had shared it with Cheryl—here, in this corner of the room. Surrounded by the tools of her trade.

Head resting on the back cushion, Yaz stared blankly up at the ceiling. "Where should I begin?"

"How about with how your father's doing?"

"*Ay*, not good. I mean, we're really not—" Her voice shook and she broke off.

"Oh, I am so sorry." Cheryl pressed a hand against Yazmine's thigh in sympathy. "I thought he was getting better."

"So did we. Rosa, Lilí, and I found out over Thanksgiving that Dr. Lopez is running some new tests. We're all meeting with him Saturday morning when the girls are back."

"Isn't that the day of the Christmas recital?"

"Mm-hmm. But Lilí gets in late Friday night for holiday break, and we didn't want to wait until Monday to know the test results." Her eyes stung and the ceiling became a blur. A tear snuck out to trail down her temple and she swiped it away, hating the sign of weakness.

"Hey, come here." Cheryl pulled her into a comforting bear hug. "I can't say it's going to be all right. But I know you'll be okay. No matter what happens. I'll be here, whatever you need."

Yaz hugged her back, relieved to have her best friend by her side again. "I'm so glad you're back. I've missed our talks."

"Me too. It's good to be home." Cheryl eased back and pulled her legs up to sit tailor fashion on the sofa. "But if your dad's not doing well, how did you wind up volunteering to take care of this little girl? I mean, you never even babysat in high school."

True, but now was different. *She* was different.

"What's her name?" Cheryl asked.

"Maria." Yaz's spirits buoyed at the thought of her little partner in crime. Tomás had dubbed them that the other day when he'd walked into Maria's room and found them in dress-up mode—complete with full makeup and up-dos. "She's actually one of my students at Hanson's. Oh, and she goes to Bright Minds. We'll stop by your room next week when you start so you can meet her. She's in the kindergarten class."

"Wait, that's my new room!"

Yaz perked up, excited about the idea that Maria might be in Cheryl's class. "I thought they gave you the three-year-olds."

"They wound up moving a few teaching assistants around. Plus, there's talk about adding another kindergarten class next year, so my plan is to apply for that teacher position." Cheryl propped her elbow along the back of the couch to rest her head against her palm. "But that still doesn't explain why you're nannying. When Mom told me, I thought she'd gotten you and Rosa mixed up."

"Funny, aren't you?" Yaz shot Cheryl a droll look and her friend stuck out her tongue.

"You know what I mean," Cheryl said. "You were always so focused. So driven. You didn't have time for anything else. God, how I envied you and your certainty."

"Yeah, well, life's not so black and white anymore, is it?" Yaz murmured. There were no easy answers. Not to the questions she faced.

"What's going on with you?" Cheryl nudged Yazmine's shoulder with her fist. "Come on, spit it out."

Yaz turned her head to look at her friend. Cheryl's gray eyes studied her.

Here was her chance to vent. Get all her doubts out in the open. Hit the release valve on the tension that had been percolating inside her for a few years now.

"Have you ever wondered how different your life would be if you'd made a different choice along the way?" Yazmine's whispered words hung in the air. As close to a confession as she could bring herself to admit aloud.

"Are you kidding me?" Cheryl huffed out a breath. "Don't you remember? I'm the girl who changed her major five times before settling on early childhood education."

"And if I recall correctly, *I* had suggested teaching to you from the beginning." Yaz tapped her chest with a finger, giving Cheryl an I-know-it-all smirk.

"I'll give you that. But you're also the one who, when you met Ronnie last Christmas, told me he and I would get married, and look how that ended up."

Yaz winced. Not one of her finer predictions. "I swear, that boy was so enamored, I figured he'd already bought your ring."

"Me too." Pain filled Cheryl's eyes, turning them a stormy gray. "Who knew that at twenty-five we'd still be sitting here on this old couch together, licking our wounds after messy break-ups, huh?"

"Well, Victor was a self-centered, cheating jerk. But Ronnie . . ." Yaz shrugged, uncertain whether Cheryl was ready to hear that Yaz truly thought her ex was a nice guy. Not with the breakup so fresh. "You're sure it's really over between you two?"

"We were together four years. I told him I needed a commitment or I was taking this job and moving three hours away. And here I am!" Cheryl opened her arms wide to encompass the entire back room.

Wow, what a pair they made. At least Cheryl's career was moving in the right direction. Yaz had sidelined herself for what many thought might be too long in her profession.

Maybe they were right. Or, maybe that was the scared, insecure side of her. The part of her Victor's harsh words had hit with a sniper's accuracy. "What would you say if I told you *I* was thinking about a major cha—"

"Good morning, girls. Staying out of trouble back here?" Mrs. Morgan swept into the storage room carrying a stack of flyers. The black curtain flapped closed behind her, essentially closing Yaz's window of opportunity to confide in her best friend.

Her frustration simmered, but relief lowered the heat by reminding her that maybe this was for the best. Once her confession was out, she couldn't take it back.

"Hi, Mom, inventory's organized," Cheryl answered. "What do you have there?"

"Something I'm hoping Yazmine won't mind taking to Hanson's for me. I'm sure she's heading there this morning to rehearse." She winked at Yaz. "I know you as well as I know my own daughter."

Yaz hoped her smile didn't look as forced as it felt. Of course Mrs. Morgan expected her to be at the studio. There wasn't any other place Yaz felt more comfortable with herself. Maybe more than a confessional session with Cheryl, she should get to the studio. Spend a few hours sweating and dancing away her uncertainties.

Shrugging into her winter coat, Yaz slung her dance bag over her shoulder, then held out a hand to take the flyers. "Sure, what are they?"

"I've been so focused on my baby moving home, I forgot to print these earlier to advertise my annual end-of-the-year sale. One of the moms from Hanson's asked me about it yesterday. Oh, what was her name again?" Mrs. Morgan rubbed her forehead as she tried to remember. "I swear old age is making me forgetful. Let me see . . . Janet . . . yes, Janet Miller."

Ha! The irony of cosmic ironies. Like fate whispering the name in Mrs. Morgan's ear, reminding Yaz she had no business being hurt about Tomás asking for Janet's number this morning.

Maybe Mrs. Morgan had interrupted them at the right time after all. The only major change Yaz needed to make involved convincing Papi to keep fighting. Then she'd head back to New York, ready to make her mark . . . for both of them.

Shortly after noon on Thursday Tomás dropped his keys into the dish by the kitchen door, disappointed to find he'd either missed lunch with Maria and Yazmine or they'd gone to eat with Rey.

After his major bust of a coffee date with Janet Miller, he'd driven home hoping to catch Yaz and Maria enjoying a picnic in front of the fireplace like they'd done yesterday, when he was working in the Chicago office.

He smiled, remembering the selfie Yaz had sent of her and Maria, heads pressed together, peanut butter and jelly sandwiches in hand. Even if he hadn't saved the picture on his phone, the image had imprinted on his brain. Maria grinning with pleasure. Yaz flashing her saucy smile.

Unfortunately, he'd told Yaz not to hold lunch for him today, thinking things might go well with Janet.

Ha, not even twenty minutes into the coffee date he could tell the divorcée was still hung up on her ex. It wasn't much longer before he couldn't help but glance at his watch, wondering what Yaz and Maria might be up to at home. Wishing he was there to join them.

Laughter rang out from the backyard and Tomás moved to the kitchen window to peek outside.

Bundled up in her black ski jacket, mittens, and a dark knit cap, Yaz crouched down, a pile of snowballs at her feet. Maria let out a whoop of joy as she tossed a handful of snow at Yaz.

The wind promptly blew the white fluff away and Maria ducked for cover.

Looked like his little girl needed some reinforcements. Joining her would be the perfect way to take his mind off his disappointing reentry into the world of dating.

"Think you can hit me with a snowball and get away with it, *señorita*?" Yazmine pitched her voice low in her best dastardly villain impersonation.

"*¡Sí!* I do!" Maria scampered around the wooden swing set in the spacious backyard, her cry trailing off with laughter.

"Think again! You are soooo mine!"

The little minx poked her head around the slide's edge. She shook her head no, the pompon on top of her pink cap jiggling before she disappeared behind her hiding place again.

Adrenaline pumping, Yaz crouched down to scoop up a snowball. A giggle bubbled up in her throat and she rose, ready to attack.

Something smacked against her back and she stumbled forward. She spun around, shocked to find Tomás standing near the back door.

"Take that!" he challenged, bending down to grab more snow. A sexy grin spread across his face and Yaz's pulse skipped.

"Papá!" Maria cried. "*¡Sálvame!*"

"Stay where you are, *m'ija*. I'm coming to save you!"

Before Yaz could react, Tomás sprinted across the yard, the ends of his navy scarf flapping in the wind.

"Two against one?" she called out. "No problem. Lilí and I are reigning snowball champs on our street. I can take both of you. Easy!"

She scurried behind the bushes under the kitchen window and quickly began assembling an arsenal.

"Hey, where'd you go?" Tomás yelled.

"Wouldn't you like to know?" His laughter answered her taunt and she found herself grinning like a fool.

"So it's gonna be like that, huh?"

"We Midwesterners take our snow battles seriously."

"Well, coming from south Texas, I may not have much experience, but I know how to win. *¡Mujer, eres mía!*"

Woman, you are mine?

His battle cry sent a thrill of excitement down her spine. "Bring it on!"

Through the bushes she spied Tomás belly crawling from the slide to the nearby picnic bench in search of protection. Snow dusted his dark hair. Determination clenched his jaw muscles.

Carefully, Yaz took aim, crying out in triumph when her snowball splattered against his hip. He paused, sending a narrow-eyed glare in her direction. She launched another, missing slightly high of his shoulder.

"She's hiding in the bushes, Maria!" Tomás called, rolling behind the picnic table. "I'll draw her out and you get her."

"Okay!" Maria answered.

Yaz snickered at his simple plan. Silly man. How little he knew about winter war tactics.

Suddenly Tomás jumped out from behind his lame

hiding place—please, a wooden picnic table?—to stride directly toward her. He made an easy target and she wasted no time in shellacking him with snow.

She aimed for his broad chest, bombarding him with pinpoint accuracy again and again. Yet he kept coming, completely undeterred. Darn his tenacity.

Then she realized. *Ay no!* If she didn't change position ASAP, he'd have her cornered between the bushes and the house in seconds.

Scooping up as many balls as she could, Yaz slid out from her hiding spot, intent on running to the side yard for better protection.

"Get her, Papá! Get her!"

A snowball smacked against her butt, the force pushing her forward. She let out something between a laugh and a scream and tried to pick up her pace. Unfortunately, in six inches of snow, she wasn't as fast as Tomás.

Peeking over her shoulder, she saw him gaining on her, looking all Abominable Snowman-ish with his navy wool coat covered in the white powder. He gave her a devilish grin that sent heat pulsing through her.

Time for Plan B. Forget about retreat!

She swiveled around to face him, arm cocked back to let her ammunition fly. Instead, she found herself body-slammed to the ground.

The thick blanket of snow cushioned her fall, but Tomás's heavy weight landing on top of her knocked the breath from her lungs.

"Holy sh—. *Ay*, Yazmine, *estás bien?*" Tomás struggled to get off her, but his arms sank up to his elbows when he tried to brace himself.

Her knit cap had been knocked askew and she peered up at him with one eye. The slack-jawed, wide-eyed look of utter shock on his face was absolutely priceless. Obviously she wasn't the only one floored by his tackle.

She started to laugh, then winced at an ache in her back.

"O-owwww," she groaned.

"Are you okay?" Tomás repeated, his voice gruff with concern.

She closed her eyes, gingerly shifting her body, taking inventory of any pain points. Hyperaware of his full length on top of her.

"I'll get the Band-Aid box from the bathroom!" Maria cried.

"*Estoy bien*." Yazmine's voice came out a scratchy whisper.

"Huh?" Tomás bent his head closer to hers.

"I said—" She cleared her throat, tugging her cap back in place. When she opened her eyes Tomás's handsome face filled her view, the cloudless sky above framing him. "I'm fine. I think."

"Damn, that's good."

He heaved a sigh, his body sinking more heavily onto hers. Desire furled through her, curling her toes in her boots.

Yaz held her breath, allowing herself to enjoy—at least for a few precious moments—the sensual feel of him pressed so intimately against her.

"Why the heck did you stop like that?" he asked.

"Hey, you're the one who tackled me."

"I was aiming for your feet, trying to trip you up a little. I didn't expect you to stop and come at me like some crazy commando."

"You should know by now to expect the unexpected

with me." She grinned, her smile wavering when he pressed his forehead against hers.

"You are unbelievable."

His minty breath warmed her face. Sent prickling heat to all parts of her body.

Suddenly the snow beneath her didn't feel quite so cold. The crisp winter breeze lifting the white fluff in tiny whirls around them could have been a summer gust for all she knew.

"Most people would have kept running for cover. ¿Tu?" He nudged her nose with his. Awareness tightened her belly. "You come right at me like a crazy woman. You're really something, you know that?"

Unfortunately, she wasn't enough for him, and she couldn't let herself want to be.

Guilt and despair sluiced in to fill her chest.

"I'm one of a kind," she answered, longing for him to agree. Then get to work devising a plan for how they could be together.

He'd called her crazy. Maybe she was.

Tomás pulled back a fraction. Far enough for her to watch his gaze slide down to her lips, then back up to meet hers again. Heat flared in his dark mahogany eyes.

Her lips begged to taste his. Her fingers were desperate to run through his hair, pull his head down to hers.

"This wouldn't be wise, would it?"

No, it wouldn't. Still, she couldn't bring herself to speak. Didn't trust herself to make the smart choice.

He must have read her indecision, or sensed the desire she held on an insanely short leash.

With a muffled curse, he swooped down to cover her mouth with his. She welcomed him, wrapping her arms around his strong back.

His tongue coaxed her to open for him. Willingly, she did. He tasted like coffee and mint, and she laved it up, their tongues twisting and dancing together. He nipped at her lower lip before sucking it between his. Desire crested, crashing over her. Making her want more. Need more.

She moaned with pleasure.

All of a sudden he pulled back, rolling to his left to land in the snow next to her. The cold wind hit her, jarring her back to the reality of her situation.

She gasped for breath, her only consolation the sound of Tomás doing the same beside her.

"I shouldn't have—"

"That shouldn't have—"

They spoke at the same time, each breaking off to let the other finish. Yaz slapped her gloved hand over her face, mortified by her inability to control her impulses. *Dios mío*, had she ruined things between them? Please don't let them slip into some awkward, uncomfortable place now.

"I'm sorry," Tomás said. "I wasn't—"

"Stop," Yaz ordered. His apology would only make her feel worse. "This was a joint venture. So, equal blame. Equal pretending it never happened. Deal?"

There was a beat of tense silence. Her heart raced with fear. Would they not be able to go back to the easy camaraderie they'd shared before?

"Deal."

Her body sagged with relief when he finally answered.

Tomás sat up, brushing off the snow as he stood. "You know, I came home hoping for a little consolation after my catastrophe of a coffee date. Instead, I wind up covered in snow, worried I might have injured everyone's favorite dance instructor two days before the Christmas show. You definitely know how to make life interesting."

"Hey, you're the one doing the Chicago Bears line-backer imitation. Not me."

"Whatever. I like my version of the story better. Commando Yazmine, that's what I'm going to start calling you. Come on, let's get inside." Reaching for both her hands, Tomás carefully pulled her to her feet.

She couldn't help but notice how quickly he let go of her once she was steady.

"I've got work to do," he said. "And no telling how many Band-Aids Maria's already ripped open."

Yaz chuckled, gingerly moving through the snow. Her back felt a little achy, but she'd shake it off.

"You okay?" he asked again, his concern touching her in ways it might not have moments before.

"Yeah, but . . ." She stopped, waiting for him to turn and look at her. "Back there?" She nudged her head toward the ground behind them, at the deep impression their bodies had left in the snow. "We're, we're good, right? Friends?"

He shook some snow out of his hair, his dark gaze unreadable.

"Sure, friends." One corner of his mouth curved up in the barest hint of his sexy little half smile. Sadly, Yaz couldn't help but notice that his dimple didn't wink at her this time.

As she started walking toward the back door again, disappointment weighed down her steps. Then she remembered something he'd mentioned earlier. "Hold on a minute, did you say *catastrophe* date?"

"I sure did. And FYI, your services as a matchmaker are terminated."

The world dropped out from under her, leaving her

wobbly-kneed and shell-shocked. "You and Janet hit it off?"

"Uh, no. A catastrophe isn't usually a positive thing." Tomás grimaced, stomping his feet on the cement porch to clean his shoes. "And I don't want to go through another painful experience like that again."

"So you're giving up on your Perfect Partner Plan?"

The excited butterflies in her belly were not a good sign. Still, they took flight.

"No, but I'll find my own dates from now on."

That easily he hit the stop button on the happy dance music playing in her head. Of course he wouldn't give up so easily. Maybe Janet Miller wasn't the right person for Tomás, but neither was she.

His Perfect Partner was out there, and sooner or later he'd find her.

Chapter Eleven

"I'm sorry, girls. There's nothing more I can do."

Yazmine heard Dr. Lopez's words, but her mind couldn't seem to make sense of them.

"That's—that's not—not acceptable!" Lilí cried, voicing the words they were no doubt all thinking.

Yazmine's gaze darted to Lilí, standing behind Papi's cushioned chair in front of the doctor's desk. Her younger sister's pixie hair framed an angry, belligerent face, hazel eyes flashing at Dr. Lopez.

A tsunami-sized wave of nausea slammed through Yaz as the magnitude of Papi's diagnosis hit her. Beads of sweat popped up on her brow. She swiped at the moisture and pressed her lips together, desperate to hold back the cry of pain building in her throat.

Dr. Lopez had to be wrong. This couldn't be happening.

Papi's slumped shoulders told Yaz much more than the doctor's prognosis. His face was lined with fatigue and sorrow, giving him a worn, haggard look. She stared closely at him and saw something in his eyes that scared her even more. Acceptance.

Everything else in the room faded from her vision except for Papi. Seated in the chair next to him, Yaz put her hand over his, feeling his death grip on the armrest. "How long have you been struggling with this truth on your own, Papi?"

He closed his eyes, took a deep, shuddering breath. Somehow it felt like he'd sucked the breath out of her, too.

Her heart cracked, in danger of shattering into a million jagged pieces right here on the floor in Dr. Lopez's office. "Two weeks ago at Thanksgiving you said the cancer *might* have returned, and if so, you didn't want to fight it. Did you already know then?"

"No, this is wrong," Lilí cried, desperation in her voice. "All wrong. Call the lab. Maybe they gave you someone else's results. Not Papi's. It's a mistake. It has to be. Damn it, this is a mista—"

"Shhhh, shhhh." Rosa wrapped her arms around their younger sister. "*Está bien*, you hear me? It's going to be okay."

Yaz glanced over her shoulder, making eye contact with Rosa who, until now, had stood silently behind her.

"Why don't you take Lilí out in the lobby to get a drink of water?"

Rosa shook her head. "She'll be fine. I think we need to hear this together."

Yaz caught the flash of fear in Rosa's eyes, but it was quickly tempered by her middle sister's habitual calm. Rosa was always their port in a storm. Yaz gave her sister a slight nod, fighting back tears of her own, then turned to face Dr. Lopez.

"When you say 'nothing more,' what do you mean?"

Yaz asked the doctor. "We give up? Stop fighting? The girls and I aren't ready for that."

Dr. Lopez looked from her to Papi. Out of the corner of her eye, she saw Papi incline his head at the doctor's unspoken question.

His expression grave, Dr. Lopez continued. "About six weeks ago we found—"

"Six weeks!" All three girls cried in unison.

Papi winced at their outburst.

Yaz willed herself to find some sense of control. Freaking out wouldn't help their situation. She gave Papi's hand a love squeeze, like they'd always done during the "Our Father" at mass and after their meal blessing. "*Perdón.* I'm sorry, continue."

"About six weeks ago I noticed something that seemed a little off, but Rey wanted to wait until we had more definitive results to share with you." Dr. Lopez's voice remained calm, his eyes gentle. "Unfortunately, we found traces of cancer in several places. His left lung, his pancreas, and his left hip."

From behind her, Yaz heard Rosa's gasp, Lilí's sob. She longed to turn around, gather them into a group hug and let the tears flow. She was the oldest though, which meant she had to be the strong one, undaunted by life's challenges.

"Okay, so this—" She broke off to clear the scratch in her throat.

Papi sandwiched her hand between his, returning her love squeeze of moments ago. Tears stung her eyes, burned in her nose at his gesture. Even during this terrible, terrible moment for him, he offered his support and strength to her.

"Okay, so this—" She tried asking her question

again, willing away the quaver in her voice. "*¿Qué quiere decir?*"

"It means it's very aggressive," Dr. Lopez replied. His mouth a grim line, his gaze slowly traveled from Yaz to each of her sisters before he spoke again. "Your father doesn't have much time."

Her sisters moved in closer behind her and Papi, closing the ranks. Lilí's sobs continued in earnest as she grabbed Papi's shoulders. Rosa cried quietly, tears streaming down her cheeks, her arms tightly embracing their little sister.

Suddenly Yaz's anger kicked in. She clenched her jaw, desperate to rail at someone, something.

They'd been fighting this damn battle for too long. Papi had fought so freaking hard. None of them were ready to say good-bye. This wasn't fair.

The childish rationale cut off her inner argument. Life wasn't always fair. She'd learned that the hard way in New York.

Coming home had been for her as much as for Papi. Helping him heal had allowed her to do the same. Still, she wasn't ready to let go. Wasn't ready to leave again. Wasn't ready for *him* to leave.

Fear skittered down her spine like a banana spider on a plantain stalk, shimmying her shoulders with a nervous shiver.

"I did not want to say anything until after the holidays," Papi said. He turned in his chair to face Yaz and the girls.

Lilí sank to her knees in between the two chairs. "*¿Por qué*, Papi? Why? We're in this together. That's what you always say."

He cupped her face with his hands. "*Sí, nena*, we are.

For as long as we can. But my body is tired. *Mi alma*"—
he put a fist to his chest—"my soul is weary."

Yaz swiped at the hot tears cascading down her
cheeks, not even sure when they'd started.

"We can fight this," Lilí insisted.

"*Sí*, Papi, together," Rosa added softly.

Papi shook his head slowly. "I cannot do this anymore, *nena*."

"*Te podemos ayudar*," Yaz argued.

"I don't want you to *help* me. I want to *enjoy* being
with you, not feel tired and nauseous, or feverish and
weak all the time. With little chance the chemotherapy
will work. *Eso no es vivir*." The desperation on his face
was like a knife thrust to her already battered body.

"That is not living," Papi repeated. His gaze pierced
Yaz, and she sensed his plea for her to back him up.
Help him convince her sisters. "This is the right thing
to do. Now I can focus on making sure that you girls
will be okay."

"I'm not going back to school after the holidays."

"Me neither," Lilí chimed in after Rosa.

"*Basta. No hables de tonterías*."

"We're not talking foolishness!" Rosa objected, her
raised voice and uncharacteristic back talk to Papi
shocking Yaz. "I want to be here with you."

"I agree with Rosa," Lilí said, "I think we shouldn't—"

"*¡Silencio!*"

All three girls jumped at Papi's outburst. He rarely
raised his voice at them. When he did, they knew better
than to keep pushing.

"I refuse to spend the final months of my life with
you *nenas* hovering around, putting your lives on hold,
waiting for me to die!" Papi pushed himself to his feet.

He stood proud before them, shoulders back, his

expression unyielding. The tiny tremble in his chin was the only sign of his inner turmoil. Yaz swore she felt his anguish to the marrow of her bones.

"Papi, *por favor*, take it easy," she begged, worried he might be getting too upset. "We can discuss this at home, okay?"

"There is nothing more to talk about." His no-nonsense attitude had her morphing back to her junior year of high school when he'd grounded her for a month for taking the train into Chicago without permission. No amount of her pleading had made him budge then either. "Yazmine, you have your own life to live. And you have already given up enough of your career for me. I will not put us through months of chemotherapy when it would be pointless. And Rosa, *te falta un solo semestre.*"

He held up a finger to make his point. "Only one semester! If you do not graduate, the Queen of Peace Academy will not hold the job for you. Lilí, you cannot"—he slashed a hand through the air like a machete cutting off any arguments at their roots— "put your scholarship in jeopardy. *¡No lo permito!* Do you hear me? I will not permit it!"

He staggered back a step.

"Papi!" Yaz and her sisters lunged forward to grab him.

"*Estoy bien*," he muttered, leaning on Dr. Lopez's desk for support.

"Okay, okay, we get it." Yaz's fear for his well-being drove her to say whatever would calm him. "We won't talk about this anymore. Right, girls?"

She turned to her sisters. Rosa's pale face was tear-streaked, her eyes dark pools of worry. Lilí ducked her head and snagged a tissue from a box nearby. Neither said a word.

"We'll do whatever you want, just, *por favor*, Papi, *cálmate*."

"Yazmine's right, Rey, you need to calm down. This anxiety and stress is not good for you."

Yaz gave the doctor a look of thanks, praying Papi would at least listen to him.

Papi sank down onto the edge of the desk with a heavy sigh. Shoulders sagging, he dropped his head to his chest, the picture of a man accepting defeat.

Yaz pressed a fist to her mouth, trying to push back the sob building in her chest.

When Papi finally spoke, his tone was measured, his words eerily steady. "We have the entire winter break to be together. Once school starts, you girls may come home on the weekends, *if* it will not compromise your grades. But I cannot—" He looked up at them, a sadness so profound pinching his features, Yaz shuddered with pain. "I will not go to your mother with the guilt of having stopped you girls from achieving all you have worked so hard to achieve. *¿Entienden?*"

The ostrich egg–sized lump in her throat kept Yaz from speaking, so she nodded her understanding.

Her sisters, eyes downcast in shame, followed suit.

"Now, tonight is Yazmine's Christmas recital. It should be a happy occasion, the same way it has been every year before. You promise me this one will be no different."

Tomás peered around the stage curtain at the standing-room-only audience, his palms sweaty with nerves. He swiped a hand over his clammy brow, then rubbed the moisture on his tuxedo pants.

Damn, all these weeks of practicing, not once had he given serious thought to the idea that he'd actually be standing on a huge stage, white lights glaring down on him like supercharged sunlamps, his limited dance skills on display for all the world to critique.

"Are you excited or what?"

Tomás turned to gape at the burly dad standing next to him. His beer belly protruding over his cummerbund, his chubby cheeks framing a gregarious grin, the dad fussed with his bow tie while they waited to go on next.

"Uh, I'll go with 'or what.'" Tomás tugged at his shirt collar, feeling like it had somehow managed to shrink since he'd put it on a few minutes ago.

"Dude, we're gonna kill it. Katie's my youngest of three girls so I've done this plenty of times, and you caught on pretty quickly after those no-shows. It's in the bag." The dad punched him playfully in the arm and Tomás tried to offer him a reassuring smile.

Obviously he hadn't done a very convincing job because Yaz sidled up to their group and the dad shook his head, jabbing his thumb toward Tomás.

"Looks like we've got a spooked one, Ms. Yazmine. You may need to talk him off the ledge."

Yaz stepped closer to Tomás, a question drawing her brows together. "What's up? You look—"

"Nervous? Petrified?"

Her mouth spread in the reassuring smile he'd seen her give her students countless times, her eyes crinkling at the corners. She put her hands on his chest and leaned in closer. Her violet scent filled his hyperventilating lungs.

In a sound-barrier-breaking hot second his situation went from bad to worse.

Since their sanity-blowing kiss in the snow two days ago, he'd made a point of *not* getting too close to her. Trying *not* to ogle the curve of her neck as she tilted her head, listening closely to one of Maria's stories. *Not* to notice the way her full lips twitched a millisecond before she laughed. *Not* to remember how delicious she tasted and how amazingly good their kiss had made him feel.

Now here she was getting all up close and personal and in his face.

His hands fisted at his sides.

This was the opposite of helping.

"Yazmine—" he ground out.

"I was going to say you look handsome. Maria will be so proud of you. I am." She straightened his bow tie, then smoothed her hands down his lapels. That quickly his libido flicked into overdrive.

His blood surged south and he willed his body to slow down. He was already stressed about the curtain going up, no need to add to his discomfort.

"You'll be marvelous," she continued. "I'm sure of it."

"*Gracias.* I appreciate the pep talk."

She stepped back, but Tomás trapped one of her hands with his against his chest. Crazy as it might be, he needed a little more of the reassurance she offered.

At least that's what he told himself.

"In case I don't get a chance to tell you later," he said, "your number with the senior class was beautiful."

"Thanks. I appreciate you saying so." She peered up at him, batting her wispy fake eyelashes.

Man, who knew those things would be a turn-on?

He did now.

She was breathtaking, both on stage and off.

He'd seen her dance at the studio, but watching her come alive on stage tonight had been absolutely astounding. She could have been dancing a solo for all the notice he gave the other girls performing with her. As soon as she moved, all graceful arms and sexy legs, wearing another one of those figure-hugging dresses, this time in red, a wispy skirt flowing around her thighs, he'd only had eyes for her.

If there'd been any doubt about the level of her talent before, it'd been erased mere seconds into the dance number. Yazmine Fernandez was meant for bigger stages, bigger crowds, and bigger things than Oakton, Illinois, or he could ever offer.

She was incredible, but the reality had been sobering.

"Now"—Yaz slid her hand from under his to give his cheek a playful pat—"you go out there and enjoy this special moment with your daughter. Hopefully it's the first of many. Treasure them. It goes by fast."

He started to fire off a smart remark, feeling more confident thanks to her. But then he looked into her eyes, saw a hint of sadness lingering behind the go-get-'em, professional persona she maintained at the studio.

"What's wrong?" he asked, grabbing her shoulders to keep her close to him.

She shook her head and looked away, though not before he saw the shimmer of tears.

"Yazmine?" He cupped her chin, turning her face back toward him.

She bit her bottom lip, the white of her teeth glaring against her red lipstick. "I can't—I can't talk about it now. I promised Papi that it wouldn't ruin the evening. But it's not good. He's not—"

The jazz music for the group on stage surged to a climax signaling that the routine neared its end. The father-daughter dance was next.

Yazmine clasped her hands in front of her chest. Her shoulders rose and fell on a deep breath as she stared out at the stage. When she looked back at him, her gaze was steady and clear. All trace of her personal turmoil wiped away. She was a professional, cognizant that the show must go on.

The music drew to a close. The dancers curtsied at the applause, then sashayed off to the opposite wings.

"Time for me to wow the crowd, right?" He winked, hoping she'd gift him with one of her appealing smiles. His anxiety eased when she did.

Seconds later Maria joined him at their spot on-stage, wearing a pink shimmery gown with tiny roses circling the waist. She looked like a little princess, which he knew pleased her immensely. She'd probably sleep in the outfit for the next week. Or try to convince him to let her wear it to school on Monday.

Out of the corner of his eye he caught sight of Yaz, ready to mime their steps behind the side curtain. Like always, there to lend a helping hand and a measure of support. But who was there for her?

The music started, grabbing his attention. He concentrated on remembering the moves and not making a fool of himself. Throughout their number there were a few flubs in the routine, none by him, thankfully. From the wings Yaz emphasized her steps so whoever was off could catch on again.

Before Tomás knew it, he and the dads were bowing to a standing ovation and then hurrying off. Yaz greeted them in the wings with high fives as they moved out of the way for another group to find their places on deck.

Backstage, the daughters scurried away to the dressing rooms to change and the dads headed to the men's bathroom in the lobby. Tomás hung back in the hallway, intent on talking to Yaz before she returned to oversee things.

She was a dynamo, this woman. From their first dress rehearsal, to the pre-show "break a leg" talk earlier this evening, to keeping the dancers organized during the recital . . . not once had he seen her ruffled. Except for that moment right before he'd gone on for their number.

"Hey!" he called.

About to grab the stage door handle, she glanced over her shoulder. She arched a brow in a *You want something?* kinda way.

Man, there were a million things he wanted from her. None he could have.

Knowing she was busy, he strode back to her quickly.

"I told you things would be fine. You were great," she said.

"Yeah, well, I have this amazing instructor . . ."

They shared a grin, him marveling at how astoundingly ready to conquer the world he felt around her. "So are we still on for hot chocolate at your house after the show?"

"Of course. I had a surprise visitor show up tonight, so he's coming over, too. He's a great guy. I want you to meet him."

The stage door opened and they stepped to opposite sides of the hall, making room for the group of dancers exiting.

"Anyway, I should run. Make sure the stage moms have the next groups wrangled and in place. You did fabulous! See you after!"

"Sure, good lu—break a leg!" he called, but the door was already closing behind her.

He turned and trudged toward the hall leading to the lobby. Now he couldn't help wondering who Yazmine's "surprise guest" might be. And exactly what this "great guy" meant to her.

Chapter Twelve

Tomás sat in a dining chair he'd dragged into the Fernandez living room, eyeing the interplay between Yaz and her friend from New York. The life she couldn't wait to return to. Jealousy tinged his vision.

"Jeremy is one of the few sane people I know in the City," she said, clinking her mug of hot chocolate against her friend's.

"Probably because I'm not in the entertainment business."

The guy's response earned him a smack on the knee from Yaz.

Their easy camaraderie tightened a knot of envy in Tomás's gut. From the moment Yaz had greeted him and Maria in the theatre lobby after the recital, her arm around Jeremy's waist, Tomás had noticed the light of pleasure shining in her eyes when she looked at the guy.

There'd also been a young blond woman in the group Tomás had quickly learned was Yaz's best friend, Cheryl. Her parents were waiting, so she hadn't stuck around long, though frankly, Tomás had been more concerned with sizing up Jeremy.

Something about the guy had seemed familiar, but it wasn't until Yaz mentioned their tie to New York that Tomás remembered the bin of photos Maria and Rey had been going through a couple of weeks ago. Jeremy was the blond IT guy with a football-player build who'd been in several pics with Yaz. One in particular had stuck out. The two of them cozied up together at some fancy event, all smiles and hugs for the camera.

Tomás really didn't want to like the guy, but when Jeremy had hunkered down to Maria's eye level and praised her "awesome dance moves," Tomás knew he couldn't fault him.

If Jeremy Taylor were a schmuck, Rey and the other two girls wouldn't have welcomed him into their home. Especially not Rey, the ever watchful, vigilant father.

"I'm glad you made it," Yaz told Jeremy. "It's been too long since I've had a connection to New York."

She leaned back on the sofa, seated next to Rey. Lilí flanked their father on his other side and Rosa had settled on the armrest. Since his arrival, Tomás had noticed that none of the girls strayed far from Rey. He'd also lost track of the number of worried glances furtively sent in the older man's direction.

"Yazmine has been working hard at the dance studio, practicing while the little one is in school, to keep up her form and technique," Rey said. "I don't want her to lose her skills or any opportunities because of me."

"Enough, Papi," Yaz mumbled. "I'm not losing anything. I chose to come home. I don't regret it."

Rey opened his mouth to respond, but must have decided otherwise because he pressed his lips together instead.

Yaz laid her head on her father's shoulder. Lilí followed suit with the other. Rosa leaned forward to finger-comb Rey's hair lovingly. Surrounded by his girls, Rey relaxed back into the sofa cushions, eyes closed.

Maybe this was his cue to leave. Tomás glanced at Jeremy. Mouth downturned, eyes questioning, Yaz's friend also seemed to catch that something was going on. Too bad neither of them knew what. Tomás had a good idea it had to do with Rey's health though.

"'Rock-a-bye baby, in the tree top, when the wind blows, the cradle will rock . . . '" Maria cuddled with an old baby doll someone had unearthed for her to play with, her song cutting through the stilted silence.

"Would you like to see the other toys in the box I found?" Rey asked Maria. "They belonged to my girls when they were your age."

Maria clambered to her feet. "*Sí, por favor.* And maybe we can have some *florecitas* for a snack?"

Rey laughed. "I'm sure we can. *Ven.*" He pushed himself off the sofa, grimacing at the effort it took. "I might even have a pair of Yazmine's old ballet shoes. I am saving them to put on display when she wins her first Tony award. Some day soon, right, *nena?*"

Yaz rolled her eyes at her father's confidence in her abilities.

Rey chuckled, then started shuffling toward the basement door, his steps more measured than usual.

"Maybe I'll go take a look at those treasures, too." Lilí jumped off the couch to take her father's arm.

"I am fine," he argued.

"Humor me."

"*Ay*, you girls . . ." Rey groaned, but he hooked arms with his youngest and continued walking, Maria skipping along in front of them.

The moment the basement door closed behind the trio, Jeremy scooted to the edge of the recliner and zeroed in on Rosa and Yaz.

"What's going on? Everyone's been tripping over each other trying to pull off this one-big-happy-family show since I got here. Even Lilí and you." He pointed a finger at Rosa. "And I know you two usually get under each other's skin. Something has you all walking on eggshells. What gives?"

Rosa slid off her perch on the couch armrest to plop down beside Yaz, her expression grim. She glanced from Yaz to Tomás, then back again.

"Should I join them downstairs?" Tomás asked, uncertain whether Rosa felt comfortable discussing a private family matter with him. He might not like it, but he had to admit they'd known Jeremy for much longer.

"No," Yaz answered. "Since I'm taking care of Maria now, you should be aware of things, too."

Her watching Maria wasn't exactly the main reason why he wanted to stay. He'd gotten attached to this family, more than he'd anticipated. When it came to Yazmine, more than he should have. However, Yazmine's role as Maria's temporary nanny was the safest explanation, so he'd go with it if it meant he could stay.

"We met with Dr. Lopez this morning. Papi's cancer is back. More aggressive this time, and it's spread." Yazmine's voice shook, sending an answering tremor of fear through Tomás. "Papi doesn't want to fight. It's so advanced now, he wants to simply let things take their course."

"What?!" Shock tore the word from him.

"It could be a matter of months, maybe weeks." Rosa's normally soft, round features were pinched with pain.

Tomás stared at the two sisters, despair a palpable force surrounding them. No matter the dismay he felt, he knew it was nothing compared to what they must be going through.

The thought spurred him to action.

"So what's the plan?" he asked. "What do you need me to do to help you?"

Yaz's sad semblance of her usual grin was like a chisel driving a crack in his heart. "Make a plan. Of course you'd say that."

"Same here," Jeremy added. "Count me in."

"Thanks," Yaz told them. "Right now, I'm not sure—"

"I want to stay and help care for him. But Papi won't let me or Lilí take the semester off." Rosa's lower lip quivered and she caught it between her teeth.

"He's right," Yaz said bluntly. "That's not an option."

Rosa jerked back as if her sister had slapped her. "How can you say that?"

"Because you've worked so hard for your degree. If you stop now you'll lose your job here. Who knows where you'll end up working then?"

Still processing the news of Reynaldo's diagnosis, Tomás couldn't follow the sisters' argument. Yaz must have understood his confused frown because she turned to him in explanation. "The librarian at our Catholic school wants to retire, but she's waiting for Rosa to graduate so they can hire her."

Yaz grabbed her sister's arm. "It's your dream job. You and Mrs. Patterson have talked about this since you started volunteering at the library your sophomore year. Why would you throw that away?"

"You think I can go back to Champagne alone, worrying about Papi?"

"You won't be alone."

Everyone turned to Jeremy. The questioning looks on Yaz and Rosa's faces told Tomás they didn't know what their friend meant either.

"I'll be at the University of Illinois main campus in the spring," Jeremy explained. "My company's been working on a project with the U of I computer division for the last year. I'll be there for a semester, then move to our Chicago office afterwards."

"You're leaving New York?"

Yaz didn't say it, but Tomás bet the rest of her question, if voiced, would have been something along the lines of *Where else would anyone want to live?*

"The lights shine equally as brightly in other cities, Yaz," Jeremy answered. "At least they do for me. Besides, it's time to come back home. My mom's thrilled."

She looked skeptical, but didn't argue. "Well, while you're at U of I, you can look after Rosa for me."

"I don't need a babysitter." Rosa's cheeks bloomed with a blush of embarrassment. "I can take care of myself."

"I know. But Jeremy's a great guy to have in your corner when things get to be too much."

Yaz and Jeremy exchanged a private glance that spoke of shared experiences. Close ones. That green-eyed snake slithered through Tomás again.

"I've got great shoulders to lean on if you need

them, Rosa. Yaz knows I'd do anything for her. And that goes for you, too."

Still keeping her grip on Rosa's forearm with one hand, Yazmine reached out for Jeremy with the other. He gave Rosa a solemn nod.

Tomás watched the exchange, ashamed at his infantile jealousy in the face of Jeremy's offer. Damn if he wasn't a stand-up guy.

"I appreciate it," Rosa told Jeremy, her voice softly polite. "But what would really help is if I were here, taking care of Papi."

"But you can't be!" Yaz argued.

"I was the one who stepped in after Mami died. When all you could focus on was getting into that dance program in New York after high school. Why does now have to be any different?"

"Because now you have too much to lose."

"And you don't?" Rosa shot back. "You've put your career on hold for too long."

The sisters faced off against each other on the sofa, Tomás uncomfortably unsure how or even if he should step in.

Yaz tossed her head, sending the end of her high ponytail flying over her shoulder. Frustration smoldered in her caramel eyes.

Rosa, who Yaz had described as the quiet and mild-mannered one, obviously knew how to hold her own. Chin jutted out at a pugnacious angle, she stared Yaz down.

Neither sister appeared ready to concede.

Feeling like an unwelcome eavesdropper, Tomás caught Jeremy's gaze. Tomás tilted his head toward the kitchen, silently asking if they should step away and give the sisters some privacy. Jeremy gave an almost imperceptible shake of his head.

"Oh, come on, Rosa, my time away probably doesn't matter," Yaz continued. "You've said so yourself, me making it in New York is a crap-shoot."

"*Ay, por favor, una vez.* Only once!" Rosa held her hands out, palms up, frustration oozing from her voice. "And I immediately took it back."

Yaz shrugged. "Papi's dream of me winning a Tony, or any other award, is probably just that, a dream. I know that, but I'm killing myself out there to give it to him because I owe him that much."

The desperation and self-reproach in Yazmine's words caught Tomás by surprise. What about her drive and desire to succeed for herself?

"In New York—hell, I'm one in a million there," she went on, swishing her hand through the air like she was brushing aside her self-worth. "You, you're perfect for your job. The students and faculty at Queen of Peace can't ask for a better, more dedicated person. They already know you from your volunteer work. I can't even count the number of kids who've stopped me in the grocery store to ask how you're doing, when you're coming back. You know how awesome that is?"

"Whatever." Rosa grumbled, mouth drawn in a disbelieving sneer. "I'm a librarian. Believe me, I know how boring that sounds to most people. But here, in this house, I'm important. I know how to keep things running like Mami did, how to cook the food Papi likes. Here I matter. Out there . . ."

She lifted an arm to the front windows, then listlessly let it fall back to her lap.

"Quit selling yourself short," Yazmine countered. "Why do you always do that?"

Rosa didn't answer. Instead another charged silence filled the room.

Tomás kept quiet, letting the sisters dictate what would happen next. The whole time he waited, he couldn't stop the nagging thought that maybe Rosa wasn't the only sister short-changing herself. He'd never heard Yaz outright doubt her skills and talent.

He was suddenly ashamed to realize that while she'd listened to him confess some of his darkest secrets, she'd remained tight-lipped about hers. Sounded like she had her own baggage to unload in order for her to move on.

While he had no idea if she'd confide in him if asked, he sure as hell planned to try.

One thing he *did* know is that right now Yaz and her sisters should be leaning on one another, not fighting.

"Before this, when Papi needed something, I'm the one he turned to," Rosa said, her voice a ragged whisper.

Eyes wide with pain, she pressed her hands to the sides of her face. The picture of a young woman at her wit's end. "My place has always been to keep things running smoothly. Step in where Mami was supposed to be. Lilí can always be counted on for a laugh. You bring the star power and awe. Everyone wants to be by you, like you. But me?"

"You're perfect." Yaz smoothed her sister's shoulder-length hair.

"I'm *dependable*," Rosa scoffed. "The one people count on to get the job done. In reality, for me it's more about trying to keep things the same. Stop things from changing so none of us feel the difference, or the pain. But they *are* changing, and I can't do anything about it."

She sucked in a shuddering breath. The stark anguish on her face brought out Tomás's protective older brother instinct, making him want to put his arm around Rosa's shoulders and tell her he'd take care of everything, like he did with Maria.

"All I needed was one more semester and then I'd be home," Rosa murmured. She spoke almost to herself rather than to the rest of them. "While you girls were busy being the life of the party, out conquering the world, I'd be here, making sure Papi was okay and everything was fine. Now, th-that's being taken away fr—"

Rosa broke off with a hiccupping sob. She sprang off the couch and raced toward the front door where she snatched her jacket off the coatrack and stormed out.

Yaz rushed to follow, but Jeremy was quickly by her side, stopping her before she got to the foyer. "I'll go. Maybe she needs to talk with someone who's not so close to the situation."

Yaz hesitated.

"He's right," Tomás said. "Let Jeremy try."

Yaz looked at Tomás, indecision and confusion furrowing her brow, swimming in her beautiful eyes. He gave her a nod of encouragement.

"Fiiine." Yaz drew out the word, her shoulders slumped in defeat. "I appreciate you checking up on her, Jeremy. Good luck. I've never seen her like this."

Seconds later, the door closed softly behind him. Down in the basement, someone started beating the bongo drums. Based on the off-tempo rhythm it wasn't Reynaldo, but at least it meant the rest of their party was occupied.

"You okay?" Tomás asked.

Lame question. He didn't want to push though and find Yaz headed out into the cold like Rosa.

One hand on her hip, Yaz pressed the other to her forehead. Her mouth opened and closed without a sound, as if she was at a loss for words; then, heaving a sigh, she strode into the kitchen.

Tomás debated following her, uncertain whether she'd want his company or not.

When he heard the soft sound of her muffled sobs he knew there was no decision to be made. No way could he ignore her need for comfort.

He found Yaz at the kitchen table, her head on her folded arms, her slender shoulders shaking with the force of her tears.

He remembered that day at Luigi's Pizzeria when she'd told him she needed to be strong for her family, especially her sisters. It seemed like a lifetime ago, instead of barely a month.

Today had packed a whopper of a punch for her family. It was crazy for her to think she had to take all this on herself. No way could he sit back and let her crumble under the overwhelming pressure and fear.

Not alone anyway. He admired her too much.

Hell, who was he kidding, he *cared* for her too much.

This was a woman who ruled her studio with a steel backbone and a friendly grin. Who stepped in to lovingly care for his daughter with no questions asked. Who made him feel alive without a single word, only the hint of her saucy smile and the promise of a witty remark.

She didn't deserve this.

Desperate to comfort her, to ease her pain, Tomás

gently grasped her shoulders from behind, letting her know he was there for her.

Yaz froze at his touch. Her breath caught on a hiccup.

He waited, refusing to consider that she might not want his help.

Hoping she wouldn't brush him off.

Before that thought settled over him, she was up and out of her chair, her arms encircling his waist, her face buried in his chest.

Relief loosened the knot choking his throat and he looped his arms around her, holding her tightly against him.

He drew in the scent of her violet perfume, caught the hint of the industrial-strength hairspray he'd smelled earlier tonight in the little girls' dressing room. It would forever remind him of her.

Yaz's sobs continued, wracking her slim frame. Slowly, rhythmically, he rubbed a hand up and down her back, praying for the right words to soothe her. "*Está bien*, it's okay. I'm here for you."

Dios mío, how he wanted to be here for her.

The depth of his emotion, the need to be her port in this stormy sea, built inside of him, scaring him more than anything else ever had. Despite that, he didn't back away. He couldn't. Not now. Not when she needed someone so desperately. Her grief, her fear, had to come before everything else.

"Why?" she murmured in between shuddered breaths. "Why does this have to happen?"

"I don't know, *querida*. It's beyond any of our comprehension. Rey's a good man. He deserves better. Longer."

Her tears flowed and he squeezed her tighter,

anxious to reassure her of his presence. Willing her sorrow to seep into him so he could carry the burden for her.

"You're going to be okay. I'm here for you."

He repeated the words over and over, rubbing a hand up and down her back until her tears finally subsided.

Then he smoothed a hand down her silky ponytail and bent to kiss her forehead. She took a deep breath, her chest pressing against his.

That quickly his thoughts jumped to how good it felt to hold her, be close to her. To how much closer he wanted them to be.

Yaz hiccupped, then rubbed her nose on his shoulder.

"Uh, can I offer you a tissue instead?" he teased, hoping he might lighten the mood, maybe get one of her infectious smiles.

She gifted him with a watery version of it. "Sorry. Your sweater's so soft though."

She stroked her fingers over the material. Tomás held his breath. Now was not the time for him to think about how right she felt in his arms, her soft curves melded with his frame.

"Cashmere?"

It took him a full second to understand her question. "Uh, yeah. Here—" He reached in his back pocket and pulled out a handkerchief.

"Thanks." She turned away to blow her nose.

It was difficult, but he stopped himself from tugging her close again.

"Keep it," he said when she tried to hand him back his handkerchief. "You can give it to me later. Clean."

She narrowed her eyes at him, but, yep, there it was,

a hint of the sassy, you-don't-wanna-mess-with-me expression he knew and loved.

His pulse skipped at his word choice and he took a mental double take.

It was a silly expression. No need for him to overreact. *Gracias a Dios* he hadn't said the words out loud.

"All that stuff you said about yourself to your sister—no, let me finish." He put a finger over her lips when she started to argue. Her eyes flashed in what he figured was annoyance. Too bad.

"You're an incredible woman, Yazmine Fernandez. I've seen you in action—with your family, your students, pushy parents, on stage tonight. More importantly, with Maria. You amaze the audience, and you light up a room. You make people feel good about themselves. Like you said to Rosa, don't short-change yourself."

Yazmine's eyes welled with tears once more.

"*Ay, por favor.* I didn't want to make you cry. *¿Qué pasa?*"

She pressed his handkerchief to her mouth and shook her head.

"What's wrong?" he repeated, wiping a tear from her cheek with the pad of his thumb. "I'm trying to cheer you up."

Yaz grasped his hand, linking her fingers with his. "You did. You are. Thank you." She lifted up on her tiptoes and pressed a kiss to his cheek.

Desire blew through him, stoking the fire he kept trying to bank. Instinctively he put his other hand on the small of her back, keeping her near him.

Yaz arched away a little, a mix of surprise and longing on her beautiful, tear-streaked face.

There was no way he could resist.

Tomás dipped his head, half expecting her to withdraw. Praying she wouldn't.

Gloriously she met him halfway.

Her lips were soft, sweet. Perfect. Heaven and hell all wrapped into one explosive package he longed to rip open. He tightened his grip on her waist, pulling her closer still. She ran a hand up his biceps to the nape of his neck, fanning his desire when she dug her fingers into his hair.

She was like fresh water to a man stranded in the desert, lost and wandering alone for too long. Only, he didn't crave just any woman. It had to be *this* one. The one who'd been driving him crazy, earning his admiration, burrowing her way into his life and making him smile and feel more alive the entire time.

Hungry for more, he deepened their kiss. Yaz moaned, a deep, guttural sound that spurred him on. He sucked her lower lip, savoring her taste of hot chocolate and marshmallows, along with a shot of something sinful and spectacular. Something that went straight to his head.

She leaned into him, pressing against his arousal. Seconds from going over the edge, he broke their kiss, bending to press a trail of tiny kisses down her neck. He nibbled along the edge of her low-cut sweater, licked the swell of her breast.

"*Sí, por favor,*" Yaz murmured, her voice breathy and heavy with desire.

Damn, she was so sexy, so open. So perfect.

A door opened and Rosa and Jeremy's voices carried in from the front of the house.

Tomás and Yaz sprang apart like two teens afraid of getting caught by their parents. Chests heaving, they wound up on opposite sides of the kitchen. Yaz's lips were swollen from his kisses, her eyes wide with . . . shock? Dismay? Fear?

Crap, he'd crossed the line. Again! Had he ruined the friendship they'd so carefully begun to build?

"*Perdóname*, I'm so sorry—"

"No, don't say that." Yazmine shook her head in short jerky motions over and over. "I shouldn't have—"

"It wasn't you. *I'm* the one at fault here. I know better." No way would he let her take the blame. He'd initiated the kiss. He'd enjoyed it way too much. Taken it too far. The same way he had after the snowball fight in his backyard.

Guilt soured his stomach.

"Fine, it was both of us," she said. "But it doesn't have to mean anything. You were offering comfort. I took it. No big deal. Right?" Her voice went up an octave on the last word.

He stared at her warily, surprised she could brush off their attraction, the passion they'd shared, so easily. Then he noticed that she wouldn't meet his gaze.

Her eyes at his chest level, she gave him the polite mask she used with difficult parents at Hanson's. "I was a mess. You were—Maybe we got a little—whatever." Hands stuck in her back jeans pockets, she edged away from him, like she was afraid he'd pounce on her again. "We both know this can't really happen. I'm not Perfect Partner material. And that's what you're looking for."

Tomás slumped against the door to the backyard, thankful for the support. There was no possible way he could feel like a bigger jerk than he did right now.

"Yazmine?" Rosa called from the living room.

Yaz flinched before answering. "In here! We were,

we're about to, to make more hot chocolate. Want some?"

She scurried over to the fridge, pulling out the gallon of skim milk. She busied herself with filling the pot and fiddling with the knobs on the stove. Not once glancing in his direction.

Disappointed in himself for bringing them to this uncomfortable place, Tomás strode to the basement door. Rather than wait for Rosa and Jeremy to witness Yazmine's obvious awkwardness around him, Tomás called for Maria to come up. No use sticking around if his being here made things worse.

Come Monday, when Yaz arrived to take care of Maria, he'd keep things polite, platonic. Hopefully by then any awkwardness would have passed.

Sure, he needed her help with childcare, and Maria enjoyed spending her days with Yaz, but he'd come up with a different solution if she felt uneasy around him because he couldn't manage to control his impulsive desire.

Heart heavy, he quickly bundled up Maria and left, crossing his fingers that he hadn't totally screwed things up.

Chapter Thirteen

Yaz tugged open the oven door in Tomás's kitchen late Monday afternoon, ducking her head at the wave of heated, sweet-smelling air that hit her in the face.

"Careful," Maria cautioned from her perch on a stool at the island.

Yaz chuckled at Maria's serious tone and the reminder she'd given each time Yaz opened the door. Apparently Tomás hadn't been careful the night before and had burned himself when cooking a frozen pizza.

That probably explained the large Band-Aid she'd noticed on the back of his left hand this morning. She'd wanted to ask him about it, but that was kind of hard when she was busy trying to keep communication to a minimum.

It was day two P2K—Post 2nd Kiss—and she was still figuring out how to cram her attraction and growing attachment to him back into a dark corner in her heart where they belonged. So far, not so good.

"No worries," she told Maria. "I'm using oven mitts. Here, don't they look and smell delicious?" Yaz set the last tray of Christmas cut-out cookies on the stovetop to cool.

"Good job! Can I eat one yet?" Maria wiggled excitedly in her seat, making Yaz rush to put a steadying hand on her shoulder before the stool toppled over.

"I'm sure the first batch is ready for a taste test. Let's see, you want a stocking, a Christmas tree, or a snowman?"

Maria oohed and aahed over the rows of cookies spread out on the cooling racks, while Yaz glanced around at the mess they'd made. Flour dusted the counters and the island. Bowls, stirring spoons, a rolling pin, and cookie cutters filled the sink. Salt, sugar, and other ingredients were piled off to the side, waiting to be put away.

She wasn't necessarily the neatest baker in town. Something Rosa had often complained about when they were growing up. What mattered most, though, was how the cookies tasted. Based on Maria's "mmmmming," the afternoon's baking session was a success.

"Tasty?" Yaz snagged a snowman of her own. "Mmmm." Definitely a success, and doubly so for her.

The baking had entertained Maria while also keeping Yaz's thoughts on something other than Papi's health or how she was going to forget Tomás's kiss. Or the desire that sparked every time she was with him.

Since their steamy interlude—when she'd gone all animal instinct on him—Saturday evening she hadn't been able to get him off her mind. Or out of her dreams.

His touch, his taste, the scent of his musky cologne. The sensual feel of his tongue along the rise of her breast. The sense of security she felt in his strong arms.

All of it took her breath away, blasting coherent, rational thought to smithereens.

That could not continue. Their mind-numbing kisses had done nothing to change their situation. He was still intent on staying in Oakton and going through with his Perfect Partner Plan. She was still obligated—no, scratch that—destined to fly off to New York in search of success for her and Papi.

They were simply on two completely divergent paths that happened to merge for this short period of time. That's all. She'd do well to remember that.

The door to the garage swung open and Yaz jumped in surprise.

"Papá!" Maria yelled, hopping off her stool to run to her dad.

"Hey, *chiquita*!" Tomás grinned, bending down to scoop Maria up in his arms.

The bottom half of Yaz's snowman cookie slipped from her grasp onto the counter, contributing more crumbs to the mess already there.

She threw a harried glance at the digital display on the stove, where 4:15 glowed in green numbers. "You're home early."

"Apparently you weren't expecting me." Tomás's gaze scanned his usually tidy kitchen. "You girls have been busy."

"We're making cookies for my class. We have a party tomorrow," Maria said.

"And this flour?" Tomás brushed at the dusting on Maria's cheek. "Are you saving it for later?"

Maria giggled. "No, silly. Ms. Yazmine says the bigger the mess, the better the cookies."

"Then yours must be delicious." He winked at Maria,

then turned his attention to Yaz, including her in his teasing compliment with his lazy grin.

Ay, but he was irresistible. Watching him tease Maria, ignoring the floury handprints she'd left all over his suit jacket, made him even more endearing.

His grin suggested there might be hope for him and Yaz. They'd been painfully, if politely, distant this morning—she getting a feel for where they stood after Saturday night, he seeming to wait and take his cue from her. Thankfully the morning rush had left little time for chitchat.

Now that he was home, the true test would come.

Picking up the spatula, she started transferring the last batch from the cookie sheet to the cooling racks on the island. Tomás set Maria down and stepped closer, checking out the fruits of their labor.

Suddenly the kitchen shrank in size. Yaz felt boxed in between the counter, the stove, the island, and his hulking frame. The mix of sweet cookie batter and his woodsy scent blended together, creating an unusual mix. One she found oddly stimulating.

If they were a normal family, he'd drop an affectionate welcome-home kiss on her lips. She'd lean in for a hug, a brief tease of what would come when they headed off to bed together later that night. If only . . .

The spatula wobbled in Yazmine's hand, clanging against the metal baking tray. The sound snapped her out of her daydream.

"My class is having two parties together!" Maria held up two fingers to emphasize her news.

"How did you get so lucky?" Tomás asked.

"'Cuz it's Christmas aaaand we have a new teacher! Ms. Yazmine's friend. And she ate lunch with us!"

Tomás's "ooh" hit the right note of awe and Maria

bobbed her head in agreement. His deep baritone intermingled with her high-pitched voice, the sweet sound a melody and harmony in sync. A welcome tune to Yaz's ears.

Watching them interact, Maria's little hands waving through the air as she spoke and Tomás's devoted interest in her story, both surrounded by the mess of the day's baking extravaganza, brought memories of Yaz's own childhood. Papi leading them in a Christmas carol from the kitchen table. Mami stirring a pot on the stove. Lilí and Rosa squabbling about something silly. *Ay*, what bittersweet times.

Tomás and Maria would create other memories like this, too. Though she wouldn't be a part of them. Another woman would be here with Maria, excited for Tomás to walk through the door. Welcoming him home with a kiss.

The thought dragged her spirits down, bringing her to a low point she hadn't felt since the last time she hadn't made an audition cut. That realization scared her.

He shouldn't be this important to her.

This life he was creating with his daughter shouldn't mean so much to her.

Rattled, Yaz picked up the empty baking tray with trembling hands. She turned to the sink, her back to Tomás and Maria and the scene she didn't belong in.

Maybe she wouldn't be here with them, playing a part in their special family moments, but she'd be doing something else even more important—honoring Papi's legacy. Especially after he was gone.

That responsibility weighed heavily on her, but she'd continue carrying the load, proving she was strong enough to handle it.

"So, Yaz, your baking strategy is a bit unique," Tomás said, drawing her into his conversation with Maria.

"Hmm?" She gave him a questioning look over her shoulder.

"The bigger the mess? Somehow that piece of advice didn't get handed down in my house growing up." The corners of his mouth quirked up in a teasing smirk.

His grin eased her worries about how they'd move past their awkwardness. The teasing, flirty Tomás she could deal with. The sensual, passionate one she had a hard time resisting.

"Hey, you're home earlier than normal. I thought I had several hours left for frosting and cleanup." She nudged the faucet lever on with the back of her hand to start washing the dishes. "What happened, they get tired of you at the office and send you home?"

"Cute. I knew there was something I liked about you—your twisted sense of humor."

"I'm here every day all week. You should have seen the earlier show."

His chuckle sent shivers across her shoulders, scurrying off to places in her body that had no business keying on his sexiness.

"Maria, will you please put my suit coat on my bed? I'm going to help Ms. Yazmine clean up a little."

"I've got it, you two go—" Yaz broke off when she turned to see Maria already skipping into the dining room, Tomás's flour-dusted coat draped over her arm.

Tomás stepped around the island, the muscles in his forearms flexing as he rolled up his light blue shirt-sleeves. Her heart stutter-stepped, her imagination jumping ahead to him slipping off his shirt completely.

His hands untying the frilly apron she'd found in a drawer and—

"Hand me that rag and I'll get started on the counters."

Yaz spun back around to the sink, mortified at her mind's meandering. Focus, focus. She squeezed her eyes closed, desperate to get her thoughts on a more appropriate track. This seesaw of emotions was going to make her a nervous wreck.

He seemed to have moved past their post-kiss awkwardness. Obviously it hadn't affected him as powerfully as it had her.

Pues, she'd been able to move on from more earth-shattering experiences, too.

"Go for it. I'm all for pawning off chores on someone else. Here." She tossed him a wet dishrag, her throw a touch more forceful than she intended.

The rag hit him square in the chest, leaving a dark blue wet mark on his shirt. Tomás blinked in surprise, grabbing the rag before it fell to the floor.

"Oops, sorry."

He arched a brow. "Everything okay?"

"Yep."

"Anything you want to talk about?"

"Nope." Inside her stomach quaked with nervous energy. "You?"

Tomás eyed her like a specimen under a microscope. "The other night . . . ?"

"Water under the bridge. Already forgotten." *Ay, qué mentirosa.*

Well, not a liar, more like a self-preservationist.

"The thing is, you were right. I've got my plan here.

And you've got yours . . ." He gestured toward the doorway. "Out there."

She nodded. Her throat clogged with tears she had no business crying.

"So, we're good?" He dragged out the words, the first note of hesitation she'd heard in his voice since he'd gotten home today.

She nodded again. In reality, though, she really wanted to ask *him* if he was sure. Only, she was too chicken.

Instead she watched him swipe at the island with his rag, sending flour cascading onto the floor. When he didn't seem to notice, Yaz frowned, puzzled. He was Mr. Type A, cleaning up messes was his specialty, not making them.

"We both had momentary lapses in judgment. That's all," he said, sending another shower of flour onto the floor.

She wondered if his calm, measured tone was the same one he used in the boardroom to sway clients who were on the fence. And whether he was trying to convince himself or her now.

"You don't have to worry about that happening again," he continued.

"Okay."

"Good." He gave a brisk nod, then stopped to frown at the flour dusting the tile floor. "Hopefully we can get back to normal then."

Whatever normal was. She didn't know anymore.

When he continued wiping down the counter, this time scooping the debris into his palm, she got back to work on the dirty dishes. "So, um, how was your day?"

She sensed him moving around the island behind

her and she pressed against the sink, giving him more room to get by.

"We heard from the Linton representative. We made the first cut and will present our final mockups in mid-January."

"That's great!" Yaz rinsed off a handful of cookie cutters and dropped them on the drain board. "It's nice they're still interested in you. Or, I guess, your firm, right?"

"We're in the top three. Excuse me." Tomás leaned in to rinse off the rag, his shoulder bumping against hers. Even through her sweatshirt she felt the electric shock of his touch.

Yaz sidestepped, removing herself from the pleasurable tingles. "Any lunch dates this week? Since your coffee date with Janet last week, you haven't said much about your Perfect Partner search."

"Because I'm not calling it that. You are." He flicked water at her with his fingers and she swatted at his hand.

"¡Oye! Be nice."

"You asked for it," he teased.

"By your deflection of my question, I take it you're in a holding pattern." Not good. While the thought of him going out with another woman rankled, it was also a reality check for her. A reminder that she didn't fit his needs. "No new prospects?"

She caught his nervous swallow and she narrowed her eyes at him in suspicion. "Are you holding out on me?"

He flashed a sheepish grin that made him look more like a mischievous little boy caught with his hand in his *mamá*'s cookie jar.

"Come on, spit it out," she urged.

Sliding over near the fridge, he opened the small

junk drawer where they kept pens, scissors, and other loose items. He withdrew a pink sticky note and two other small pieces of paper. Rolling his eyes, he held them out to her without a word.

"What's this? Who—?" She stopped when she recognized the name scrawled above a phone number on the sticky note. Pamela Starnes. One of the moms at Hanson's Academy. The other two slips held familiar names and numbers as well. "How did you . . . ? When did you . . . ? The recital."

Hands in his pockets, Tomás flashed his sheepish grin again. His dimple winked hello. "Two of them walked right up after the show, introduced themselves, and handed me the paper. The other must have slipped it into my pocket in the crowd."

Yaz snorted her disbelief. "No way!"

"I didn't even notice. I got home from your house—" He paused.

Was he remembering their interlude in her kitchen? How she'd nearly come undone in his arms? She couldn't tell. Darn his well-practiced boardroom face.

"Anyway, I got home, cleaned out my pockets, and found the third one."

"Have you called any of them?" Her breath lodged in her chest, wanting him to say no.

"Not yet. I'm not sure what to think. The third one"—reaching out, he flicked the smallest of the three papers—"if she couldn't bring herself to say hello, even if she was aiming for mysterious, kind of weirds me out. I'm not really into playing games."

"Good, I know this mom." Yaz crumpled the paper he'd indicated. "Cindy's not right for you. She's a barracuda. Looking for husband number four." Yaz pursed her lips, nodding at Tomás's raised brow.

She tossed the paper in the trash can with a spurt of satisfaction.

"And the others?" he asked.

"Not too bad. I can do some digging for you if you'd like."

"Uh, no." Tomás tugged the papers from her grasp. He placed them back in the drawer and pushed it closed. "Let me think about it. Now, about this Christmas party for Maria's class." He tapped the flyer Yaz had stuck on the refrigerator door. "You know the new teacher?"

"Yes, and she's fabulous!" Yaz laughed when he blinked at her exuberance. "You met Cheryl the other night after the Christmas show. Petite blonde, a little shorter than me."

"Oh yeah, I remember. We chatted briefly. Seems nice."

"She's been my best friend since high school. Cheryl got her degree in early childhood education and has been working in southern Illinois since graduation."

"High school, huh? I bet she has some fun stories to share about you." He grinned when Yaz wrinkled her nose at him.

"She's a great teacher. And an even better person." As soon as she said the words Yaz froze, her hands deep in the soapy water.

Cheryl loved kids, wanted to settle down and get married, and enjoyed living in Oakton. She was clearly Perfect Partner material. Not only that, now that Ronnie was out of the picture, she was available.

Jealousy sparked in Yaz. Just as quickly, reality and the truth doused the flame.

She glanced at Tomás under her lashes as he cleaned

the island. *Dios*, with his chiseled jaw and aquiline nose, his profile alone made a girl feel all wobbly kneed. Those good looks were only a small part of the package that made up this amazing man. He deserved more than a woman who couldn't figure out where her dreams lay, or how to make both herself and her family happy.

As much as it might hurt, she knew someone who fit Tomás's ideal far better than she ever would.

"Can you get away for an hour or so tomorrow, mid-morning? Maybe come to the Christmas party with us?"

The indecision in his eyes made her increase the pressure with a little guilt trip. "Maria would be thrilled, and it'll give you an opportunity to meet Cheryl. A lot of the parents stopped by during drop-off and pick-up today to introduce themselves."

His island cleaning paused as he stared off into space. Yaz figured he was picturing his color-coded planner in his mind. The guy could give Rosa a run for her money when it came to organization.

"Hm, I can probably do that." He stepped toward the sink, still pensive, to drop more crumbs down the drain. This time Yaz edged away before he bumped her. Better to be safe than stupid.

"Yeah, I can swing it," Tomás said, turning the water on. "I'll do a few things tonight, get ahead of the game. If you have any errands you need to run, I can take Maria on my own." He rinsed off the rag, then hung it over the faucet.

Before she realized what he meant to do, he tugged the kitchen towel off her shoulder, his knuckle brushing against her collarbone. Her breath hitched in her chest. Her eyelids fluttered, mimicking the butterflies taking flight in her belly.

"You need to take the morning off?" he asked. "Spend time with your dad or go to Hanson's and practice?"

"N-no, I can make it." She cleared the shakiness out of her voice. "I volunteered to help. Pablo is taking Papi to eat breakfast with some of their *compadres*."

Besides, how could she orchestrate setting up Cheryl and Tomás properly if she wasn't there? This required a delicate touch. Both of them were newbies to the dating scene again, so they were a little gun-shy. It might take a few gentle nudges to persuade them. But she would.

Finding Tomás his "perfect partner" might be the best way to convince herself that in his arms, in his life, was not where she belonged.

"Sounds good then. We'll go together." Tomás flicked the end of the towel back over her shoulder with an easy grin. "Let me see what Maria's up to. She's been awfully quiet."

Yaz sagged against the counter and watched him stride away. "Going together" sounded good to her, too. For entirely different, completely inappropriate reasons.

She straightened her shoulders, annoyed with her schoolgirl-crush behavior. This self-sabotage wasn't healthy.

Starting tomorrow, Operation Perfect Partner Search would kick into high gear. Identified target? Cheryl Morgan, kindergarten assistant teacher and best friend extraordinaire.

If Yaz couldn't be Tomás's perfect partner, she'd

let someone better, someone she loved like a sister, have him.

And she'd have to find the strength to stand by and watch that happen.

Yaz shrugged out of her peacoat and hung it next to Tomás's jacket on a wooden peg in Maria's classroom. Maria hadn't even bothered to take her jacket off before she started weaving through her classmates, anxious to bring Cheryl over to meet Tomás.

The little girl's excitement over the fact that her father was cutting work to join them for her party reminded Yaz of how easily a parent could lift their child's spirits by simply showing an interest in them. Taking the time to be there for and with them. It's what Papi and Mami had done for her as a child.

This time caring for Maria was allowing Yaz a chance to savor a little taste of being a parent, filling a void she would never admit existed. Though he didn't know it, she owed Tomás for giving her this opportunity.

She could repay him by finding him a suitable match. Not a "life partner" like he planned. That was a dumb idea. He deserved more, and so did Maria. With Cheryl, he'd find a woman who met all his needs, one he was safe giving his heart to.

"Man, it's noisy in here." Tomás bent toward her so she could hear, his breath tickling her ear. "They need some pointers from you on how to run a quiet class."

She grinned, wrapping his compliment up to enjoy again later. "They don't run a tight ship like I do, but the kids settle down. And they already love Cheryl. She has that effect on people. Wait a minute." Yaz reached up to brush a few wayward flakes of snow from his hair.

"Thanks, Mom." His dimple flashed, giving rise to thoughts that were anything but mom-like. "Do I look presentable?"

Presentable?

Yaz slid her gaze up his strong frame, taking in his brown boots, khaki corduroy slacks, navy cable-knit sweater, and model-gorgeous face. *Ay bendito*, presentable didn't even begin to describe him.

"You'll do," she deadpanned, laughing as she side-stepped the elbow he tried to poke in her ribs.

"Yaz, I'm glad you could make it!" Cheryl opened her arms for a hug, then stepped back and held out her hand with a welcoming smile. "Hi, Tomás. It's nice to see you again. Maria's an absolute joy in class, and she's already shared quite a lot about you."

"Only good things, I hope," he answered.

Yaz barely stopped herself from rolling her eyes at his deepened timbre. *Por favor*, he didn't need to lay the schmooze on so thick.

She did, however, notice that he only gave Cheryl his "charming" smile, not the relaxed grin Yaz couldn't resist.

"I'll add that he's not a bad guy to temporarily nanny for, either," Yaz said.

"I wouldn't doubt it, if he talked you into baby-sitting." Cheryl put her hand on Yazmine's shoulder and leaned conspiratorially toward Tomás. "This girl has been *all* dance, *all* the time, for as long as I've known her. It's nice to see her branching out a bit."

"But we won't have her for long," Tomás said, his lips inching more toward that comfortable grin he didn't share with everyone. "She's on to bigger and better, while we little people stay behind."

Cheryl laughed, the tinkly sound mixing with

Tomás's husky chuckle. Yaz knew she should join in. She wanted to, but she suddenly felt like the outsider.

"I guess we 'little people' need to stick together," Cheryl teased.

"I hope so."

Tomás's response brought a dull shade of pink to Cheryl's cheeks, the color highlighting her gray eyes. "Um, sure."

Unbelievable! Yaz blinked in surprise. Her friend was already smitten, and Yaz couldn't blame her in the least. Nor could she be jealous. Cheryl didn't deserve that.

"Well, as you see, we can always use an extra pair of hands around here." Cheryl extended an arm to indicate the classroom, overrun with excited kids. Some were dressed for the occasion in Christmas sweaters, others sported the rumpled, bed-head look from what was probably a mad dash out the door.

"It's a little like controlled chaos," Tomás noted. "I have to admit, I've always thought it takes a special person to teach kindergarten."

"That's our Cheryl alright," Yazmine said, finally feeling like she could trust her voice not to give away her conflicting emotions.

Cheryl shot her a secretive look, her eyes screaming "Wow!"

"Class, let's meet at the reading corner," the head teacher called.

Most of the kids followed the instructions. A few dragged their feet.

"Joey, Stephen." Cheryl cautioned two boys who had stopped to play with the math manipulatives on a table near the far window. "That's not the reading corner."

The boys dropped the varied geometrical shapes and trudged to join their teacher on a multicolored rug near a short bookshelf and several beanbags.

"I was about to set up the cookie decorating station. Would one of you like to help?" Cheryl asked.

"Here, that sounds like a job you can tackle." Yaz thrust the plastic container with their homemade goodies at Tomás.

"You sure?" he asked.

"Of course. That'll give you two time to get to know each other before the craziness begins. Hey, don't give me that look. You and I both know it's about to get crazy in here," Yaz said, intentionally misreading Cheryl's puzzled expression.

The last thing she needed was either one of them thinking she was trying to set them up. Tomás had already told her he didn't want her help and Cheryl had a tendency to clam up if she was nervous.

"You two work on that together and I'll back up Mrs. Morris in the reading circle."

She flashed them a bright smile, realizing she might have overdone it when Tomás and Cheryl exchanged a dubious look.

"Go on." Yaz shooed them away.

"Well, if you're game, Tomás, let's get started," Cheryl finally said.

"Sure, I don't want to brag or anything, but Maria's told me I'm a pro at decorating cookies." He winked at Cheryl, eliciting another tinkly laugh from her.

Yaz watched her best friend lead Tomás to one of the round arts and crafts tables filled with cookies, plastic knives, tubs of frosting, and food coloring. They bent over the table, Tomás following Cheryl's instructions for how to organize the supplies. His dark coloring next to her light skin and hair made a striking contrast. Cheryl said something and Tomás's laughter rang out.

A yearning ache for what couldn't be and a wistful pang at her friend's good fortune swirled in her chest and Yazmine turned away, unable to watch anymore.

She tiptoed to the kids and their teacher, needing the distraction. Maria's eyes lit up and she scooted over, patting the floor beside her. As soon as Yaz sat, Maria scrambled onto her lap. She linked their fingers together, then crisscrossed her arms in front of her so they wound up in a big hug.

Maria angled her head to shoot Yaz a sweet, chubby-cheeked grin. Yaz pressed a kiss to the little girl's forehead and a welcome peace settled over her.

This was what mattered most. Her time with Maria and her time with Papi. Because as much as it pained her, she knew those moments were limited.

Behind her, Cheryl laughed, a familiar bubbly sound that usually made Yazmine join in the fun. She refused to turn around though and check on the potential lovebirds. If the way Tomás had charmed her friend earlier was any indication, neither one needed any more nudging from her. And she was more than willing to give them their space.

It was too painful otherwise.

Chapter Fourteen

Late Friday afternoon Tomás set his briefcase on the kitchen counter with a tired sigh. Rush hour traffic drained even the best of men.

"We're in my room, Papá!" Maria's voice carried down the hall from the back of the house. "I'm showing Ms. Rosa my Barbie dolls. Come play with us!"

Now that was a demand he could easily give in to. He strode through the living room, ready for some together time with Maria before he headed out for the evening.

Tonight was his first date with Cheryl Morgan. He had enjoyed chatting with her during the class party, then again one day when he'd picked up Maria after school because Yaz had been waylaid at the dance studio. He knew Yaz was matchmaking. Thankfully, he'd also learned enough about Cheryl to recognize that his temporary nanny might not necessarily be looking at her "fabulous" best friend through rose-colored glasses.

He'd be lying to himself, though, if he didn't admit he was a bit nervous about potentially having to sit through another disastrous date. When he'd gotten Yaz's text earlier, letting him know Rosa would be staying with Maria, he'd read it with mixed emotions. Partly relieved Yaz wouldn't be waiting for him when he returned home from an evening with another woman. Partly disappointed she wouldn't be there to send him on his way with some flip remark about not blowing it right out of the gate with her best friend. Her sassiness kept him on his toes, and he wanted to be on his game when he picked up Cheryl.

"Hello, ladies," he greeted as he stepped into Maria's doorway. "How's it going, Rosa? Thanks for filling in tonight."

"Oh sure, I'm glad I could help." She worried her lower lip before adding, "I hope you don't mind."

"Of course not. You're doing *me* a favor, remember?" He pushed away from the door frame to shrug out of his suit jacket. *"Mi casa es su casa."*

"Gracias." Rosa spoke softly, her mouth curving up in a shy smile. The marked difference between her quiet, reserved personality and Yazmine's bright lights, big-city confidence must have made life quite interesting for Reynaldo when his girls were growing up.

"Papá, can you help me get this dress on my Barbie?" Maria held out a dark-haired doll with a scrap of shiny purple material stuck around its shoulders.

"Here, mama, I can do it." Rosa's nimble fingers made short work of the task. She obviously still knew her way around a Barbie, something Tomás's large hands couldn't seem to grasp.

"I can't remember the last time I played dolls," Rosa told Maria. "Thanks for letting me join you."

Tomás hunkered down near them in front of the pink and white plastic two-story dollhouse. "I got the condensed version of why you had to fill in tonight. What's Yaz up to again?"

Rosa slid over to make room for him on the princess-crown throw rug. "Jeremy called to say he'd won tickets to a concert in Chicago. Pablo was visiting, and when he said he'd keep Papi company, I told Yaz I'd sit with Maria."

"I think I would have volunteered to take Yazmine's ticket instead."

Rosa smiled demurely and ducked her head. Her shoulder-length black hair fell in a wavy curtain to hide her face. "That would have been fun, too, though I think Jeremy wouldn't enjoy my company as much."

"Oh, somehow I doubt that." Rosa might be quiet, but last weekend he'd seen firsthand the feisty side she kept hidden most of the time. He doubted any moment with a Fernandez sister would be dull.

"I never apologized for my behavior the other night. After the recital," Rosa said, her expression an endearing mix of discomfort and guilt.

"Are you kidding? You don't have anything to apologize for. You girls are dealing with a lot. Better to let it out than to bottle it in and wind up blowing like a volcano at the wrong time."

"*Bueno*, I think I blew like a volcano last weekend. And I shouldn't have done that in front of you and Jeremy."

"It's all good. You don't have anything to worry about."

He grasped her hands as she struggled with shoving a pair of ridiculous-looking plastic high-heeled boots on a Barbie. "I'm serious. And Jeremy seems pretty close with your family, so I doubt he minded either. Thanks to how Yazmine and your dad have stepped in to help with Maria, I feel like they're family now. That includes you and Lilí, too."

"*Gracias.*" Rosa murmured the word, her gaze coming up to meet his briefly before dropping back down to the doll.

"As for you not going to the concert . . . Jeremy would be a bum if he didn't have a good time with you, Rosa," Tomás said, giving her jeans-clad knee a quick squeeze. "And he doesn't strike me as a bum."

She tucked her hair behind her ear, offering him another one of her Mona Lisa smiles.

He winked back at her. "I think I heard a wise woman tell you recently not to sell yourself short."

Rosa wrinkled her nose much like Maria did when she didn't care for something he said. "Don't you dare let Yaz hear you call her wise. She'll never let the rest of us hear the end of it!"

Tomás laughed. "There's the feisty Rosa I saw last weekend. You need to let her out more often."

"I think you have a pretty smile, Ms. Rosa," Maria added.

"*Gracias,* spending time with you makes me feel happy." Rosa ruffled Maria's hair playfully.

"Yes, she does have a pretty smile, *chiquita.* And so do you." Tomás dropped a quick kiss on top of Maria's head, then stood. "I'm going to wash up before I leave for dinner. You girls need anything?"

"No, we're good," Rosa assured him. "I'm ordering Luigi's pizza and I don't have any other plans, so don't rush home."

Luigi's. Merely hearing the restaurant's name made him think of Yaz. The last time he'd eaten there had been that Saturday they'd run into each other at the dance store. Ironically, he'd found out yesterday that

Cheryl's mom owns Center Stage. It was almost like he'd come full circle.

That day at Luigi's he'd known Yaz was a special woman. Since then his opinion hadn't changed. If anything, he was more certain now that she was one of a kind. Too bad she was also the leaving kind.

"Cheryl's a nice girl, by the way," Rosa said, her words stopping him in the doorway. "I hope it works out for you."

"Thanks, we'll see." He wasn't committing to anything, but he hoped this date went better than the one he'd had with Janet Miller. God help him if it somehow didn't.

"Are you coming to the *parranda* tomorrow night? Our caroling party is a holiday tradition for Los Paisanos."

"I haven't decided yet," he answered.

"You should come. It'll be fun. We start the caroling at Pablo's house with drinks, move to André's for appetizers, on to José's for dinner, and finally to our house for desserts and more drinks. Lots of music, dancing, good food, and friends."

He caught a flash of Yaz's sassiness in Rosa's inviting grin. "Sounds like a long night for Maria. It depends on whether or not I can get her to take a nap."

Not to mention whether or not he felt up to being around Yaz. Watching her dancing with someone else, laughing with her friends while he tried to keep his distance. Hell, it sounded like a long, stressful night if you asked him.

"It's really fun, and it'll mean a lot to Papi if you join us." Rosa's smile faded, a hint of the sadness she hid welling in her eyes. "It's probably his last *parranda*, so we're not shutting down until he gives us the sign."

"We'll see." Tomás took a backward step toward his room.

"Seven o'clock at Pablo's. One of us will text you the address, and you can invite Cheryl. Though Yaz probably already has anyway."

"Maybe," he hedged. Rosa drove a hard bargain, but he wasn't one to be swayed easily.

"I'll tell Papi that I reminded you about it. He'll be excited to see you and Maria."

Tomás laughed at her determined expression, a hint of self-satisfaction tingeing her smile. Man, the apple did not fall far from the tree in Rey's family. Rosa may not have Yaz's flair or Lilí's energy, but her father's strong will lay within her, too.

"Okay, okay, I give in. Let Rey know we'll be there."

He closed his bedroom door, chuckling at Rosa's "Yes!" of satisfaction.

"So how'd it go with Tomás tonight?" Yaz tucked her cell phone between her ear and her shoulder, shimmying out of her jeans and into her flannel pajama pants.

"Girl, it's nearly one o'clock in the morning," Cheryl grumbled in a sleep-heavy voice. "Why are you calling me?"

"Because I just got home from the Harry Connick Jr. concert with Jeremy, and I wanted to get the dirt from you." Yaz hopped onto her bed to sit cross-legged under the covers.

"We're too old for this."

"Bite your tongue!"

Cheryl snorted in response.

Yaz grinned, sensing her friend was about to give in.

It'd been a while since they'd sat on the phone sharing first-date details. It almost felt like old times. Almost, because in the past, Yaz had never had the hots for any of Cheryl's guys.

Now she tried to squelch her misgivings over hearing about Tomás's night out with her best friend. They deserved to be happy. That's all Yaz needed to remember.

In the grand scheme of things, her feelings couldn't matter.

"Tomás is an amazing guy," Cheryl said.

Of course. Yaz already knew that. "And?"

"Aaaand, we had fun." Cheryl's tired yawn punctuated her response. "The conversation was nice."

Nice? Yaz shuddered at the lame description. "That's it? Did dinner include dessert, or drinks, maybe a nightclub after?"

"Oakton isn't really hopping with nightclubs, Yaz. For a first date, I enjoyed it."

Yaz leaned back against her headboard, pulling her covers up to her chest. Her idea of living vicariously through Cheryl wasn't working out so well. Not with her friend's lukewarm response. "Did he ask you out again?"

"Actually, he asked about the *parranda* tomorrow, well, tonight now, seeing as how it's already early Saturday morning . . ."

"Don't be an old lady. You've called me later than this before."

"Yes," Cheryl said through another yawn. "But usually not when you've got to be up at the crack of dawn to catch a flight for a friend's bachelorette party."

"Ooh!" Yaz winced, her cell phone nearly slipping off her shoulder. "I completely forgot! This is that girl you roomed with your junior and senior years at Southern Illinois, right?"

"Uh-huh. 'Member, I planned to drive down after work today. But when Tomás asked me out I checked and got a good deal on a last-minute flight. Flying makes my trip easier. Though I didn't think about you calling for a play-by-play in the wee hours of the morning."

"Sorry." Yaz felt bad for waking Cheryl, but not enough to wish she hadn't called at all. "So you can't make the *parranda*, but did you two set another date?"

"We're playing it by ear. By the way, seems I'm not the only one who has a way with kids. He raved about how much Maria loves spending time with you."

Yaz squeezed her phone to her cheek, Tomás's praise warming her heart. "I hope you didn't spend your dinner talking about me."

"No, not really." Cheryl's voice was groggier. She was fading. Then again, she'd always been the first to nod off when they had sleepovers as kids. "He's sure impressed with you. And Maria talks about you a lot at school. She'll miss you when you head back to New York."

The last part was somewhat distorted by Cheryl's loud yawn. Still, Yazmine got the gist of it and her forced excitement over hearing Cheryl's date details faded.

Yaz sank lower under her covers, cushioning the phone between her ear and her pillow.

Maria might miss her when she was gone, but someone else, maybe even Cheryl, would take her place. Sure, Maria would think of her fondly, but she wouldn't feel the same keen sense of loss Yaz knew awaited her when she arrived in New York, alone. She wouldn't wish that misery on anyone, especially not this sweet little girl.

Tomás was right to shield Maria from feeling abandoned. He'd gone through that when his wife had walked out on them.

"You still there?" Cheryl asked.

"Yeah, I'm here."

Tomás wanted to ensure that Maria was in good hands. As far as Yaz was concerned, Cheryl's were perfect.

"Maria's an angel," Yaz said. "You're gonna love her."

"I'm sure I will. But I gotta go now."

"Have fun on your trip. Give me a call when you get back. And do lots of fun stuff I wouldn't do at the bachelorette party."

Cheryl snickered. She mumbled her good-bye and disconnected.

Yaz turned off her lamp, then rolled over in bed.

As her eyes drifted closed, she wasn't thinking about life as a dancer in New York. Instead, she was remembering evenings with Tomás and Maria, helping them practice the father-daughter dance in his living room, laughing at his missteps, cheering his successes. The nights she and Tomás would drink a glass of wine and chat about their day. She sharing something funny Maria had said, he going over ideas for the Linton ad campaign, asking for her opinion. Dancing with him in front of the fire, kissing him in the snow, losing herself in his embrace downstairs in her kitchen.

The memories flowed through her mind. All memories she'd cherish when she left. Because they were all she could have.

* * *

Two a.m. and the *parranda* was in full swing. People of all ages milled about the Fernandez home. Drinks flowed. Countless glasses of *coquito*, the rum-imbued, coconut and creamy Puerto Rican version of eggnog, were still being toasted. *Quesitos* and an array of other delicious pastries and finger foods filled the dining room table. Music blasted from the basement.

Tomás figured as long as the neighbors were participating in the revelry, there wasn't any worry about a noise complaint being called in to the cops.

Standing near the bottom of the basement stairs, he took in the scene before him with awe.

Despite the late hour, Los Paisanos had been persuaded to play a few tunes for their fans. Really, it hadn't been difficult to convince the men to pick up their instruments and treat the guests to an impromptu show.

Watching Reynaldo at the microphone, his guitar in his arms, his smooth voice serenading the crowd with a story of romance and life well-spent, lent a heart-breaking note to the evening. The love and pride tinged with sorrow on Yaz's and her sisters' faces was agonizing to watch. Damn if Tomás's admiration for those girls didn't inch up another notch.

He lasted through several of the trío's songs, but the crush of people and the uncomfortable knot of sorrow in his chest forced Tomás up the basement stairs. He slipped out the back door, braving the winter weather for some fresh, albeit frigid, night air.

Snow blanketed the lawn and flowerbeds, weighing down the bushes and the stark branches of the oak trees. He peered up at the night sky, unable to stop thinking about the unfairness of Rey's situation and the heartache ahead for Yaz and her sisters.

Through the light snowfall, Tomás gazed up at the

scattering of stars above him. In the distance one seemed to blink on and off and he recalled something Maria had shared on a trip to the park before the last snowfall.

"When a star winks at you, it's really an angel saying hello. Did you know that, Papá?" she had said.

Maybe his precious baby was right. Maybe that star up there *was* Rey's Marta, letting Tomás know she patiently awaited her lover.

Tomás shook his head. He was being silly. Letting emotions clog his brain.

The star twinkled again. Mocking him.

Who was he to scoff at anyone lucky enough to find an all-consuming love like Rey and Marta's. Or his parents'. Hell, even his brother's and sisters'.

The sharp wind gusted, sending a flurry of snow swirls dancing across the yard. Tomás shivered, huddling deeper into his coat.

Laughter seeped through the back door. He peeked in the kitchen window to spot a couple dancing to the romantic ballad. Their bodies pressed close together, they swayed to the sensual beat.

Despite the crowd and high spirits inside, he couldn't kick this strange desolation lingering within him. Couldn't get Rosa's "it's Papi's last *parranda*" out of his head.

Ever since last night, there'd been this . . . this sense of impending doom on the edges of his consciousness.

He'd returned home early from his date with Cheryl, which had gone well. She was friendly. Peppy, but not in a bad way. More like a kid-friendly, energetic kindergarten teacher way.

Maybe no bells or whistles had gone off when he was with her, but he wasn't looking for that anyway.

Cheryl was a nice girl. They had a lot in common. They were both close with their families, both enjoyed living in suburbia, and both were interested in having a family. So what if at the end of the evening he hadn't felt the urge to kiss her? Everything else with her seemed promising.

Yet, on his way home he'd thought about calling Yaz to chat about how the night had gone. Certain she'd tease him if he admitted the uncharacteristic nervousness he'd felt on the drive to Cheryl's apartment.

He'd found himself pulling into his garage craving the lightness Yaz's smile made him feel and her smart-ass remarks that made him laugh.

Only, she was out on her own date, with Jeremy. Not home waiting for him.

Inside it was sweet, shy Rosa who had greeted him in his living room. His disappointment had been sharp. A bittersweet reminder that if he let himself get more attached to Yaz, the prick of disappointment when she eventually left would be much worse.

The wind shifted again and the snowfall increased. Large, fat flakes drifted through the night air. Inside the Fernandez home, the band kicked off another song. Not for the first time that evening, Tomás marveled at the volume. Outside he could hear the music clearly, feel the thump of the bongo drums like a second heartbeat.

He craned his neck to peek at the darkened upstairs windows. Maybe he should check on Maria, make sure she slept comfortably through the *parranda*'s noise.

Moments later he took the stairs by twos, pausing near the top step when Yaz emerged from one of the front bedrooms facing the street.

A palm tree–shaped nightlight cast a shadowy glow

in the hallway. Surprisingly, the strains of music were muffled on the top floor, the mix of voices more like a soft rumble in the night.

Yaz slowly pulled the door closed.

"Is she still asleep?" he whispered.

Yaz jumped like he'd poked her with a live electrical wire. "¡Ay, Dios mío! Give a person some notice next time. You scared the buzz right out of me."

He grinned at her cheeky reprimand. "Is she good?"

"Out like a light. You're lucky she's such a sound sleeper."

The muted lighting in the hall, mixed with their whispered conversation and the notes of another Spanish ballad drifting up the stairs, lent an intimate feel to their surroundings.

Yaz moved closer, edging around the banister but stopping a few feet away from where he stood a couple steps down. Moonlight filtered in through the front picture window, giving him a better view of the hesitation in her eyes. He frowned, hoping she wasn't thinking about the last time they'd been alone at her house.

The night she and Rosa had argued after the recital and he'd wound up comforting her in the kitchen. When he'd crossed that invisible line between wanting and taking, again. The last time he'd held her in his arms and kissed her lips, tasted her sweet skin.

"How was the concert last night?" he asked, hoping the reminder of her night out with Jeremy would ease her discomfort. While prolonging their conversation because he wasn't ready for it to end.

"Ah-mazing." Her shoulders relaxed and she leaned back against the wall near the steps. "I can't believe Jeremy actually won tickets on the radio. I've been dying to see Harry Connick Jr. for years."

"I didn't know you liked jazz."

"I'll listen to almost anything. But, Harry? Mmmmm, his voice is like velvet." Head resting against the wall, she closed her eyes on a sigh.

Tomás crooked an elbow on the banister, enjoying the private moment with her. Their first all week. She'd been fleeing his house the second he walked in the door, off to some outing with her sisters or Cheryl, or to the dance studio to get in a few hours of practice.

"Like velvet, huh?" he repeated.

"Oh yeah. I can never get too much of Harry." She stepped out of her heels, losing about four inches in height.

He watched her alternately draw a circle in the air with each foot, then she curled her toes into the carpet and lifted each heel. Stretches he'd noticed her go through at night when her feet were sore after dance class.

"Here, sit down a minute. Let me help." He lowered himself to the stair landing, motioning for her to join him.

The question in Yazmine's frown tugged at his conscience.

He'd lost count of the number of times she'd put others before herself—to help him, to care for Rey, at the dance studio. She was under a ton of stress and deserved a little TLC.

He could give her that. Wanted to give her that. At least for a few minutes.

Tomás stretched out an arm to hook one of her shiny silver stiletto pumps with a finger. "Your feet are sore, probably from all that dancing in these uncomfortable contraptions you call shoes. Sit down. I'll give you a free massage for checking on Maria for me."

And maybe because he was a glutton for punishment, welcoming the opportunity to touch her.

Yaz took her time considering his suggestion. The need to break through the wall wedging itself between them drove him to push more.

"Come on. It's a special offer. You better grab the chance while you can." He patted the floor beside him, hoping she'd give in. Afraid she wouldn't.

Chapter Fifteen

"Fine, if you insist." Yaz huffed out a breath, dropping down onto the floor beside him.

Tomás bit back a satisfied grin. "You don't *have* to take me up on my offer, you know."

"Do I look like a fool to you?"

"Foolish" was probably the last word he'd use to describe her.

He scooted farther back so Yaz could stretch out her trim legs to place her feet on his lap. Adrenaline revved his pulse and he realized "foolish" might be a better word for him.

"*Sabes*, I've been taking care of Maria for weeks now."

"Yeah, I know," he answered.

"So how come this is the first I've heard about free massages?"

Beneath her petulant tone he caught a hint of the spunkiness he was relieved to hear. He'd only seen flashes of that side of her since they'd shared those explosive kisses. He missed the Yaz who threw a mean snowball in a battle, made a man crave an evening of dancing and drinks, or told him flat out she didn't like an idea he bounced off her for a campaign at work. The one he could relax and be himself with, especially at the end of a hard day.

"You're lucky. I'm in a giving mood tonight. Must be the Christmas spirit." He grasped her foot, her skin cool and soft. Deftly he set his hands to work kneading the tight muscles. "Or maybe I'm an easy target for a good-looking woman in skinny jeans and high heels."

"Yeah, right. Oooh!" She winced, then moaned, low and throaty.

He nearly swallowed his tongue.

Yaz leaned back, setting her hands behind her on the carpet for support. The position thrust her breasts out toward him, the material of her red V-neck sweater stretched taut across her chest. His imagination, along with other parts of him, twitched to life.

Man, it would be so easy to slide his hands up the length of her legs, past her trim hips, across her toned stomach, not stopping until he cupped the weight of her breasts. He'd nudge her back to lie on the floor, then take her mouth in a kiss meant to rock her world. The way she rocked his.

"*Ooh, sí,*" Yaz murmured.

His hands froze.

"Don't stop." Head cocked to the side, she looked at him through sexy, heavy-lidded eyes. "It's like pleasure and pain, all mixed together."

Exactly.

He gulped, but started massaging again. Her skin was silky smooth beneath his hands, her soft moans of approval driving him closer and closer to the edge of insanity.

Jaw clenched, he worked to keep his breathing even, measured. Slowly in, slowly out.

Maybe this hadn't been such a good idea after all. When it came to Yaz, far too often he found himself acting impulsively. Winding up in a precarious position. Like now.

His friendly gesture, a bid to get back in her good graces, had morphed into a test of his willpower.

"So you had a good time on your date with Jeremy?" he asked, grasping for a reminder as to why he couldn't act on what his body craved.

"Hmm?" came her drowsy response. Her head lolled to the side, the ends of her long satiny hair brushing the floor by her hands. "Date? *Dios, no.* Jeremy and I are only friends. We've never been—ooh, there!"

Tomás pressed his thumbs into the arch of her foot again.

"Yeah. Riiight . . . there—oh, you are good."

He swallowed. Hard. Stopping himself, barely, from uttering an inappropriate response.

"Okay, now this one." She wiggled her other foot. "It's feeling neglected."

"Pushy, aren't you?"

In the dim lighting, he caught the flash of her teeth as she grinned. Impudent woman.

"I'm glad you had fun with Jeremy," he said. He meant it. Even if on some level he hated the idea. "You deserved a night off. I certainly didn't miss your wisecracks on my way out the door for dinner."

"That's right, I forgot to ask—Oh!" Yazmine slapped her hand over her mouth, her eyes wide with surprise when he shushed her. A beat later, she slowly dropped her hand, a chagrined look on her face as she whispered, "Sorry. That was pretty loud. I hope I didn't wake Maria."

"With all the noise downstairs?"

Still, they listened quietly for a couple of minutes, waiting for any sounds from Yaz's room. Tomás continued massaging, his hands moving up her leg, applying pressure to her shapely calf, careful not to stray much farther.

"So how *did* it go with Cheryl?" Yaz eventually asked.

"I think it—wait." He broke off as a thought occurred to him. "Did you ask her the same question already?"

"Maybe . . ."

"Of course you did." He shook his head, certain no amount of pushing would get her to share any of Cheryl's secrets. Equally certain he didn't want Yaz giving Cheryl details about him. "I'll simply say the evening was enjoyable, and we'll leave it at that."

"Enjoyable? That's it?" She sat up, eyeing him like he'd grown a third eye or something.

"What?"

"How did she measure up to all those criteria in your Perfect Partner Plan?"

"Would you quit calling it that?" He leaned a shoulder against the banister, embarrassed because when she said it that way his plan sounded a little crazy.

"I call it like I see it. Now quit dodging the question. How'd it go? Did she pass?"

He scowled at her with resignation. "There was no test to pass. Come on, you make it sound like I'm a robot, taking feelings out of the equation."

"Oh, you've got feelings. Look at how great you are with Maria. It's like you don't trust love. Or, maybe it's yourself you don't trust."

His hands stilled, shock robbing him of the ability to deny her claim. She'd hit a little too close to home, her intuition shining a bright light on a fear he didn't want to acknowledge.

He'd messed up with Kristine, big time. That had been a difficult enough pill to swallow—knowing he'd let his lust-fogged brain ignore the truth.

From the beginning she'd admitted she wasn't mother material. He'd stupidly thought she'd change.

"Cat got your tongue?" Yaz teased.

Suddenly he realized that, once again, she was shining the spotlight on him and his issues. What about hers? He knew she had her own hang-ups.

"Well, if I'm the pot, you're the kettle, right?" he challenged, interested in seeing how she liked having the tables turned. "I'm not the one who's dodged any relationship questions thrown at him. So far, I've been pretty much an open book. You, on the other hand, have shared next to nothing about your love life. Why's that?"

Yaz's gaze cut away to the picture window overlooking the front yard. Her lips pressed together in a straight line, proof she didn't plan on sharing any private details now.

"I rest my case."

"Whatever," she muttered. "Look, if you're not comfortable talking about Cheryl, fine. But if you're not interested, you have to promise me you'll let her down easy." Even in shadow he caught her scowl. "Though you'd be an idiot not to give things with her a shot."

Before, their talk about him finding a partner had seemed more like playing pretend. Somehow, now that Cheryl had entered the picture, it had gotten more real.

It felt weird. Almost like he was cheating on Yaz. Silly. Especially since she'd set him up with her friend in the first place. Any signs of guilt only proved that he was messed up.

Yaz was right, Cheryl did seem like a good fit for him.

"If you really must know, we already decided that if we can't get together this week, we'll connect when Maria and I get back from Texas after Christmas. Satisfied?"

"Good." Yaz stared down the length of the stairs to the empty foyer below, her expression pensive.

"Speaking of Christmas." She pulled her feet off his lap, scooting closer to sit beside him on the stair landing. "Have you heard from Mrs. B about whether she'll be back at the beginning of January?"

He nodded, more excited about the pressure of Yaz's shoulder against his than by the thought of his nanny's imminent return. Mrs. B coming home meant no more Yaz hanging around the house.

That should be a good thing. No more fighting off an attraction headed toward the inevitable fork in the road.

"She arrives late on January first," he said.

"Mrs. Hanson returns full-time at the beginning of the year, too. That means I'll have plenty of time to spend with Papi and get some extra practice in at the studio during the day."

"Have you started making plans to go back to New York?" he asked.

"No, Papi comes first right now. New York will always be there. Besides, without him . . ." She paused, uncertainty painting her words. "I'm not sure."

"About what?"

"Anything. Everything." Shoulders hunched, she rested her chin on her bent knee. "If I should even bother trying anymore."

Tomás started with surprise, knocking his elbow against the banister.

What the hell? This was the second time she'd hinted at indecision regarding New York or her dance skills.

"*¿Qué pasa?*" He bumped her shoulder with his own. "Where is this coming from?"

Head bowed, she didn't answer.

"Yaz?" He tucked her hair behind her ear, squinting in the soft lighting to get a good look at her face. "What's going on inside that stubborn head of yours?"

"I'm not stubborn."

"I'm not stubborn." He mimicked her pouty tone. "And you're still evading my questions."

When she didn't respond right away, he bumped shoulders with her again. "Come on, spit it out. I bared my soul about Kristine. Now you level with me."

"I can't." She groaned, pulling her knees up to bury her face on them. "It's stupid."

Tomás put his arm around her shoulders, unable to stop himself from offering her comfort any more than he could stop himself from breathing. "Spill it. You know me, I have no problem telling you if you're being stupid."

Her body gently shook with laughter. Good, that was more like it.

For a few moments the only sounds were the chatter of partygoers in the living room and the bass-filled strains of a Top Forty hit blaring from the basement stereo speakers. Apparently Los Paisanos were taking a break.

"Spit it out." He squeezed his arm around her as if he could squeeze out her confession.

"I haven't really told this to anyone before." Her voice was so low he had to strain to hear her. "Not my sisters. Not even Cheryl."

He gulped, torn between his head warning him to stop the sharing of intimate confidences and his heart pushing him to do whatever he could for her.

Who was he kidding? It wasn't even a fair contest. Making her feel better easily won over protecting himself.

"I'm a great secret keeper, you know. Ask my older brother Eddie. Our mom never found out about the stack of adult magazines he kept stashed under his bed. Of course, he had to share them with me to pay for my silence."

Yaz rolled her head to look at him, her temple resting on her knees, a familiar glint flashing briefly in her eyes. "You're incorrigible, you know that?"

He winked, pleased to see her little half smile in response. Unfortunately, it faded away too quickly.

"Life in New York isn't the same as it is here. I know—" She stopped, her face scrunching up in a wry grimace that reminded him of Maria when he made her eat her broccoli. "That sounded dumb. I didn't mean it that way."

"What *did* you mean?"

"I want to do what's right, for Papi, for me."

Tomás's arm slid off her shoulders as she twisted around to face him. She crossed her legs tailor style, her knees resting intimately on top of his thigh. Reason told him to scoot back, break the connection binding him to her. The pain and confusion in her eyes kept him from doing anything but being there for her. In whatever way she needed.

"Papi gave up so much for us. He didn't tell you this, but if Mami hadn't been sick when she was pregnant with me, he wouldn't have felt compelled to apply for that job with the post office. Wouldn't have had to put aside his dream to provide for us."

"He didn't *have* to," Tomás stressed. "He did it because he's a smart, responsible man. The music industry isn't the most stable profession. Especially if you have a family to feed and care for."

Yaz heaved a sigh, lolling her head back to stare at the ceiling. He imagined himself leaning closer to press a kiss to her elegant jawline, breathing deeply of her provocative violet scent. If he was crazy enough—dumb enough—to do it.

Gracias a Dios, he wasn't.

"Intellectually I know you're right." Her rough whisper interrupted his meandering thoughts. "But Mami was okay with him giving his music a shot. Then she started having complications with her pregnancy. Don't you get it?"

Yaz skewered him with a look dripping with so much anguish she might as well have reached inside his chest and grabbed ahold of his heart with her fist.

"If I hadn't come along so soon, who knows what kind of success Papi and the guys would have attained."

"Or not. That can't be predicted."

She shook her head, her mouth twisted with derision. "You don't get it. I owe him. He wants me to succeed so badly. All I've ever wanted was to give that to him, do that for him. That's what drives me. But if he's not here anymore, what good is it? And what if I don't have it in me to try?"

"You were right, that's dumb."

Yaz jerked back. Her mouth a little "oh" of shock.

Good, he'd gotten her attention.

"That's a jerky thing to say." She pushed away from him with a huff.

Even better. Pissed off beat the hell out of the pity party she'd been throwing herself a few seconds ago. "I told you I'd be honest, didn't I?"

She rolled her eyes, her shoulder shrug the epitome of a teen's "whatever" attitude.

"Look, I may not know much about dance or how the dance industry works, but when I see you on stage there's no doubt you're incredibly talented. You're at Hanson's before the sun comes up, and back again after you drop Maria at school. I don't have any problem seeing you make it on a stage in New York, or wherever you want to go. The thing is, do *you* see yourself making it?"

He grabbed her hands when she tried to wave off his words. "Listen to me, damn it. You can't pursue something this demanding only for your father. Rey wants you girls to be happy on your own terms. Not his."

"You don't understand."

"Make me, then."

His frustration mounted when she responded by shaking her head.

Her entire body vibrated with a palpable tension like an electric fence warning him to stay away.

But he couldn't. He wouldn't.

Tears pooled in her eyes and she blinked several times, stubbornly trying to keep them at bay. He held his breath, knowing if she gave way to them he'd be a goner, in danger of repeating last weekend's debacle in the kitchen.

More importantly, he honestly believed she'd benefit more from a kick in the pants than some coddling.

"I'm not sure if I have it."

"It?"

She sighed heavily, piercing him with an are-you-a-moron glare. "Papi has such faith in me. But he doesn't know how cutthroat it is. How lonely it can be. What if Victor was right and I don't have what it takes?"

Tomás frowned at her declaration. "I don't know who Victor is, but I'd venture to guess he's the phantom ex-fiancé I've only heard about in passing. If so, and he actually said that to you, he's an even bigger idiot than I thought, and you're better off without him."

"You sound like Lilí, and she doesn't know the half of it."

"I knew I liked that girl."

They shared a grin and his heart lightened.

"Tell me, what did this fool Victor do to make you doubt yourself so much? That's not the Yazmine I know."

She closed her eyes, her entire body sagging with dejection.

After several moments had passed, he squeezed her hands to get her attention. "Hey, I aired all my dirty laundry about my ex weeks ago. Now it's your turn."

"Talking about Victor reminds me of how gullible I was," she grumbled. "I should have realized he was such a jerk."

"Happens to the best of us."

"Yeah, well, I should have known better." She tugged her hands free of his grasp, sliding across the carpet a few feet to lean back against the wall.

He wanted to close the distance between them, stay close to her, but if she needed space to share her story, he'd give it to her.

"Papi had to choose. Me? I let myself believe I could have it all. Success *and* a family. Only, I failed to realize there are far too many people willing to do whatever it takes to make it. Even sleep with a show's producer, in their fiancé's apartment, if it gets them ahead."

"Ouch." Tomás winced. Whoever Victor was, he sounded like a colossal dunce.

"It gets better," she said dryly. "Apparently, I was the one at fault, for not knowing that's how you're supposed to play the game. For not having thicker skin. According to him, I'd gotten my latest role because of his maneuverings. I was supposed to be *thankful*."

She sneered the last word and Tomás couldn't tell if she was angry with herself, with Victor, or with the dance industry as a whole. Neither was productive, though she probably didn't want to hear that right now.

"Victor kept hurling the blame at me and I—I freaked. I ran for my sanctuary, a rehearsal hall nearby where I could lose myself in dance and music and motion. Block out the world. Pretend no one else, nothing else, existed. Only, for the first time in my life, that didn't work."

She speared her hands through her hair, holding them against the side of her head like it might explode. "All I could think about were the times he'd supposedly been out late for a rehearsal. The overnights and weekends. The people who must have known, but didn't say anything."

She hopped to her feet, then began pacing down the hall toward the back of the house.

"Come on, give yourself a break," Tomás said, following behind her.

"I don't deserve one." She stopped at the end of the hall and pressed her forehead against the window overlooking the backyard.

Tomás moved closer, gently combing his fingers

through her silky strands, anxious to calm her. "Yazmine, I think you're being too hard on yourself."

She blew out a breath, the warm air fogging the window. "The signs were there. I ignored them."

"Why?"

When she didn't respond, he gently pressed on her shoulders, turning her around to face him.

"Why?" he repeated.

"Because I was lonely," she whispered. The despair in her eyes gutted him. "Honestly though, unless Victor and I were in the same show or taking a dance class together, our schedules were often at odds. I was fooling myself, clinging to the silly idea that eventually we'd get in a good groove, get married, maybe have a child. Hearing him admit that he'd been using me and my connection to another choreographer . . . something died in me that day. Not even dance could take the pain away."

She slumped forward, laying her head against his chest. Instinctively he wrapped his arms around her, pulling her to him in a tight hug.

"What you were feeling is natural," he said softly, trying to assuage her anguish. "Believe me. I put myself through the same mental gymnastics, blaming myself. Blaming Kristine. Sounds like you left that traumatic experience and jumped into another one, coming home to deal with Rey's cancer."

He pulled back to grasp her upper arms, waiting until she looked up at him and he was sure he had her attention. "Keeping all of that inside isn't helping you deal with it. I'll say this, though, don't give that prick Victor the satisfaction of beating you down. You're better than that."

"What if I'm not? What if I've been wrong all these

years? But then I—I guess it doesn't matter because Papi won't be around for me to disappoint." A tear slid down her cheek, leaving a silvery trail of hurt that shone in the glow from the hallway nightlight.

"*Ay, querida*, don't do this to yourself," Tomás said, his voice gruff with a well of agony he hadn't known he was capable of until he'd met her.

He cupped her face with both hands, swiping her tears away with his thumbs. "Forget about your ex. Don't think about your dad for a minute. I know you have it within you to do great things. I've seen you in action, remember? But *you* have to believe it. *¿Entiendes?*"

He held her gaze with his, willing her to see the woman he saw when he looked at her.

After a few tense seconds, she finally offered him a watery smile. "Yeah, I understand."

"That's my girl."

The moment was ripe for him to lower his head, steal the kiss that his mind, his body, his *heart* craved. Damn, there were few things in his life he'd wanted more than to taste her sweet lips again. Only, she wasn't really his girl, and stealing a kiss would break the fragile trust they'd begun to rebuild. That wasn't a risk he was willing to take.

"You'll know what to do when the time is right. Like I said, don't be so hard on yourself. Okay?"

She nodded, but didn't say anything in response.

"Good. Now come on, let's rejoin the party." Rather than pull her in for a kiss, he slid his hands down her arms to link their fingers together. He tugged her toward the stairs, pausing for her to slip on her heels. "They're playing my song, and I think you owe me a dance."

"Oh really? Since when?"

"Since I talked your butt off the ledge a minute ago. Look, I learned early on that if there's something you want, you make a plan and keep taking steps in that direction. Eventually you'll get there."

They reached the bottom of the stairs, but before they were sucked back into the crowd of revelers, Yaz pulled him to a stop.

"*Gracias*," she whispered, stepping near so only he could hear. "I hadn't shared all that with anyone. Ashamed to say most of it out loud. You're right though, talking to you helped. I appreciate it."

"That's what friends are for, right?"

She nodded.

"Now quit stalling. I'm ready to put Lilí's dance moves to shame." He did a quick little salsa step, then spun full circle, coming to a stop with his hands pointing gun-style right at her. Yaz rewarded him by throwing her head back with a gusty laugh. The low, throaty sound wrapped around him like a lover's embrace. As close to the real thing as he'd ever get with her.

He'd have to learn to deal with that.

Yaz looped her arm with his to drag him through the throng of partygoers. For the first time all evening he felt a spring in his step. They were finally back in a good groove.

Maybe the time they had left together would be spent trying to foster a friendship, but he'd take whatever he could get.

Chapter Sixteen

The signal for an incoming phone call trilled through Yaz's laptop speakers, drawing a smile to her lips. She minimized the audition website she'd been reading and clicked the icon to enlarge her Skype program. Several clicks later Maria's inquisitive face appeared on Yaz's computer screen.

"*¡Hola!*" Maria's dark brown eyes lit up and she clapped her hands with a grin. "*¡Feliz Navidad!*"

"Merry Christmas, *mamita*! It's great to see you." Yaz hadn't realized how much she'd miss her little companion until Maria and Tomás had left for Texas a few days after the *parranda*.

His pep talk that night had really opened her eyes. He was going after what he wanted—a stable family life for himself and his daughter—in what she'd thought of as a methodical way, but he was happy. More importantly, he was succeeding. If she applied that same focus in New York, the rest would fall into place for her, too.

"Look!" Maria leaned closer to the computer screen, opened her mouth wide, and pointed to where her top right front tooth had been before they'd left. "Ih-feww-ou."

"It fell out?"

"Uh-huh." Maria's curls bobbed at her energetic nod. "And the tooth fairy bringed me three whole dollars!"

"Wow, you got visits from Santa *and* the tooth fairy. Lucky girl. Are you having fun with your cousins and all your new toys?" Yaz figured the atmosphere in Tomás's crowded family home, with his three siblings and all their kids, had been much rowdier than the Christmas morning she'd spent with Papi, Lilí, and Rosa.

"You should see what Santa bringed me!" Maria's enthusiasm could have convinced Scrooge to change his ways, forget the three ghosts. "I got a new baby doll, with her own cradle and bottle and diapers. I can take care of her like my very own real live baby! You can teach me when we get home. Will you?"

"I'm sure I can figure it out. But you know who will be a much bigger help when it comes to babies? Mrs. Buckley. She'll be home soon, too."

"*Sí, pero . . .*" Maria frowned, her earlier excitement dimming. Yaz tried not to show her own disappointment that their time together would soon end.

"But," Maria repeated, "that doesn't mean I won't get to see you. Does it?"

"Of course not. Maybe not as often, but we'll still hang out together as much as we can."

Maria still didn't look convinced.

"You know what I really wanna know?" Yaz asked, hoping to change the somber mood. "What did you name your beautiful baby doll?"

Maria perked up again. "Flor! But I call her Flower, too, so she knows her name in English and Spanish."

"Smart girl."

"My doll family's gonna be like yours, all flowers—Yazmine, Rosa, and Lilí. I asked Papá if I could change my name to Daisy so I could be a pretty flower like you. But he said no."

Yaz laughed so hard she had to wipe a tear from her eye. *Ay*, she missed Maria's childlike imagination.

"Here, I'm gonna get Flor so she can meet you!" Maria hopped out of the desk chair and raced out of view, her little-girl voice calling out to Tomás. "Papá, I'm on the 'puter with Ms. Yazmine!"

Yaz grinned. Wait until she shared this flower story with Papi. He always got a kick out of the funny things Maria came up with.

Now that the little girl wasn't filling the computer screen, Yaz noticed the camera's view of the room. A poster of a football team was tacked up on the wall next to a bookshelf. Trophies, a scuffed football, and a collection of books filled the scarred wooden shelves. A framed picture caught her attention.

She leaned closer to her laptop, straining to get a better view. Squinting, she made out what looked like a younger Tomás in a graduation cap and gown, flanked by a tall gentleman with dark good looks and a short, plump-figured woman with a welcoming smile.

A guilty thrill trickled through her. This was obviously Tomás's childhood bedroom. If only she could manipulate the computer camera to scan the entire area and sneak a peek. See a bit of what a young Tomás had treasured.

Had he been as focused, as goal-oriented as he was now? He'd certainly been a cute young man, though age and maturity had molded those round boyish looks into the chiseled hunk he was today. She wondered whether, if she could zoom in on that photograph, she would find the same intensity, the same charisma she saw when he gazed at her now.

A dark shadow passed across the screen, momentarily blocking her view.

"You know, the camera usually works best if you don't partially cover it with your hand."

Tomás's teasing voice made her jump back in her desk chair.

"That's better." He chuckled. "You look more attractive with two eyes rather than one."

He winked, his dimple flashing her a hello.

Why did he have to be so adorable?

She stuck out her tongue at him. "I knew there was something missing around here this morning. Your smart mouth."

It'd been missing in the days after the *parranda*, too. He'd worked like a dog trying to get ahead with the Linton campaign before his trip. They'd barely seen each other, Maria mostly hanging out at Yazmine's house because of his late hours. He'd even stayed overnight at his office a couple nights, sleeping on his couch, showering in the building's gym.

He'd left for Texas tired and worn down, though determined to win that account. Three days into his visit and he looked refreshed already. His posture relaxed, his voice and face radiating happiness. Spending time with his family obviously agreed with him. Like hers did, too.

"Before Maria gets back, how are things at home?" He sobered, his expression serious.

Yaz sighed, wishing harder than she'd ever wished for anything else on Christmas morning that this subject could be avoided, simply ignored until it went away. "Papi's doing so-so. More tired than normal, but

Dr. Lopez said that's to be expected. He's taking a nap now."

"And your sisters?"

"Rosa is reading a new book she got in her stocking, go figure. Lilí headed out to the sled hill in the park where she can act like the crazy kid she still is."

A corner of Tomás's mouth curved. "I know another Fernandez sister who can get a little crazy in the snow."

"Yeah, Rosa makes a mean snow angel if you can get her to put her book down and join you outside." Pleasure bloomed in Yazmine's chest at his lazy chuckle.

"Seriously, you holding up okay?" Even through the video display she felt the heat of his gaze honing in directly on her.

"I'm fine." She tossed her ponytail back over her shoulder, trying hard to be nonchalant about the fact that Papi was fading, faster than any of them were ready for. "I'm either at the studio practicing or hanging out at home with Papi."

"I want you to know—Hey, there you are!" Tomás glanced to his left. Probably toward the bedroom door because Maria had run off in that same general direction.

"I'm ba-ack!" Yaz heard Maria's sing-song tone before the child appeared in the computer screen.

"And you brought almost *all* your gifts." Tomás winced, shooting Yaz a sorry-about-this look. "Great idea, *m'ija.*"

Maria scrambled up onto his lap holding a life-sized baby doll and its bottle, a Barbie wearing a blue and pink tutu, a child-sized matching tutu Yaz had given her, and a red envelope Yaz recognized as her gift to Tomás.

"I see you got my presents. I hope you like them."

Shopping for Maria had been easy. Choosing something for Tomás had been about as mind-boggling as one of Rosa's crossword puzzles. Yaz had struggled with what to get a man who made you want to be a better, stronger person, without revealing how much you'd come to care about him.

"Oh, I loooooove my presents!" Maria answered. "My costume fits perfect! I look like a real dancer! Abuela even said so!"

Yaz grinned. "I totally agree!"

"And, and, and I showed them part of our dance," Maria continued, bouncing with enthusiasm. "Abuelo said I did awesome!"

"Of course you did." *Dios*, it was unthinkable to even imagine someone not loving this little girl. Not wanting to share these special moments with her. It boggled Yaz's mind how Tomás's ex didn't even want to be in contact with Maria over the holidays. Yaz yearned to hug her right now. "You are super talented. And if you work hard, you'll keep getting better. Look, even your dad did okay at the Christmas recital once he started practicing."

"Wait a minute!" Tomás leaned to the side so he could see around Maria and her armfuls of gifts. "I did better than okay. I rocked it! Plenty of the moms even said so."

Yaz snorted at his self-satisfied smirk. Yeah, quite a few of the single moms had, especially those few who'd slipped him their numbers. With Cheryl in the picture now, he wouldn't have to worry about that.

Though come to think of it, Cheryl had seemed out

of sorts when she'd come back from her friend's wedding, and their second-date plans had been nixed because of Tomás's late work hours before he'd left.

"*Pues*, I'm glad you liked my gift, *mamita*," Yaz told Maria. "I can't wait to see you wear your tutu on free-for-all day at the studio."

"Me too! I hafta go now. 'buela said I could help mash the beans for dinner." With a wiggle of her fingers and a flounce of dark curls, Maria hopped off Tomás's lap and out of view. "*¡Te quiero!*"

Yaz couldn't have replied even if she'd been given a chance. Maria's off-the-cuff "I love you" had snatched away her voice, ensnared her heart in a grip that was far stronger than a child's hastily spoken declaration should warrant.

Yaz fell back against her seat and closed her eyes, imprinting Maria's words on her heart to treasure when she returned to New York.

"What's wrong?" Tomás asked.

She smoothed a trembling hand over her hair, tucking a few loose strands behind her ear. "Nothing. In the midst of everything, it's uplifting to be around her."

"I hear you." He picked up the red envelope Maria had left behind. "Now it's my turn to say thanks. A monthly bottle of wine for three months? Nice idea."

"I'm glad you like it."

He leaned forward, resting his forearm on the edge of his laptop. She could see the dark springy hair on his arm, the muscles flexing as he tapped his screen with the envelope.

"I love it."

She slid her gaze down to her keyboard, not wanting him to see how much his words meant to her.

"Did you get my gift?" he asked.

She picked up the autographed collector's edition of a Harry Connick Jr. Greatest Hits CD and concert DVD she'd opened earlier. "Already uploaded on my iTunes. The autograph earned jealous 'ooohs' from both my sisters. Thanks."

"'You can never get too much of Harry,' isn't that what you said the other night?"

Her chest tightened at the memory of their quiet talk on the second-floor landing. "I'm surprised you remembered."

"That's the kind of guy I am." He laid a hand over his heart, a saccharine-sweet, Eddie Haskell expression on his face. "Maybe you can bring your CD over and we'll listen to Harry croon a few tunes while we open the first bottle of wine."

"You're going to share with me?"

She edged forward in her seat, his magnetism reeling her in despite the thousand-plus miles separating them. *Dios*, she must be going a little insane because she would swear she smelled his musky cologne, felt the heat of his touch as if he held her hand instead of the gift certificate she'd given him.

"Of course I'll share, why wouldn't I?" A tiny V furrowed between his brows.

She voiced the one reason that was easier, safer. "I guess I figured Cheryl would get that honor. I know you guys had a hard time connecting before you left."

"If things work out, she'll get to taste a bottle, don't worry. I was thinking that with Mrs. B heading back on the first, maybe you could come over for dinner. She'll want to see you, do her mother hen act to say thanks herself."

Yaz bit the inside of her lip, focusing on that discomfort rather than another. His suggestion of them sharing a bottle of wine and a little Harry had nothing to do with romance, more like a friendly good-bye.

"Speaking of getting back, Maria and I land mid-morning on the thirty-first. Are you sure you don't mind watching her that evening?"

"Of course not." Yaz waved off the question. "We're planning dinner at seven followed by an early Happy New Year celebration before Papi and Maria get too tired. You're welcome to stay and eat if you have time before you pick up Cheryl."

Yaz tried to think happy thoughts when the picture of him and Cheryl kissing at midnight flashed in her head. She and Tomás would be starting off the new year as they should—him in the arms of a woman who offered the family life he wanted, she practicing at the barre in her basement, preparing for New York.

"I'll have to let you know. Cheryl and I have been playing phone tag."

"Sure."

He cut another quick glance toward the doorway. "I better let you go. But Yaz, if you need anything, if Rey or your sisters need anything, don't hesitate to call me."

She swallowed past the lump in her throat, at the same time tamping down her desire to keep him on the video chat longer. It was only borrowed time.

"Don't worry. I've got you on speed dial," she answered, but she knew she'd only call him as a last resort. It was better that way.

Mrs. B arrived back on the first. Tomás wouldn't need Yaz's help anymore. It was time she stopped relying on him to bolster her confidence. Time for her to stand on her own.

* * *

Two weeks into the new year, Yazmine stood at the kitchen sink watching the snow fall outside the window, while Rosa finished clearing the dining room table.

"I'm glad Lilí's friends made her join them," Yaz said. "I didn't think she'd put up such a fuss about catching a movie."

"She's hardheaded. Like you." Rosa set a stack of plates on the counter.

Ignoring the jab, Yaz started filling the sink with warm water. "She's hurting. Struggling with memories of Mami's death."

"What makes you say that?"

"She told me so this morning. I took a cup of coffee to her room and we shared it while you were hogging the bathroom."

"I'm never the one hogging the bathroom. That's you two." Rosa leaned a hip against the counter. Arms crossed, she frowned at Yaz. "And why hasn't she said anything to me about how she's feeling?"

Yaz heard the hurt in Rosa's voice and she rushed to soothe her. "I was surprised she mentioned it, really. She's been so sullen and moody since Christmas. Don't take it personally. We're all in this together, okay?"

A tense beat passed before Rosa nodded. Evidently she was still struggling with her need to fix everyone's problems. Good luck with that idea.

"Look, I've got Lilí's kitchen duty covered tonight so your fancy schedule's not in jeopardy of disruption." Yaz glanced pointedly at the "organizational chore chart" Rosa had created and hung on the side of the refrigerator, like she'd done when they were in high school.

"I don't know what you have against being organized,"
Rosa complained, probably still sore at Lilí's snarky
comments about the color-coded system. "I'm only
trying to help."

"I know."

"A place for everything and everything in—"

"—in its place."

Yaz shared a tender smile with her sister as together
they finished one of Mami's favorite mottos.

"Somehow, her words stuck with you much better
than with Lilí and me." Yaz watched Rosa perusing the
pictures stuck to the fridge door. She bit back a smile
when Rosa started carefully lining up the photos in
straight rows and columns.

"From order comes peace. Serenity," Rosa murmured.

Things they all lacked now. And it was only getting
worse.

"*Mira,* I've got things covered down here. *Vete arriba
con Papi.* Go up with him." Soap bubbles flew through
the air when Yaz flicked her wet hand toward the upstairs and repeated the words. "Maybe he'll want you
to read to him some more."

Rosa pulled a picture off the fridge. Her eyes glued
to the image, she sank slowly into one of the kitchen
chairs. "*Tengo miedo, Yazmine.*"

Her sister's softly whispered words pierced Yaz's
chest like a sharp dagger. Shutting off the stream of
warm water, she took a steadying breath before turning to face Rosa. "I'm scared, too."

"It's not fair." Frustration and pain laced Rosa's
words. "I mean, I know that's an absurd, infantile complaint. Life's not fair. But I can't help it. I want more
moments like this."

Rosa turned the picture to show Yaz the candid shot of the four of them after Lilí's high school graduation. Huge smiles, arms wrapped around each other. Papi's face glowed with pride. None of them aware of the threat looming over their shoulders.

"Don't go there. It'll only make this worse," Yaz cautioned. "We have to take it one day at a time."

"You sound more levelheaded than I do. How'd that happen?" Rosa shook her head with a weary sigh.

"I guess you're rubbing off on me." Yaz strode over to wrap Rosa in a tight hug. "Now go check on Papi before I change my mind about covering Lilí's dishwashing shift."

With a wistful look at the graduation photo, Rosa set it on the table, then left the kitchen.

Biting her lip to stem the ever-present threat of tears, Yaz plopped down onto Rosa's chair. She traced the smile on Papi's lips, dragging her finger lightly over each of their faces. Rosa was right. This wasn't fair.

The new year was supposed to signal new beginnings, positive affirmations.

Only, it didn't for her. Not for any of them.

Over the past few days, Papi had slowed down considerably. He complained more of fatigue. His body ached. His breaths were more difficult for him to catch. Yaz hadn't said as much to her sisters, but she was afraid for Papi, for all of them. The downward spiral was happening too quickly. Like someone had jammed the fast-forward button on the video of their lives.

She wasn't ready to say good-bye to him. Didn't think she'd ever be ready.

The doorbell rang, dragging Yaz out of her depressing thoughts. She glanced at her watch, unable to think of who might be stopping by at eight forty-five on a Wednesday evening. Cheryl had mentioned grabbing dinner with coworkers after a staff meeting. None of Rosa's close friends were in town. Pablo had been here most of the day.

Reaching the door, she looked through the peephole, quickly drawing back in surprise when she recognized Tomás.

She hadn't seen him since the morning of January first when he'd picked up Maria from her house. Even when she'd gone over for the thank-you dinner Mrs. B had planned, Tomás had wound up working late.

She'd been anxious to see him, tease him about sharing his first bottle of wine with her. Instead, he'd already fallen back into his old workaholic routine, concentrating on the Linton campaign now that his nanny was back.

Silly as it was, she missed him. She'd tried convincing herself that going from seeing him every day to not at all was like ripping off a Band-Aid. The quicker you were done with it, the better. It hadn't worked.

Now that he stood on her front porch, snow dusting his broad shoulders, a tired yet hopeful expression in his sexy bedroom eyes, an excited thrill zinged through her.

She made short work of the dead bolt and tugged open the front door. Despite her fleece pants and thick sweater, she shivered at the winter's bite. "What brings you out in this weather? Hurry in, it's freezing out there."

"¡Gracias! No matter how long I've lived in the Chicago area, I still can't get used to this mess."

Tomás brushed passed her into the foyer, his musky scent mixing with the crisp smell of snow. Once inside, he shrugged out of his navy wool coat, draping it and his black scarf over a hook on the coatrack.

"Are you just now getting home from the city?" she asked, noting he still wore his black pinstriped suit with his red and black tie—her favorite combination.

He brushed the snow from his hair. "Linton moved up the deadline on our presentation so it's been crazy since we got back from the holidays. I've been burning the candle at both ends."

"Old habits die hard, huh?"

"I don't plan on making it a habit anymore. If I can land this account, I'll be golden. It'll only be a matter of staying on top of things, keeping in touch with the old man so we're rarely in this position again."

"Sounds like a good idea."

"A good *plan*." He tilted his head forward, a wise-guy grin on his lips. Then he quickly sobered, glancing up the stairs. "I'm sorry I haven't had time to stop by and see Rey. I've been working in the city five, sometimes six days a week, getting home late after planning meetings. Do you think he's still up?"

"I'm not sure. Rosa's sitting with him while I finish the dishes. You can go check if you want."

"How's he doing?" Tomás's face creased with worry, reminding her how his concern for her father had drawn her to him from that first time he'd come over for dinner.

"He tires easily, and his pain is pretty much constant." Yaz twisted the towel in her hands, hating the uselessness of letting the cancer run its course. "Dr. Lopez warned us it's only going to get worse."

Tomás stilled her nervous movements by placing a hand over hers. "I know it's not easy, but you're strong. And you have the rest of us to lean on."

She knew she should smile, make a witty remark, but that was beyond her capabilities right now. Not with fear, frustration, and sorrow constantly bubbling to the surface.

"If he's still awake, I won't stay long. I promise."

"He'll be pleased to see you." She stepped back, sliding away from Tomás's touch before she said something stupid like how pleased *she* was to see him. "I better get going. The dishes won't wash themselves."

She started toward the kitchen.

"Yaz!"

When she glanced over her shoulder, Tomás already stood on the first step.

"Are you driving to the studio to rehearse when you're done?" he asked. "Or will you be around?"

"I'll be here. They're calling for more snow tonight so I'm going to do my workout in the basement."

"I was hoping you'd have time to chat for a few minutes. I wanted to run something by you."

"Something . . . ?"

"An idea for Linton. Funny, as much as you love giving me a hard time, you have a good eye. I wanted to get your opinion on the final idea." He hesitated, his uncertainty a reminder of the distance that had cropped up between them the past couple of weeks. "If you don't mind."

"Sure. No problem." Two could play the just-friends game.

"Thanks. I'll be down soon."

He flashed the lazy grin that won her over every time, then he took the stairs by twos, quickly disappearing around the top banister.

Yaz strode back to the kitchen, warning herself not

to get too excited. He valued her opinion. No big deal. Not a big deal at all.

Yeah, right. Maybe if she kept telling herself that, she'd actually believe it.

"A sandy beach, sunset skies, palm trees, a hammock hanging off to the side." Tomás moved his hands through the air in front of him, trying to paint the picture for Yazmine. They sat at her kitchen table, the smell of a strong pot of coffee, freshly brewed, and warm air from the vent giving the room a cozy feel.

"The sky's a vibrant mix of varying shades of peach and blood orange with a touch of wispy purplish, light blue clouds. Two figures in shadow. A diamond ring sparkling in a box in the guy's hand."

He had counted on Yaz's teasing grin and smart-aleck comments to keep him levelheaded. Instead, her eyes filled with a dreamy expression he hadn't seen before. Her lips parted as she pictured the scene he created for her.

"Yeah," she murmured. "I can see it. Sounds beautiful."

She was beautiful.

The thought had his blood heating.

Damn! He dragged his attention back to his presentation, before things got embarrassing for him. "Emblazoned across the sky in silvery letters we have the slogan, sparkling like diamonds on a midnight tapestry."

"*¿Qué dice?*" Yaz slowly lifted her mug to her lips, her gaze pensive, considering. Alluring even though she probably didn't even realize it.

"It says: Linton—for a love that lasts a lifetime."

The dreamy look on her face vanished, replaced by a cat-who-ate-the-canary grin. "Hmmm, sounds familiar."

She remembered.

He smiled back, pleased with her reaction to the campaign and her part in it. "That night you came over after Maria had gone to bed. We talked about Linton Jewelry and shared a bottle of wine." The night they'd danced in front of the fireplace together. "You tossed out some flippant remark. Which doesn't surprise me."

She narrowed her cat eyes at him, her saucy mouth still quirked.

He arched a brow. "If the shoe fits."

"I prefer a sti—"

"Stiletto. I know."

He dodged the balled-up napkin she threw at him, his coffee sloshing out of his mug. "Easy. Seriously though . . ."

He used her weapon to soak up the spilled liquid. "You inspired me. It's nice to have an outsider's point of view every once in a while. I finally feel like this campaign is coming together, and I owe it in part to you."

She looked down at her mug, but not before he noticed the faint blush creeping up her cheeks. "You're welcome."

She was a study in contrasts, this woman. Had been since the first day he'd met her.

That was part of what kept him on his toes around her. Part of what made her so damnably captivating.

"I still owe you a glass of wine, don't I? Sorry about missing dinner the other evening."

"Forget about it." There was a beat of silence before she glanced back up at him. He caught a hint of resignation flashing in her gaze. "We both have a lot on our plates. Save the wine for Cheryl. How's that going, by the way? She and I have been so busy the past couple of weeks, we haven't connected much."

Tomás took a sip of his coffee, considering how to respond. Cheryl wasn't really a topic he cared to discuss with Yaz. He hadn't spoken much to the easygoing teacher himself lately, and while their New Year's Eve party hadn't been a dud, something had felt . . . off.

Honestly, going out on a date was about the last thing on his mind right now. "I'm not so sur—"

"Yazmine! Yazmine!"

Rosa's cry of alarm reverberated through the house. In seconds, Tomás was racing up the stairs, Yaz nipping at his heels. Together they tore into Reynaldo's room.

"What's wrong?" Yaz cried, her voice a screech of fear.

Rey still sat up in his bed, but he looked much paler than he had twenty minutes ago when Tomás had visited with him. His skin was ashen, his body in spasms as he struggled for breath.

"What should I—We have to—He needs help!" Rosa's eyes bugged out in alarm. Her hands shook as they fluttered through the air in her agitation.

"*Cálmate,*" Rey gasped.

"Calm down?" Yaz squeaked. She elbowed Rosa aside, then fell to her knees next to the bed.

Rey grabbed at his chest, tugging at his flannel pajama top. "*No puedo,* I can't, can't breathe."

"It's okay, Papi. Rosa, call 911," Yaz ordered.

Rosa stood frozen, staring at their father, tears streaking down her pale cheeks. In seconds she'd gone from an agitated mess to a mute statue. Tomás doubted she'd be able to put together a coherent sentence at this point.

"I got it." He whipped out his cell phone.

Rey shook his head. "No. Stay. Here." His words were broken up by his desperate gasps. "*Estoy. Bien.*"

"Papi, you're not fine." Yaz's voice trembled. "Tomás, please call an ambulance."

"*No, no.*" Rey's agitation increased. He waved at Tomás with jerky motions.

"Why don't I call Dr. Lopez, too? He can decide the best course of action," Tomás suggested. It was obvious Rey didn't want to go to the hospital, but his daughters needed the comfort of a medical opinion.

Rey nodded, continuing to wheeze.

Yaz looked up at Tomás. He could see her struggling to contain her panic. Whatever he had to do to help her, he would.

"How do I reach the doctor?" Tomás waited, his fingers poised to key in the digits.

Yaz rattled off the number, rubbing a hand up and down Rey's back.

Tomás stepped over to Rosa so he could put an arm around her stiff shoulders. Pale-faced, her expression shell-shocked, she looked like she might shatter into a gazillion pieces if someone didn't hold her together.

Moments later they'd been reassured that Dr. Lopez and the ambulance were on their way. Rey had slid down to lay in bed, his breathing shallow, but steady. Yaz carefully adjusted the pillows behind his head.

Tomás gently led Rosa over to sit on the end of the bed.

"*Está bien,*" he told her gently. "Help is on the way."

Noting the sheen of sweat on her face, he pulled his handkerchief out of his pocket and placed it in her hands. "Take a deep breath. Hold it in for a couple of seconds. There you go. Release. Now slowly take in another."

Rosa gazed up at him, her brown eyes huge orbs filled with terror.

"It's okay," he repeated, sinking down to sit beside her. He brushed her hair out of her face, seeking to comfort her like he would his own sister. "It's scary, I know."

Yaz laid a hand on Rosa's shoulder. "Hang in there with me. We'll be okay. You hear me?"

"Lilí," Rosa whispered, her lips barely moving.

"I've got it covered." Scrolling through his contacts, Tomás tapped Lilí's name, thankful he'd thought to save her number the one time she'd relayed a message about Maria. This wasn't a call he wanted to place, but no way would he make Yaz or Rosa do it.

"Hi Lilí, it's Tomás," he said when she picked up on the third ring.

"Tomás?"

He stood up, lowering his voice and stepping out into the hallway when he heard Lilí's surprise. "I'm sorry to call you like this, but you need to head home. Now."

"What's wrong? Is Papi—"

"He's holding his own, at the moment," Tomás rushed to reassure her. "Dr. Lopez is on his way."

"What happened? Where's Yaz? Where's Rosa? They're both supposed to be there!"

"They're here, we're all here." He worked to use a soothing tone in an effort to stop the rising hysteria he heard in her young voice. "But they want you with them. Can someone else drive you? If not, I'll come get you."

"No, no, that's okay. One of my friends will do it . . ." Lilí trailed off, probably like her sisters, her thoughts scrambling in different directions, unable to make sense of anything. Hell, his own heart was racing, and Rey wasn't his father.

"The most important thing is for you to get here safely. We'll be waiting for you." He turned when he felt someone touch his elbow. "Hold on a minute."

He passed the phone to Yaz, her hand trembling as she lifted it to her ear.

"Come home, Lilí. We need you." Yaz's voice caught on the last word. Tomás heard Lilí's tinny "okay" through the speaker before Yaz silently cut the connection.

Tomás enveloped her in his arms, wishing like hell he could shield her from this pain. Hating the impotence of it all.

He felt a shudder go through her, knew she fought to pull herself together for her sisters' sake as well as Rey's. *Dios*, how he admired this strong, passionate woman.

"Hold on to me if you need to. I'm here," he said, tightening his embrace.

She responded by sliding her arms around his waist, burrowing her face into his chest. His breath caught as he felt her burrowing deeper into his heart. Panic flared, his flight instinct kicking into high gear.

Doggedly he ignored it. The only thing that mattered right now was this woman, her family, and the support they needed. Anything else slipped off the radar of importance.

The front doorbell rang and Yaz flinched.

"I'll get it. You stay here with Rosa." He combed a hand down her silky hair, swiped a tear from her cheek with the back of his hand.

"Gracias. I don't know if I . . . without you . . . *ay,* thanks."

"There's nowhere else I'd rather be." Bending down he pressed a kiss to her brow.

Things were about to get even more difficult for her and her sisters. God help him, he'd do anything he could for them. He may have already been burning the candle at both ends, but the flames were about to get bigger.

As much as it pained him to say, Rey's time was drawing to an end. No way would Tomás leave Yazmine to deal with everything alone. If it was the only thing he could do for her, he'd be there for her to lean on, for as long as she needed him.

Chapter Seventeen

Yazmine sat on the edge of Papi's bed, smoothing the damp washcloth across his brow, wiping away beads of sweat. He shivered underneath the layers of blankets covering him, murmuring incoherent words in his sleep. She shushed him soothingly, then went back to humming along with the Los Paisanos tune playing softly through the speaker on Papi's dresser.

It'd been five days since they'd had to call Dr. Lopez and the paramedics to the house. Papi had refused to go to the hospital, but thankfully a hospice nurse had come to show Yaz and the girls how to care for him. She was still afraid of being in over her head, drowning in what-ifs, but if Papi wanted to be at home, then she was determined to do whatever she could to make him comfortable.

Despite her best efforts, each day he'd progressively gotten worse. The blood when he coughed meant the cancer had metastasized to his lungs when it had already begun attacking his liver. The nurse had bluntly told them that it was only a matter of time.

Yaz blinked back her tears. She refused to give in to

the despair threatening to drag her under. Papi's lucid moments were few and far between now. If he woke up, she didn't want him to find her a blubbering mess of tears and snot. It would only make him worry more.

She was rinsing the washcloth in the bowl on his nightstand when the bedroom door creaked open. Rosa slipped through, a tray of food in her hands.

"Has he woken up again?" she whispered.

Yaz shook her head, afraid her voice would give away her anxiety. She didn't want to worry Rosa. Papi's quick decline was already taking a toll on her sisters.

None of them had slept much. They'd eaten even less. Their days and nights had been spent here in Papi's room, sleeping on the floor or in the recliner Tomás had helped her lug up the stairs from the living room.

Rosa set the tray on the dresser, carefully lining it up so all the edges matched precisely. She fidgeted with the knickknacks Papi kept. Angling this picture a little, straightening that comb. She turned the music down, then back up again before brushing at some nonexistent dust on the speaker. Her neat-freak compulsion, by her own admission her coping mechanism, was in fine form. But looking at her sister, Yaz could tell her coping mechanism wasn't helping much.

Rosa's normally wavy, shoulder-length pageboy cut looked more like a bird's nest of brown sticks. Dark circles framed her sad eyes. Worse, she'd been wearing the same blouse for two days, even though she'd spilled tomato soup on it yesterday.

Rosa moved around the room, tucking in the bottom edge of a sheet, bending down to pick up Papi's house slippers. Busying herself with mundane tasks to avoid reality.

Yaz gnashed her teeth, this close to screaming at her sister to stop. Sit down. Quit fussing.

Yet she knew that would only upset Rosa, and then Yaz would feel worse.

"*¿Donde, donde está?*"

Yaz sucked in a sharp breath at Papi's raspy-voiced question, her attention immediately zeroing in on him.

Rosa dropped a slipper, hurrying over to the other side of the bed.

"Where's who, Papi?" Yaz combed her fingers through the graying hair at his temple.

His gaze shifted from her to Rosa and back again. "*Necesito—*"

His body convulsed in a fit of coughs, and Yaz pressed a tissue into his hands to catch the speckle of blood.

It was several minutes before he fell back against his pillows. Exhaustion and pain left his features haggard and drawn. His eyes fluttered closed.

Yaz wiped his brow with the wet washcloth again, murmuring soothing sounds. "It's okay, Papi. Don't talk. Get some rest."

Rosa clasped his hand, her face a mask of fear and desperation. "*Estamos aquí, Papi.* We're right here."

"*Necesito a las tres.*"

He needed all three of them. That's why he'd been asking for someone a few minutes ago.

"Rosa, go get Lilí, please. She went to her room to check her email, see if she'd heard back from her professors."

Rosa scrunched up her face in a mutinous scowl, looking more like a preteen Lilí when she hadn't gotten her way. "I don't want to leave him. What if he's asleep again when I come back?"

"*No, nena, estoy bien.*" Papi's coughing attack resumed,

deep hacking sounds that did nothing to make the girls think he was "okay." When he finally spoke again he had a hard time catching his breath. "I need, to see, all three, three of you. *Por favor.*"

Her sister was out the door before Papi took another shallow breath.

Yaz stayed at his side, grateful for whatever time she had left with him. What she really wanted was to curl up next to him, like she'd done as a little girl when she'd had a bad dream. Mami and he used to let her climb into their bed, and he would sing softly to her until she fell asleep.

Grief overwhelmed her and Yaz leaned down to place a kiss on his brow.

His eyes fluttered open as she sat up. "*Eres una nena buena.*"

"It's Yaz, Papi, not Rosa. She's the good one, remember?"

His dry lips curved in a sad smile. "I know who you are." He stopped, wincing with pain. When he spoke again, his voice sounded scratchy and raw. "*Mi estrellita.*"

"*Sí*, Papi. I'm your little star." Yaz bit her bottom lip to keep it from trembling. "You and me, headed straight to the top."

"I am headed, higher, now."

Anguish knifed through her. Yaz pressed a hand to her mouth, trying to stifle her moan of desperation.

"Papi, I'm here." Lilí raced into the room, skidding to a halt at the end of the bed. Dressed in sweatpants and a ratty long-sleeved T-shirt, her pixie hair a spiked mess, her younger sister looked like a typical college coed. Only her hollowed eyes and tearstained cheeks gave away the fact that she wasn't coping too well either.

Papi patted his bed, their sign that they had permission to hop on. Years ago the gesture evoked screeches of delight and a little mattress bouncing. Today the girls gingerly sat down, afraid of jostling their father and causing him any undue pain.

Once they were settled, Rosa and Lilí on Mami's side of the bed, Yaz on the edge by Papi, he motioned toward his nightstand.

"What is it?" Yaz asked.

"In the drawer, *por favor*." His arm flopped back onto the bed, as if fatigued by the simple movement.

Yaz pulled open the drawer to find three envelopes, each labeled with one of their names. "These?"

"*Sí*. For you." He gave the slightest of nods as she handed her sisters their letters, pressing hers to her chest in a painful mix of grief and gratitude.

She knew what these were. Papi's last words of advice to them. His final good-bye.

Across the bed, Rosa's shoulders shook, silent sobs racking her body. Lilí covered her face with her hands, leaning down to lay her head on Papi's chest.

"*Te quiero, te quiero*," she cried, repeating her words of love over and over.

Papi patted her head, shushing her like the little girl she still was in his eyes. A little girl losing her beloved father.

Tears streaked down Yazmine's face, her heart breaking for her sisters, for Papi, for herself. She wanted to stop this from happening. Hit the pause button so she could catch her breath, steady the shakiness rattling through her.

"I am so, proud, of you," Papi wheezed. "You are,

all beautiful, kind, strong." Lilí wrapped her arms around his waist. Slowly, he reached his hands out to Yaz and Rosa, completing the circle. "Love, each other."

His eyes drifted closed. His breathing slowed.

Yaz longed to scream out in anguish and denial.

"*Te quiero.*" Papi's words were hardly audible, his lips barely moving. His expression turned peaceful and he took his final breath.

Still, his voice lingered, crooning words of eternal love in an age-old ballad that hauntingly played through the speaker.

Abject pain and misery and loss jackknifed in Yazmine's chest. The moan she'd fought so hard to stifle forced its way up her throat in a gut-wrenching howl.

Papi was gone. Finally joining their beloved mother.

A Los Paisanos CD played on the stereo. Neighbors and friends roamed the first floor of the house. The dining room table was filled with food and sweets, one corner weighed down by bottles of wine and Puerto Rican rum. To an outsider it looked like a regular party in full swing.

Yaz sat in a chair in the corner of the living room, struggling to maintain a peaceful smile. People stopped to offer their condolences and she wondered for what felt like the millionth time if this was what hell would be like.

This was supposed to be a celebration of Papi's life. But all she wanted was to sneak up to her room, curl into a ball on her bed and pretend none of it was happening.

Today signified the ending of a part of her life she wasn't ready to give up. Her parents were gone. Her sisters were busy working on their own dreams and goals. There was nothing to tie her to Oakton anymore.

She heard Maria's giggle and she turned to follow the sound. The little girl, dressed in a black long-sleeved gown with a Peter Pan collar, flipped the pages on a family album she and Tomás were perusing together. One of the albums Papi had sat and stared at for hours over the last few weeks.

Tomás must have felt her gaze because he glanced up, a question in his dark eyes.

"¿*Estás bien*?" he mouthed.

She wanted to lie, tell him she was fine, but she couldn't pretend anymore. She gave him a slight shake of her head, then rose to escape. Threading her way through the crowd, she reached the kitchen, then slipped outside.

With the wind gusting and snow falling, few would venture out here. It was freezing cold, another arctic Chicago day, but she finally had a moment's peace.

She stepped to the back-porch railing, realizing too late that she hadn't even bothered to stop for her jacket. Dumb, but right now she'd rather freeze than go back for it.

The door opened behind her and she glanced over her shoulder, annoyed by the interruption.

Tomás didn't say a word, he simply held up her coat for her to slip her arms into the sleeves.

She burst into tears.

The next thing Yaz knew, his strong arms were around her, the sound of his reassuring voice whispering in her ear.

"He'd be proud of you, and your sisters. You did a beautiful job at the ceremony. Hold on a little while longer and I'll clear the house for you. Send everyone home so you girls can relax together."

"*Estoy tan cansada,*" she mumbled. "Tired of people, tired of forms and legal questions. Tired of pretending I'm fine."

"I know." He rubbed his hands in a circle around her back, the motion soothing her raw nerves.

She sniffed, reaching into her skirt pocket for the handkerchief he'd given her earlier.

"Thank you, for everything." She stepped back to wipe the wetness from her cheeks, hoping her tears hadn't done too much damage to her makeup.

"Like I said, whatever you need."

"You're a good man, Tomás Garcia."

His face actually flushed at her compliment.

"Of all the dance studios in all the world, I'm glad I walked into yours." He winked, drawing one of the few true smiles she'd given someone in the week since Papi's death.

"You're an old romantic, you know that?" she said.

"I have my good moments."

She sobered, needing to say something she should have said earlier this week, but she'd avoided calling him. "I'm sorry things didn't work out with Cheryl."

He shrugged. "No worries. She's a good person. I hope she's happy."

"I thought she and Ronnie were finished. I guess he finally saw the light and came begging for another chance."

The wind picked up and she shivered into her coat.

"Come on." Tomás crooked an elbow for her to grasp. "The sooner you face everyone, the sooner I can help them on their way. You're almost done. Hang in there."

She *was* almost done.

As soon as Rosa and Lilí went back to school, and she worked things out with Pablo to ensure the house was taken care of, she'd be on her way to New York.

Done with Oakton except for holidays. Done spending time with Maria and Tomás.

Dios, that thought only made her sadder.

Chapter Eighteen

Tomás kneaded his aching neck and shoulder muscles with one hand and reached for his ringing cell phone with the other. He blinked in surprise at the caller ID number flashing on the screen. "Hi, Rosa, how's my favorite librarian?"

"Oh, you know. I'm doing the best I can."

The worry lacing her words told him otherwise. "What's going on?"

"I'm sorry to bother you at work . . ." Her voice trailed off and he could picture the hesitancy on her face.

"You are never a bother. Call me anytime, I mean it. What's up?"

"Thank you, I appreciate that. Well, I was, I was wondering if you've seen or heard from Yazmine this week?"

His computer dinged, a reminder box popping up on the screen with the words "Call print department!" in red letters.

"No, I haven't actually. I'm on an extremely tight deadline at work for a big presentation tomorrow. I've been going into the office early and coming home long past Maria's bedtime. Today's the first day I've worked from home in weeks."

"So Yaz hasn't touched base with you?"

"Not since the funeral." He swiveled his chair to face the snow-covered backyard, ignoring the reminder blinking obnoxiously on his screen. "I've left her a couple of messages over the past two weeks, but she hasn't called back. I figured you girls could use some private time. But I'm hoping to see you and Lilí before you head back to school."

Rosa's heavy sigh didn't send out any positive vibes. "Pablo made us leave over the weekend so we wouldn't get too far behind. We'd already missed the first few weeks of the semester."

"Aw man, I'm sorry I missed saying good-bye in person. Wait a minute—" Tomás sat up, spinning back around to look at his desk calendar with alarm. Today was Thursday. "So Yaz has been home alone all week?"

"Yeah. We left Sunday. I thought she'd call you, maybe go over to see you and Maria."

No, she hadn't.

Disappointment coursed through him like a line of gasoline lit with a match. He sank back into his chair, unable to stop the emotion from blazing unchecked.

During the memorial service Yazmine had been a little withdrawn. With Pablo, his wife Dolores, and the rest of Rey's *compadres* gathering around the girls for support, Tomás had hung back. They were more like family than he was.

Feeling like an outsider had grated on his spirit, but he understood that those men and their families had been in the girls' lives for decades, while he'd only enjoyed being welcomed into their inner circle for a few months.

Later, at the wake, he could tell by her rigid posture and strained smile that Yaz was only holding on by a thread.

She'd continued keeping him at arm's length until he'd caught up with her on the back porch. After their conversation, he'd thought they'd turned a corner and could remain friends.

But she'd been on her own the past four days, probably going crazy in that empty house, bombarded with memories, and still she hadn't reached out to him. Hadn't called to talk, to vent. Hadn't needed him for anything.

If there'd been any doubt in his mind about where he'd stand with Yaz once Rey had passed and there was nothing keeping her in Oakton any longer, Tomás knew now.

"I'm a little worried about her," Rosa said, interrupting his thoughts. "Maybe it's nothing. But when we left she seemed a little too quiet and withdrawn. When I called to let her know I made it to my apartment she was really cryptic, cutting our conversation short. It reminded me of the months right after she and her ex broke up. The last time we spoke she barely said a word."

"When was that?"

"Monday morning when I was walking to class. Oh, excuse me." He could hear a door opening, people talking in the background. "Sorry, I arrived at my building to meet with a professor. Anyway, I haven't been able to get in touch with her since then."

Antsy, Tomás rose and crossed to the window. Gray, billowy clouds filled the sky, threatening more damn snow. He shivered, the cold barrenness of winter seeping into his bones. Man, he could not wait for spring. Warmth, sunshine, new life.

"What about Lilí?" he asked.

"Same thing. Yaz hasn't returned either of our calls since Monday. I don't know what to do."

This was not a good sign, but the hint of panic in Rosa's voice made him keep the comment to himself. Damn Yazmine and her stubbornness. "Let me see what I can find out. Hang in there and try not to worry."

"I'm sorry. *No quiero molestarte.*"

"It's no bother. I could use a brain break from work. I'll be in touch, okay?"

There was a beat of silence before Rosa's relief-filled response came through the line. "*Gracias, Tomás, te lo agradezco.*"

"Don't sweat it," he said, brushing aside her appreciation. "You can count on me."

Tomás hung up, then immediately tapped the speed dial number for Yaz. It went straight to voice mail. He called the house phone, experiencing a jarring sense of déjà vu when Rey's voice answered on the machine. Frustration mounting, Tomás hung up without leaving a message.

It was one thing to push him away. Something completely different to do that to her sisters. What happened to *familia primero?*

Damn her independent streak.

Frustrated, he leaned his forehead against the windowpane. The frigid glass cooled the heated anger building inside him. As he worked to calm his thoughts, he focused on where she might be instead of why she kept pushing everyone away. If Yaz was upset, in need of getting away from what she wanted to avoid, where would she—

In a flash of recollection, he realized where Yaz was probably hiding.

Striding out of his office, he went in search of his nanny. He found her in the laundry room folding towels. "Mrs. B, I got a call from Rosa Fernandez a few minutes ago, wondering if I'd touched base with Yazmine. How did she look when you dropped off Maria at dance this week?"

"There's been a substitute covering Yazmine's classes since they started back after the holiday break. I thought you knew."

Tomás shook his head, a sinking feeling in the pit of his stomach.

Mrs. B paired the ends of a towel together as she continued. "I've heard a few mothers wondering how much longer she'll stay in town now that her father has passed."

Join the club. He'd been wondering the same thing. Though certain her departure was inevitable.

Somehow he knew his first hunch was right. Yaz was at the studio, practicing, preparing to leave. Not before he talked to her about shutting out her loved ones, even if she didn't include him in that group.

"I've got an errand to run, Mrs. B. Don't hold lunch for me after you pick up Maria from school. I'll grab something when I get back."

Seconds later he was on his way to Hanson's Academy of Dance, grumbling at the icy road conditions slowing his pace, cursing every red light, tapping impatiently on his steering wheel when he got stuck behind a city bus for several blocks.

He pulled into the studio parking lot to find Yaz's

blue Ford Focus with the familiar miniature ballet slippers dangling from the rearview mirror, parked in a space next to a mound of snow left by the plow truck.

Relief and gloom warred within him.

Huddled in his winter jacket, he banged on Hanson's locked front door until Yaz emerged from one of the back studios wearing a pair of figure-hugging black leggings and a spandex crop top. Her face flushed, she looked beautiful. Even with her brow furrowed in confusion.

She unlocked the bolt and pushed open the glass door. "What are you doing here?"

He shoved his way inside, out of the bitter cold. "Looking for you. Is your cell phone not working?"

"Excuse me?"

"Is your battery dead? Did you lose your power cord?"

She drew back, eyeing him like he was one tortilla short of a dozen. "What are you talking about?"

"Or are you just being stubborn and refusing to answer my calls?"

Guilt flittered across her face before she pursed her lips and spun around to march back to the studio. "I'm busy. Did you need something?"

"Yeah, to make sure you're all right."

"Peachy."

Normally her smart-ass attitude made him laugh. Today, he'd caught the vulnerability in her caramel eyes, seen the fatigue on her classic features. He'd heard Rosa's pain over the phone. A pain he saw mirrored on Yaz's face.

"How come you're not communicating with your sisters? What's going on?"

Yaz snatched a hand towel from her dance bag in the front corner of the room.

"Who dragged you into this?" She narrowed her eyes at him. "Never mind, I know. Rosa the worrier. Look, I'm fine. Like I said, I'm busy."

"Too busy to talk to Rosa and Lilí? They're hurting as much as you are."

"Tell me something I don't already know." She tossed her head, her ponytail flicking across her shoulder blades as she turned to fiddle with her iPod.

"So what gives?" he pressed.

She adjusted the volume on the stereo speakers and Tomás used the opportunity to take a good look at her. His concern for her mushroomed.

She'd lost weight in the last two weeks. Her collarbones protruded under the delicate straps of her black crop top. Dark smudges circled her eyes above her sunken cheeks. She looked fragile, breakable. A delicate china doll wearing a tough-girl façade.

When she still hadn't acknowledged his question, he unzipped his jacket and tossed it in the corner next to hers, digging in for a fight.

"You look like hell," he said, hands on his hips.

"Thanks, I always appreciate your honesty. If that's all you came to say, I've got a lot of work to do. It was great seeing you though."

Her tone was snarky, dismissive. It matched the personality he'd typecast her with when they'd first met—uppity, dance snob. He knew differently now.

Now he'd seen and experienced the loving, passionate, caring woman she really was. The one who wanted so badly to make her father proud, and had finally decided she wanted it for herself, too.

His admiration for her rivaled the strength of his

attraction. Because of that, he wouldn't allow her to brush him off that easily.

"What are you doing, Yaz?"

"What does it look like?" She spread her arms wide to encompass the entire room. "It's what I *do*."

"Push people away?"

"Yes! No! Uggghh!" She threw her towel into her dance bag with a muttered curse. "*¡Déjame en paz!*"

Sure, he could do what she wanted and leave her, but she wouldn't be at peace. Not by a long shot.

"I'm dealing the best way I know how," she grumbled.

"Uh-uh, that's a cop-out."

She winced, her face turning an even whiter shade of pale.

He didn't back down though. He couldn't.

Her happiness, her sisters' happiness, depended on him being able to help Yaz move past this agonizing transition now that Rey was gone.

"You're better than this. Your sisters deserve better than this." His gaze caught hers and he swore he could see the real Yaz in the depths of her eyes, crying out for help.

He wanted to hold her in his arms and promise her everything would be okay. Unfortunately, he couldn't promise that, not to either of them.

Arms folded across her chest, she tilted her chin at a pugnacious angle. It wobbled under the pressure of her pent-up emotions, a telltale sign she was hanging on by a quickly unraveling thread.

"Well, I can tell you, whatever you *are* doing, it's not healthy."

She sucked her teeth at him like a temperamental teen, hip cocked in a kiss-my-ass jaunt. "I'm fine, working a little harder than normal, but I've been out of the game for too long now. This is the price I have to pay for letting myself go."

"Hey, you know me. I understand dedication and determination." He grabbed her hands when she tried to brush his words aside.

"Let me go."

He kept his grip on her, biting back a curse when she mutinously turned her head to the side, refusing to look at him. "You're talking to a reformed king of workaholics, remember? Pushing yourself this hard, pushing your family away when you need each other the most? That's not going to make things better."

Her hands shook under his.

"Yaz, come on. Let's be honest here. Level with me. Please."

When she finally met his gaze the look of utter anguish on her stark features nearly knocked him to his knees.

He tugged her to him and Yaz stumbled into his open arms. She grabbed his sweater, laying her head against his shoulder as her tears fell.

He wrapped her in his embrace, relieved to see her finally letting her emotions go.

Her shoulders shook with the force of her sobs and he squeezed her tighter, holding her close to his heart. After a while, when her crying quieted to a few shuddered breaths, he pressed a kiss to the top of her head, hoping she could draw strength from him.

"I feel like I'm going crazy," she mumbled. "The girls are gone. I'm here trying to respect Papi's final wish, afraid to think that no matter how much I want it, I won't succeed."

"You can do anything. I thought we established that already."

"I know, but it's—" She pulled back, raising a shaky hand to smooth a strand of hair off her tearstained face.

Her eyes were puffy, her nose a dark shade of red, yet she'd never looked more beautiful to him. "Why haven't you called me?"

"You're busy."

"Lame excuse."

"I'm a big girl." She stepped away to snag a tissue from the box on the desk. "I can take care of myself. You've got your own worries."

"I'm never too busy for you, or your sisters. I thought I made that clear. Come on, talk to me." Grasping her elbow, he gently tugged her down to sit next to him on the hardwood floor.

She settled next to him, legs crossed tailor style, and blew her nose. "I know you're working on the Linton presentation. That's gotta be coming up soon. Maria deserves your free time and attention, not me. And what about your Perfect Partner Plan? How're you going to figure that out if I'm bugging you with my problems?"

"*Mierda.*"

"Excuse me?"

"You heard me. That's bullshit."

Lips pursed, she glared at him.

Tomás raised his brows, daring her to argue. He was right, and she knew it.

"Fiiiine." She drew out the word, lifting her shoulders and dropping them like the effort had taken all her energy. "What do you want to hear about? How quiet the house is? How I can't bring myself to walk into Papi's room because I keep expecting to find him there? How it's no fun cooking for one, so I pop a frozen dinner in the microwave, when I even remember to eat? What does it matter? I'll get over it eventually."

He circled her wrist with his thumb and forefinger, the tips overlapping. "If you don't starve yourself first. I'm calling Mrs. B to let her know you'll be coming for dinner tonight."

Yaz tugged her wrist free. "Don't exaggerate."

"I won't take no for an answer."

She narrowed her puffy eyes at him.

Well, she certainly had the pissed-off glare down. It was a relief to see a flash of her old spunk.

"Why are you being so pushy?"

"I learned from the best," he replied.

Her lips curved in a wistful smile. "We both did."

A pang of regret arrowed through his chest, knowing she was remembering Reynaldo. Her father wouldn't be happy with her reaction to his death. The older man would expect Tomás to give her a nudge, even if it had to be a hard one.

Even if that nudge pushed her farther away from him.

"So, you're killing yourself in preparation for heading back to New York." The words were painful to say, but he forced himself to spit them out.

"That was the original plan." Yaz fiddled with the laces on her jazz shoes. "But I got a call Monday from a choreographer I did some work with in New York. He hired on with a new show that's touring the US. The director is based out of Chicago and they're holding auditions here, tomorrow."

Tomás's heart dipped to the pit of his stomach. "Wow, that's, that's good news. All this time you've been planning to take New York by storm and your next big break could happen right in our backyard."

"Yeah."

"I'm happy for you." He honestly was.

What more could he ask than for someone he cared about to be given the opportunity to pursue her dream? Even if that dream didn't include him.

He looped an arm around her in a congratulatory hug. "That's incredible."

"Thanks," she murmured. Scooting closer, she rested her head on his shoulder. He tilted his head to hers, then glanced at their reflection in the mirror-lined wall. Her slender figure was dwarfed by his, yet somehow they fit well together.

They sat in silence, Tomás enjoying the quiet peace he always found with her. In the hustle of his daily life, being with her felt so incredibly right it scared him.

"So you'll impress them at the audition tomorrow, then pack your bags and hit the road." Saying the words out loud made their situation more real.

She nodded. "It's time. Papi's gone. There's nothing keeping me here anymore."

Her eyes met his in the mirror.

Tomás forced himself to keep quiet. No matter how badly he wanted her to stay, he would never ask. He was smart enough to know they'd never be happy if she longed to be somewhere else, itching to leave for something better.

"Tomorrow will be a big day for both of us then."

Yaz sat up, scooting around to face him. "Both?"

"I'm giving the final Linton presentation tomorrow. We made the cut for the top two."

Her face lit up with excitement. "No way! That's

awesome! How come you didn't say anything, you big lug?"

She leaned toward him, pushing his chest with her palms, and he fell back against the floor. Yazmine landed on top of him with a squeak of surprise. She buried her face in his neck, her body shaking with laughter.

Tomás linked his hands at the small of her back, letting himself enjoy her weight, the feel of her soft curves molding with his.

"You're crazy, you know that?" he said.

"It's one of my finer character traits."

He chuckled, but his body continued its war with his brain. He needed to sit up, put some distance between them. End this madness.

He couldn't bring himself to do it. Not yet.

Yaz lifted her head to rest her chin on his chest.

Tomás gazed up at her and immediately found himself drowning in the warmth of her eyes.

"You and me, we're going to the top, aren't we?" she asked, her soft smile at odds with the melancholy tone in her voice.

He hated his next words, but knew he had to say them. For both their sakes. "Of different mountains, but yeah, we are."

Her expression sobered. Her lashes drifted closed for a few seconds before she pushed away from him and hopped to her feet, reaching out to help pull him up.

When they stood facing each other, she smiled up at him, not the impish grin he loved, but a sad-tinged wannabe. "I'll give Rosa and Lilí a call to let them know I'm doing fine. Busting my ass to prove to myself that I can fulfill Papi's wish."

"As long as it's your wish, too."

"It is." She gave a brisk, no-nonsense nod.

"We'll see you at dinner tonight?"

"No, I'll be—"

"Yazmine, you have to eat." And he wasn't ready to cut this last tie.

"It's a big day tomorrow. For both of us. How about we celebrate our success later? Maybe I can swing by your place for dinner before I leave. Tonight I need to get myself ready. Go to bed early."

"But you'll have a meal. Or do I need to send Mrs. B over with a plate?"

"You keep forgetting I can take care of myself."

Damn if he didn't want to take care of her himself.

"Thanks for the pep talk—again—but I've got this. Now get out of here. You're wasting my studio time." She spun him around by the shoulders and gave him a shove. "I'm sure you have your own last-minute details to perfect."

He let himself be pushed toward the door. Only because she was right, he did have work to do. He'd call her later tonight though, nag her about eating something.

At the doorway he paused, turning to take a final glance at her in her element.

The strains of an old Sinatra tune trilled from the speakers. Yaz strode to the center of the room to take her starting mark, her legs and arms the epitome of grace and fluidity. Her expression was now calm, focused. Devoid of the stress and anguish he'd seen earlier.

This was her calming influence. Not him. Dance brought her to a place he never could.

Tomás dragged in a deep breath, surprised at the wistfulness engulfing him.

Yazmine Fernandez was a special woman. One day she'd make some guy the happiest man on earth.

Unfortunately, it couldn't be him.

Chapter Nineteen

Early the next morning, Yaz sat in her car shivering, waiting for it to warm up in the driveway. She squinted at the sun's reflection off the snowy front yard. The juxtaposition of the icy arctic temperature with the sunny brightness mirrored her emotions.

One minute she was excited for the audition and the incredible opportunity it represented. The next, cold fingers of regret for what, and who, she'd be leaving behind tiptoed up her spine.

Annoyed with the constant ping-pong of feelings and thoughts, she pressed the gas pedal, revving the engine to warm it up faster. Wishing she could get over Tomás and her doubts as quickly.

He'd made it painfully clear that it didn't bother him one way or the other if she stayed in Oakton.

Bottom line, he had his plan in motion. He was focused on what he wanted for himself and Maria. Completely fine that it didn't include Yaz. Even when he'd called to check on her last night, wishing her luck in his go-get-'em pep-talk tone, he hadn't said anything about missing her when she left.

Over the past two weeks she'd done nothing but dance and cry and hold one-sided conversations with Papi, his letter tight in her hands. He'd known that dance had always been her salvation, and his letter had basically told her to go after her dream, pursue what made her happy.

After she'd gotten the call about the audition, she'd tucked Papi's words into her heart and used his confidence in her to fuel her determination. Then she'd taken Tomás's advice and come up with her own plan: walk into that studio this morning like she owned it and nail her audition!

The car stereo blasting her favorite warm-up music, her fingers tapping out the beat on the steering wheel, Yaz pulled out of her driveway. Minutes later, she approached Maria's school. Out of habit, she flicked on her blinker and veered into the turning lane at the school's entrance. At the last second she caught herself and swerved back into the continuing traffic lane.

A car behind her honked, bursting the bubble of nervous energy in her stomach. Regret ached in her chest.

Since her replacement had taken over at Hanson's when Papi's health started deteriorating, she'd barely spent any time with Maria. In the weeks after the funeral, Yaz had purposely kept her distance, too emotionally drained to be around anyone. Not to mention, it wasn't healthy for her to rely on Maria and Tomás's company for comfort.

Her heart a little heavy, but her determination strong, Yazmine blew a kiss in the direction of Maria's school, sending love for her one-time sidekick with it. As the building grew smaller in her rearview mirror, Yaz kept her foot on the gas pedal. This was for the best.

* * *

Tomás trudged into his office, head pounding with the threat of a migraine. He'd done a final run-through of the Linton campaign fairly early the evening before, then had gone to bed, intent on getting a good night's sleep. Too bad he'd spent the rest of the night tossing and turning, visions of Yazmine dancing on a stage, far out of his reach, invading his dreams.

Eventually, he'd given up on getting any rest and spent the last few hours of the night channel surfing, tired yet unwilling to face the disturbing vision again.

"You look like hell," his secretary greeted him when he walked in.

"Thanks, Myrna, you look lovely today, too."

The older woman tsked as she followed him into his corner office, a hot cup of coffee in her hand. Her gray hair pulled back in a chignon, his ever-ready secretary rattled off the day's schedule, passing along messages and easily dismissing the calls she deemed unworthy of his attention at the moment.

"You're an angel," he said, gladly taking the mug of hot coffee she offered him.

"The Linton pitch starts at eleven thirty sharp. Main conference room. How are you feeling? You look like you're coming down with the flu or something." She pressed a cool hand to his forehead. "Has Maria been sick?"

"I'm fine. Something didn't agree with me last night, that's all." He took a deep drink of the coffee, needing the caffeine to fuel his system. He'd been waiting all morning for his usual pre-presentation adrenaline to kick in. So far it had abandoned him.

"Give me a few minutes and I'll be good," he said.

"The drawings and everything are in the carry-case. Will you make sure it's all set up and ready to go?"

"Sure thing. I've got it covered."

The older woman hurried off, closing the door quietly behind her.

Leaning back in his chair, Tomás closed his eyes, searching for the stamina that had gotten him where he was today. He knew it was in him. Somewhere. Buried under thoughts of Yazmine.

Was she still at home, or on her way to the audition? She'd mentioned the studio where the audition would be held, but he hadn't thought to ask what time it started when he'd called to check on her the night before. He smiled now, remembering her complaint about his nagging.

"You'd make a good fishwife," she had grumbled, smart-ass that she was.

His office intercom buzzed, reminding him of what he should be focusing on.

"Yes, Myrna," he answered.

"Little Boss Man's on line one."

"Thanks." Tomás clicked over to speak with the younger of the two partners who had founded the advertising firm. "Good morning, Wayne. What can I do for you?"

The next several minutes were spent verifying that all was set to go for the presentation. Apparently, with Linton himself here for the final pitch, the partners were antsy that no surprises crop up. All hands were expected on deck, spit polished and pristine.

Tomás knew he needed to be on his toes if he wanted to pull this off. Linton might look like Elmer Fudd, with his short, portly body and balding head, but the old man had a snappy sense of humor and a shrewd mind that served him well. Far too many business opponents had underestimated his prowess and smarts over the years.

Today, Linton was looking for a top-notch team who understood his company's vision—the pursuit of perfection, one loyal customer at a time.

Striding out of his office to check the setup, Tomás was confident in his ability to lead that team. His ideas were rock solid. All the hours of hard work, of tossing out the bad and perfecting the good, of seeing how others reacted to his idea—especially Yazmine—would pay off.

She had played an integral part in getting his thoughts focused in the right direction. Helping him infuse passion into his work. Evoking emotions like love and commitment, words like *forever* . . . ideas Linton Jewelry strove to convey to their customers. Sentiments he'd blocked from his radar—until Yaz.

He reached the conference room, but paused to gather himself before going in. Yazmine was the last person he needed to be thinking about when he walked in there. Anyway, by now she was probably at the studio, mid-audition, dancing her way out of his life.

His heart slowed to a dull thud.

He felt the blood drain out of his face, leaving him clammy and nauseous.

Dios mío, he was an idiot. Letting her go could be the biggest mistake of his life.

The heavy wooden door pushed open from the inside, knocking him back a step.

"Whoa, good morning, son." Bradford Linton stood in the doorway, his bald head shining, his pudgy figure sporting a tailored suit. "I was just coming out to see if the posse was rounding up."

"Uh, yes, sir. I was, uh, about to head in." Tomás stumbled over the words, his mind still grappling with the finality of Yaz's departure and the gaping hole it would leave in his heart. In his life. A chasm he suddenly realized only she could fill.

Linton backed into the room. Tomás followed, unnerved by this new revelation.

"I've been admiring your mock-ups," the older man said. "You've been paying attention to my suggestions, but staying true to your vision as well. I noticed you didn't add the tiki bar over to the left. Didn't care for that too much, huh?"

Tomás blinked several times, trying to follow the conversation. Somehow his brain had turned to mush the moment he admitted to himself that letting Yaz go without telling her how he felt had to be the ultimate asinine move.

"Tiki bar? Uh, yes," he finally answered. "I know you made that suggestion, but when I added it, I felt it drew the eye away from the couple, and the ring."

"You're right." Linton stepped closer to the mock-up boards depicting the sunset beach scene Tomás had described to Yaz the night Rey had taken a turn for the worse. "I don't admit to being wrong very often, but that's just 'cuz I rarely am."

The older man chuckled and bent to peer closer at the boards. Tomás snuck a quick glance at his watch. Eleven fifteen.

Would the audition last all day? Would Yaz commit to something immediately? Could he wrap things up here quickly and race over to the audition studio to be there when she finished?

"You've got some beautiful imagery here." Linton tapped a picture with a pudgy finger. "The colors, the slogan. There's something about the couple that grabs me, y'know? What a man wouldn't give to find a woman this beautiful. Somehow, the way you've captured them, I know she'd be something special."

Tomás nodded, his gaze transfixed by the woman who embodied Yaz in his mind. From the graceful arms, the long satiny hair, the dreamy expression on her face—the same one she'd worn when he'd shared the ad idea in her kitchen. And he—Tomás tightened his fists, angry with himself for taking so long to recognize this—he was the man with her, down on his knees, humbling himself for the chance to have her at his side for eternity.

"Yeah, she's special, and a whole lot more," he answered.

"Ah, I see how it is." Linton's crafty smile split his round face. "After our last meeting I wondered where your inspiration came from. Reminds me of my Betty, God rest her soul. She was the best thing that ever happened to me. Married forty years before the cancer took her." His smile slipped, his voice growing wistful. Turning toward the mock-up board, he traced the figure with the pad of his finger. "If I had a woman like this still waiting at home for me . . . I don't think I'd work such late hours anymore. You're a lucky man."

Only, this woman wasn't waiting at home for him. She was getting ready to go. And he'd done nothing to try and stop her. Or at the very least, be honest with her. All because he'd been afraid of getting hurt again. Of losing in love again. The problem was, now he was losing anyway.

Regret shot through him, reverberating through his

entire body. He sucked in a quick breath, staggered by his utter foolishness.

"Son, you doing okay? You look like a kid who's lost his best friend or his dog, or both." The older man moved to the wet bar in the corner of the conference room where he poured mineral water in a glass, then handed it to him.

His mind foggy, Tomás took a shaky drink. On the other side of the door he heard the firm's partners speaking in the hallway. He gulped down more water and wiped the sweat from his brow. Damn it, he had to pull himself together or risk making a mess of everything. He'd lost Yaz, he couldn't risk losing this account, too.

"I—Mr. Linton—Have you—" He broke off, at a loss for where to begin when his career was on the line, yet the one person who could complete his future was in a studio somewhere in the city, on the verge of dancing off into the sunset.

"Son, I can see that your presentation is ready. Are you?"

"Yes." Tomás drained his glass, then set it on the conference room table with a thud. "Sir, I can knock your socks off, show you the best-selling idea you'll ever hear. But may I ask you a question? If you'd mistakenly let your Betty think you were fine without her—would you let her go, or fight to win her back?"

Linton's gaze narrowed, his keen eyes assessing Tomás. "What are you trying to tell me, son?"

"Everything needed to convince you that my campaign, this firm, is a perfect match for Linton Jewelry is right here, no problem. I assure you, there isn't anyone else in the country who can do better than what we've put together for you, now and in the future. But . . ."

"I'm listening," Linton said when Tomás trailed off. He'd never gained anything by holding back before. Now was not the time to start.

"In here," Tomás put a hand to his heart, "I'm not the man you need to represent your company's vision. Not in this precise moment. But I have been, and I will be again, if you can give me a little extra time today."

Linton frowned, the skin from his brow to the top of his bald head wrinkling in his confusion.

"I'm about to let the most perfect woman I've ever met—*my* Betty—walk out of my life."

The older man's mouth curved in a conspiratorial grin. "Your Betty, huh? Your inspiration?"

Tomás nodded, hoping his people-reading skills hadn't steered him wrong. Linton's grin, the way he rocked back and forth on his toes, hands deep in his trouser pockets, told Tomás that maybe, if luck was on his side, the old man understood. That he wasn't about to cross the firm off his list of potentials.

"She's more than my inspiration," Tomás said. "Much more. If you can give me a couple of hours, I swear to you it'll be a move you won't regret."

The door opened. The two partners' conversation came to a halt when they spotted Tomás and Linton already inside the room. Tomás silently pleaded with the old man to trust him. To give him a shot.

Linton eyed him speculatively for a few interminable seconds. Then, the sly dog winked at Tomás before striding over to cut off the partners before they entered. "Gentlemen, I missed breakfast this morning and now I'm feeling as ravenous as a lone wolf. I can't think on an empty stomach. Why don't you two join me for an early lunch, tell me a little more about your company? Then we'll rendezvous back here around,

say"—Linton looked back over his shoulder at Tomás—
"two o'clock."

The partners glanced from Linton to him and back
again. Though his stomach felt like a million Mexican
jumping beans were bouncing around inside him,
Tomás kept his expression bland.

Without waiting for a response from the partners,
Linton slapped the two men on their backs and led
them out the door.

Yaz took a long drink of water from her bottle, her
body tired but exhilarated from the exertion of the audition. She'd made the first two cuts. Now there were
ten women and ten men left. Only half of them would
be cast.

She eyed the other dancers spread out around the
studio. A few of them were in a small group, obviously
friends or acquaintances from previous auditions.
They bent and stretched while they chatted, tossing
the occasional sly glance over a shoulder at someone.
Ay, the gossip and cattiness was probably flying in that
little circle.

The rest of the dancers, like her, had kept to themselves. Of course, that didn't mean the sizing up of their
competition hadn't taken place. Case in point, the
thin blonde currently poofing her hair in the mirror.
Yaz had smiled in support earlier when the blonde had
missed a step. As a show of thanks the blonde had shot
her a mutinous glare.

The aura of egos bigger than their bodies shimmered
off many of them. The scent of blood in the water
had others gnashing their shark teeth when a fellow
dancer flubbed a combination. The negativity was

something Yazmine had not missed about auditions. The dog-eat-dog mentality of needing to be cast to make rent, to move up, to be seen by the movers and shakers who could help launch you on to bigger and better.

Gracias a Dios she'd had Murphy to greet her when she'd arrived this morning. Being out of the game for so long, her nerves had nearly turned her feet to quivering masses. Not good when you were learning new choreography.

"You holding up okay?" Murphy asked, walking up to her now.

"Yeah, it's tough, but it feels good to push myself. Where have you been?"

Midmorning, after the first cut had been made, she'd realized Murphy wasn't sitting next to the director at the front table anymore. If it came down to a close decision between her and someone else, she hoped Murphy would put in a good word for her.

"Had to run out for a bit. I've been working with a nonprofit group in New York for a few years," Murphy replied. "They're looking at branching out to open an office in Chicago. I'm doing some legwork while I'm here."

"Really?" Yaz hooked her foot on the barre, continuing to stretch during the break. "What's the program about?"

"We teach dance to inner-city kids during the school day. It's been a pretty cool experience." Murphy bent at the waist to do a stretch of his own. "I met with one of the Chicago sponsors for a quick planning session."

She thought about the time she'd spent at Hanson's, how rewarding it was to see her love of dance reflected in her students' eyes.

"I've always enjoyed teaching, almost as much as performing," she shared, before taking another swig of water. She pressed the squirt top closed, then tossed the bottle into her bag a few feet away. It landed on the edge of the opening and teetered out. "Sounds like a great idea."

"It is. And you know"—Murphy eyed her speculatively—"we're looking for instructors. *Paid* instructors. If you had turned me down for the audition, my next question would have been whether you'd like to work with us at the foundation."

"Why didn't you say anything?"

"Because I've seen you dance, and I want you in my show."

Yaz laughed at the implied "duh" in his tone. She hunkered down to retrieve her bottle of water before it rolled away. "I'd like to hear more about the organization when we're done."

"Sure, if you know anyone local who—"

"Murphy, would you mind running through the third combination with me?"

Yaz looked up from her bag to see the slender blonde who'd shown no interest in making friends earlier, hooking her arm through Murphy's. Before he could respond, the girl tugged him away, sending Yaz a satisfied smirk.

Annoyed at the girl's pettiness, Yaz shoved her bottle into her bag's side pocket. Her finger jammed against something hard and she winced.

Pushing her knit cap aside, she dug deeper and pulled out a ballerina Barbie doll. One of a trio Maria had played with at the studio while Yaz had practiced.

Ay, how the two of them had struggled with pulling the tiny pair of leotard pants over the doll's stiff plastic legs. Knowing Maria, she'd probably turned her room inside out looking for this straggler. Yaz could already picture Maria's excited eyes, feel her little arms wrapped around her for a hug of thanks when she dropped off the doll later tonight. Anticipation at seeing Maria again brightened Yaz's mood.

Grinning, she unzipped the inside pocket of her bag to tuck the doll in for safekeeping. Papi's farewell letter caught her eye. *Dios mio*, she'd forgotten that she'd put it in there last night as a good luck talisman.

Carefully she withdrew the envelope. The Barbie in one hand, her father's letter in the other, she recalled from memory the last few sentences he'd written:

Tus sueños necesitan ser tuyos. Eres una estrella donde quiera que vayas. Más importante es ser feliz y tener amor.

Fear, relief, uncertainty, and excitement coalesced into one big ball of emotions that bowled her over with its intensity. Eyes closed, she pressed the doll and the letter to her chest, repeating Papi's words to herself.

Your dreams need to be yours. You are a star no matter where you go. More important is to be happy and have love.

Ay, Papi had known her so well. Even though she'd tried hard to hide her insecurities, her doubt, he had still seen them because he was an amazing father.

Always looking out for her. Always knowing what she needed, before she even knew herself.

Behind her, Murphy called out to anyone who wanted to go over the choreography with his assistant while the director stepped outside to take a call. The other dancers immediately lined up. Yaz didn't move, her thoughts in turmoil. Questions screaming in her head.

What was she doing here? Unhappy. Surrounded by

people who cared more about themselves than each other. Other than Murphy, did she really want to spend the next however many months of her life traveling from city to city with these people? Was that the right choice for her?

Or would she rather work at Hanson's, or maybe with this new dance program Murphy had mentioned, if there was a place for her? More importantly, did she want to stay and fight for a life with Tomás and Maria?

She was still Papi's star, still shining brightly, living a life with dance. His letter was right, she could shine anywhere. Be a star in many ways, especially in the eyes of those who meant the most to her.

That's what truly mattered.

Refolding the letter, Yaz tucked it and the Barbie back into her duffel. She quickly slipped on her fleece pants and sweatshirt, changed out of her dance shoes, then rose and slung her bag strap over her shoulder.

"Murphy, I have to go," she called out.

He hurried over to her side, concern pulling his brows into a deep V. "What's going on?"

"I don't belong here, not anymore."

His frown deepened. Grasping her elbow, he bent closer to whisper, "What are you talking about? Tom's thrilled with you. You're a shoo-in."

"Being here this morning, around the audition atmosphere, it's not what I want. Not anymore." She grabbed his other hand, hoping he'd understand. "Listening to you talk about the foundation. Finding the Barbie . . ."

"Barbie? Yaz, you're not making sense."

She shook her head, embarrassed by her rambling. "I know, I'm sorry. I don't think everything was clear inside my head until a few minutes ago. I am truly grateful you called me. But I really think I belong working with your new dance program here in Chicago."

Murphy rolled his eyes and heaved a disgruntled sigh. "Damn, I knew I shouldn't have said anything about that. Especially after you told me this morning how much fun it's been working at your high school studio again."

"No, it's good that you did." She squeezed his hand, wanting him to know how important this was to her. "I was making a mistake here. And I'd hate myself if I took a spot that someone else might appreciate more than I do. I know you're busy with the show, but please, call me about the program. I'm serious about getting involved."

Her friend wrapped her in a big bear hug. "After everything you've been through, I think this is the first real smile I've seen on your face in too long. It looks good on you. I'll be in touch, count on it."

The director stepped into the studio and the dancers immediately hushed, ready for his instructions.

"Don't worry about Tom," Murphy told her. "I'll break the news to him. He can be a pain in the ass during auditions, but he's a decent guy."

"Thanks!" Yaz gave her friend another hug, grateful for his understanding.

"The show won't be the same without you, but I'm thrilled for the kids in this town. You'll be brilliant for them."

"I'll be waiting for your call. Don't forget me." She pointed a finger at him as she backed away.

"Impossible."

Yaz blew him a kiss, gave the director her thanks for the opportunity, then left Murphy to fill in the details. Once outside on the busy city sidewalk, she buttoned up her peacoat, wrapped her knit scarf around her neck, then took a deep, cleansing breath of the refreshing winter air. Strangely, despite having walked out on an audition for the first time in her life, she felt a sense of freedom. Relief.

A taxi squealed to a stop nearby and she glanced up in surprise when someone called her name. Tomás raced across the street toward her and the deep, cleansing breath she'd taken lodged in her chest.

"I can't believe I caught you!" He stepped gingerly over a pile of dirty ice and snow plowed up along the curb.

"What are you doing here?"

"Looking for you."

She gaped in confusion as he reached her. "How did, how did you find me?"

"It wasn't easy, that's for sure!"

Hands shoved in his jacket pockets, his cheeks ruddy from the cold, he stared at her with a look of apprehension and . . . hope? . . . in his eyes. "Did you know there are two studios with this name in the theatre district? I stopped at the other one first. It's closed today. Locked up tight."

"I-I don't understand. Is something wrong?"

Tomás reached for her, cupping her shoulders in his hands. "I'm rusty, and the first time I said these words, I didn't have any idea of their true meaning."

"Tomás, what are you—?"

A group of tourists hurried by, jostling them in their haste. Tomás muttered a curse and guided her to stand underneath the studio awning. He swallowed like he was trying to work up the nerve to do something.

Then she remembered today was his big day, too.

"Wait, what about the Linton pitch? Did you already finish? How'd it go?"

A frustrated scowl creased Tomás's handsome face. "I asked him to postpone it."

"You what?" Yaz reared back in alarm, her hands grabbing onto his coat lapels when her boots slipped on the icy sidewalk. "Why? You've been working on that account for months! What were you thinking?"

"That I needed to find you. That I couldn't let you walk away without telling you how I feel."

His grip on her shoulders tightened and he pressed his forehead against hers. Their warm breath mingled in a tiny fog between them.

"I've been fighting this since the day I met you. Pretending I could ignore how you affect me. Pretending we could be friends, when that wasn't enough. It'll never be enough. I love you, Yazmine Fernandez."

Blood rushed to her head, whooshing in her ears. *Dios mío*, she could have sworn he'd just said—"You— you—"

"I didn't need some master plan to find my perfect partner. I'd already met her. You're the one I want to be with. Whether it's in between shows, or if Maria and I meet up with you somewhere on the road. Or, even if I have to make the move to New York, whatever you want. It'll be enough for me. If it's enough for you."

"I—you—you think—"

Tomás grinned, his dimple winking at her. "Hell, if I'd known telling you I loved you would shush that sassy mouth of yours, I might have tried it sooner."

"No. I mean, yes." She ducked her head, her mind racing. He loved her. He loved her!

Euphoria rushed her senses, buckling her knees.

She sagged back against the studio door, tears springing to her eyes.

Tomás bent down to meet her gaze. "I'm hoping those are tears of joy?"

"*Sí! Sí!* Yes!" She cupped his cheeks, humbled by his heartfelt declaration. "I love you so much. But I was too afraid to go after what I really wanted. Too afraid you wouldn't want me."

"I do. Oh, how I do." He leaned in to capture her lips with his.

Yaz slid her arms around his neck, feeling like she'd finally come home. His tongue teased her mouth open, deepening the kiss. She moaned with pleasure, savoring his taste of coffee and mint, with a sweet dash of forever.

Tomás backed her up against the door, pressing his body into hers. She arched against him, wanting more. Needing more. Despising the thick coat that kept her from running her hands along his muscular back.

A car honked in the busy street.

Someone yelled, "Get a room!" and they broke apart on a laugh.

"We'll make this work, I promise," he said, dropping a kiss on the tip of her nose. "Did they tell you when rehearsals start, or where the production opens?"

"I'm not in the show."

"What? You were smiling when you walked out so I thought—they're crazy if they don't cast you!"

"I dropped out." She laughed at his bug-eyed expression, her breath forming a puff of warm smoke in the cool air. "I had a bit of an epiphany myself. I realized I don't want to be living out of a suitcase, traveling with a bunch of people, half of whom I don't necessarily even like. Not when I could be with you and Maria."

Tomás's expression hardened.

He dropped his arms and stepped away from her, taking his warmth with him.

"You can't give up dance because of us. I don't want you waking up five or ten years from now feeling like you settled for something less."

Too late she remembered the words his ex had thrown at him before leaving for greener pastures. Yaz's heart melted.

Grabbing his lapels again she jerked him back to her. "Let me be perfectly clear here. You will *always* be enough for me. You, Maria, and any other kids we're blessed with. Don't you ever doubt that."

Several tense beats passed and Yaz feared that words and promises wouldn't be enough. She gazed up at his dark eyes, saw the uncertainty he so rarely admitted. If her words couldn't convince him, there was only one thing left to try.

Rising up on her tiptoes, she slid her hands around his neck again and tugged his head down for a soul-searing kiss. She grinned when she felt the pressure of his hands on her waist, lifting her off the ground to spin in a circle. A thrill raced through her and she held on to him tighter.

When he finally put her back on her feet he kissed his way along her jaw, murmuring sweet endearments that curled her toes in her snow boots.

"Being with you doesn't mean I have to give up dance," she said, struggling to keep her train of thought while his mouth played havoc with her senses. "I'll keep working at Hanson's. And I've got a lead on something local."

"What do you mean?" he murmured. He blew into her ear and she shivered with desire for him.

"Later. Now I want to—" She turned her head to bring his lips back to hers.

The kiss was slow, sure. Perfect.

An alarm bell chimed and Tomás groaned, reaching for his cell in his jacket pocket. The words "Linton Pitch" flashed across the screen.

Yaz gasped, remembering what Tomás had left behind to come find her.

As much as he didn't want her giving up dance for him, no way did she want him losing an account, especially one as big as this, because of her. "Please tell me you didn't sabotage the whole pitch. Tell me you can fix things with Linton."

She started to slide her hands from around his neck, but he held on to her tighter. "Surprisingly, he's actually a softie when it comes to romance. He gave me his blessing to leave. With the caveat that I'm ready to go in . . ." He glanced at his cell phone. "Twenty-eight minutes."

A taxi turned the corner, headed in their direction. Yazmine raised her arm to hail it. "Okay, so here's the plan."

"Oh, you've got a plan now, do you?" he teased, his dimple flashing.

"I learned from the best." She gave him a cheeky grin, then stepped to the curb to open the taxi's door. "I'll head home to Maria, you head to the office and win Linton over. Tonight, we'll celebrate."

He stepped toward her. Looping one arm around

her waist, he cupped her cheek with his other hand, rubbing his thumb across her bottom lip.

She pressed against him, craving his touch. Relieved she could finally show him how she really felt.

"Sounds perfect," he said. "And you know why?"

She shook her head, lost in the love shining in his eyes. Love for her.

"Because you're my perfect partner."

"And you are absolutely mine," she murmured, tilting her head so they could seal their promise with a kiss.

Keep reading for a special sneak peek
of the next romance in Priscilla Oliveras's

Matched to Perfection series,

HER PERFECT AFFAIR

A Zebra Shout mass-market paperback and eBook
on sale in April 2018!

Rosa Fernandez stared at the sea of wedding guests whirling on the dance floor. Her toe tapped to the beat of the salsa music, but she didn't join in the revelry. Not when it was her responsibility to make sure everything was running smoothly.

Scooting around a potted palm, she made a beeline for the buffet tables and the wedding planner, relieved that so far everything had gone according to plan. Her big sister and her new husband had departed over an hour ago amidst kisses and good wishes. With huge grins on their faces and love for each other in their eyes, they'd headed upstairs to one of the finest suites the downtown historic Chicago hotel boasted.

Now, with the clock close to striking one a.m., the party would be ending soon.

And Rosa had yet to work up the nerve to ask a particular someone to dance. Her gaze scanned the crowd, looking for—

"It was a beautiful wedding, *m'ija*."

Rosa turned her attention to her neighbor, bending to accept her hug. "*Gracias*, Señora Vega."

Señora Vega smiled, the wrinkles on her face deepening. "You did a fabulous job. Just like the church senior social you organized last month."

"I'm glad you enjoyed it."

"*Bueno*, no one doubted tonight would come together beautifully in your capable hands," Señora Vega said. "Taking care of things for others. That's your specialty, *verdad*, *nena*?"

Right.

Or maybe it was her affliction.

Rosa kept the errant thought to herself, returning Señora Vega's smile with a tremulous one of her own. "Yazmine and Tomás deserve the best."

"*Que nena buena eres.*" The older woman patted Rosa's cheek, a wistful sheen in her eyes. "Your parents would have loved this," she said, leaning in for a goodbye hug.

Rosa nodded mutely, melancholy wrapping around her heart at the thought of how much she missed her parents. They should have been here. Sure, there was nothing any of them could have done to stop Papi's cancer, but her mother's car accident all those years ago . . . that should never have happened.

Resolutely, Rosa pushed aside the memories and guilt. Tonight was about her big sister. So Rosa would do her best to channel their mom and her knack for organizing the best parties anyone could throw.

As she wove through guests, the reception music changed to the heavy bass of a popular reggaeton song and the crowd on the dance floor let out a cheer.

"Hey, Rosa, come join us!" Arms raised overhead, her younger sister waved at her.

Surrounded by a crowd of her old high school friends, Lilí shimmied her hips and shoulders in reckless abandon to the Spanish rap music. Thanks to her sweaty gyrations throughout the night, her pixie haircut had lost some of its spike, but Lilí's easy grin had only widened.

One of the guys snaked his arm around her lower back and Lilí plastered her lithe body against his. They moved to the music as one, simulating an act that more likely belonged in the bedroom than on the dance floor.

Rosa shook her head in bemusement.

Lilí puckered up and made a show of blowing her a kiss.

Ay, the little brat. A cocktail dress and heels could not a properly behaved young lady make.

Lilí sent another catcall in her direction.

Rosa waved her off. That style of dancing wasn't really her cup of *café con leche.* Lilí knew that.

Lilí stuck out her tongue, then went back to her fun.

With a resigned sigh, Rosa turned away. Lilí might not understand that there were responsibilities to attend to, but she certainly did. With Papi's passing earlier this year, Rosa felt compelled to take charge. Even more so than after Mami's death when Rosa and Yaz were in high school.

Be responsible. Do the right thing. It was what Rosa did best. Even if her "good girl" reputation sometimes made her itch to break out of the mold.

She continued moving through the crowd, stopping now and then to chat with friends and guests, thanking them for their attendance, reminiscing about her parents.

She was halfway across the ballroom when a thick arm encircled her waist from behind.

"Red Rosie, you've been avoiding me."

Recognizing her former classmate's voice, Rosa bit back a groan.

"Hector!" She turned, leaning away from him, barely stopping herself from stomping on his foot with her heel. It would serve him right after grabbing her butt earlier in the buffet line.

"*¡No seas mala!*" he complained.

"I'm not being mean. I'm busy."

"One dance. A slow one. Come on, Red Rosie."

The embarrassing high school nickname grated on her already frayed nerves.

"Hector, I have to check in with the wedding planner."

"All work and no play—"

"I know, I know. But tonight is all about Yaz and Tomás. So, how about you play a little harder for the both of us, okay?" Rosa schooled her face into her understanding yet I'm-not-giving-in expression. She might only be seven weeks into her job as the librarian at Queen of Peace Academy, but she'd been practicing this look in the mirror for months. "Marisol is sitting by herself. I'm sure she'd love to dance with you." She pointed at their mutual friend.

When Hector gave her a sad-eyed pout, Rosa arched her brow, but softened it with a teasing smile.

"*Está bien,*" he finally moaned.

She watched him trudge away, part of her wanting to join him and the crowd having fun. Yet, her job wasn't done.

After a short discussion with the wedding planner, Rosa learned everything was under control. She glanced from her peers, excitedly dancing, to the older couples chatting at the circular tables. Most people here would say she fit in better with the older, more reserved crowd. She heaved a sigh weighty with resignation.

No one knew about the increasing number of times lately that she wondered how it might feel to shake up the status quo. Do something just because it felt good, without worrying about consequences.

However, shaking things up might not be what the diocesan school board at Queen of Peace Academy wanted from their new librarian. She'd worked hard to finish her MLS on time so she could take over when Mrs. Patterson retired this past summer. Now was Rosa's chance to carve her own niche amongst the staff, moving from former student to colleague. Allowing her to work on becoming a mentor to her students.

So what if she felt something was missing. It would pass.

Rosa edged her way toward the back of the ballroom near one of the portable drink stations.

"One ginger ale with a lime twist for the *señorita*, coming right up," the bartender said as she approached.

"You remembered!"

The gray-haired man filled a cup with ice and smiled at her. "Why aren't you enjoying yourself with the other young people?"

"I was just about to ask her the same question."

Rosa started at the deep voice coming from behind her.

She glanced over her shoulder, pleased to find Jeremy Taylor standing close by. His broad shoulders and football-player physique filled out his navy pinstriped suit to perfection. Even though her heels added a good four inches to her five foot seven height, Jeremy still towered over her. He grinned, his blue eyes crinkling at the corners. A thrill shivered down her spine.

"I'll have what she's having, please," Jeremy said.

"Ginger ale?" the old bartender asked.

"Rosa, Rosa, Rosa," Jeremy said. "How can you celebrate your sister's marriage without enjoying a little champagne? Share a glass with me?"

Longing seared through her fast and hot. *Ay*, little did he know that she'd share pretty much anything with him.

Jeremy tilted his head toward her, urging her to say yes. But not pushing.

Ever since Yaz had introduced the two of them almost four years ago, Jeremy had been nothing but friendly, almost brotherly. After Papi's death back in January, Jeremy had been amazingly supportive. A perfect gentleman.

Just not *her* perfect gentleman.

Now he waited for her answer, an expectant gleam in his blue eyes.

Technically she was off the clock. The wedding planner had said she'd wrap things up and touch base on Monday.

What could one glass of champagne amongst friends hurt?

Rosa nodded, pleased by the way Jeremy's grin widened at her response. He held up two fingers at the old bartender, who winked at Rosa.

She gave him a shy smile of thanks as she reached for his proffered champagne flute, then sidled away from the bar.

Jeremy fell into step alongside her and her heart rate blipped with glee.

"Where's your date, by the way?" she asked, striving for nonchalance.

The tall blonde who'd been his plus-one was the epitome of old money and high class, reminding Rosa that Jeremy came from a wealthy, established Chicago family. She, on the other hand, came from the island, her parents having transplanted from Puerto Rico to the Humboldt Park area of Chicago when they were first married, then later to Oakton in the suburbs.

Not quite the same pedigree.

"Cecile?"

"Uh-huh. Is she your . . . ?" Rosa let her voice trail off, wondering what his response might be.

"Family friend. I mean, we dated years ago, but decided we're better as friends."

Rosa breathed a soft sigh of relief.

"She ditched me a while ago anyway." Jeremy lifted a shoulder in a lazy shrug. "Her parents are hosting a charity event over on Michigan Avenue and she wanted to put in an appearance."

"You didn't want to go?"

"And miss this?" He jutted his chin out at the people dancing to a well-known merengue hit. Couples packed the floor, some more seasoned and coordinated than others, but all having a great time.

They reached an empty table and Jeremy pulled out a chair for her.

"I haven't seen you out there," he said. "How come?"

He sat down to join her, his muscular thigh inadvertently brushing against hers. Tingles of awareness danced a cha-cha down her leg.

"Um, well." Hyper-attuned to his nearness, it took Rosa a second to respond. "This is more Yazmine and Lilí's scene. I tend to be a much better party planner than a partygoer," she answered.

"I don't know about that." Jeremy narrowed his eyes, giving her a mischievous stare. "I seem to recall you play a mean game of charades."

Rosa laughed, remembering Lilí's birthday party this past spring. It'd been their first family celebration since Papi's death, so Lilí had kept it an intimate affair at home with the three sisters, Tomás, his six-year-old daughter Maria, Jeremy, and a few other close friends.

She and Jeremy had been on the same team. That night, they'd been on the same wavelength or something, quickly guessing the other's clues before anyone else.

"Anyway, Yaz mentioned how you stepped in to help so she could relax today. Everything turned out great." The pleasure in his bright smile, directed right at her, made Rosa's breath catch.

She ducked her head, embarrassed by his praise. "It wasn't that much."

"Right," Jeremy said.

She peeked at him from under her lashes. As always, she was drawn to his ruffled dark blond hair and square jaw. But even more so by his friendly eyes and the easy camaraderie they shared. At some point in the evening he'd shed his suit jacket and rolled up his shirt sleeves, revealing his muscular forearms. He took a swig of his champagne, eyeing her over the rim.

What did he see when he looked at her?

Anxiety fluttered in her chest at the thought.

No way did she measure up to Cecile, or any of the

other women who traveled in his family's social circle. Cecile's diamonds had been real. Rosa wore costume jewelry she'd found on sale. Her navy taffeta bridesmaid dress was bought off the rack, and was far from designer label.

She tugged at her hem, uncomfortable with the short style Lilí had preferred. Hating the fact that even among her sisters she sometimes felt like she didn't measure up.

They were movers and shakers, life-of-the-party people.

She was the low-key Fernandez sister.

For a long time, she'd preferred it that way, especially after . . .

It was just safer.

The thing was, safer often also meant lonely.

"How come you didn't bring your own plus-one tonight?" Jeremy leaned toward her to be heard over the music, his shoulder bumping into hers. His earthy cologne teased her senses.

She shrugged, her bare shoulder rubbing against the cool material of his shirt sleeve. "Pretty much everyone I know was already coming. Plus, I thought it'd be rude to leave a date alone if the caterer or someone needed help."

Besides, the only man she would have liked to ask was already on the invite list. With his own plus-one. And probably way out of her league.

Not that Jeremy had any inkling of her crush on him.

"Always thinking of others, huh? You're pretty amazing, Rosa Fernandez." Jeremy raised his glass in salute, with a playful wink.

"Thanks," she murmured, his flattery and sincere

tone causing heat to flood her cheeks and reminding her of Hector's earlier Red Rosie comment. She despised the nickname that dated back to her freshman public speaking class and the vicious blushing episodes she'd suffered.

Rather than press her flute to her warm face, Rosa settled for a gulp of the cold champagne.

"*Mis amigos*, it's almost closing time." The deejay's rich baritone elicited a groan of disapproval from the partiers. "We'll play our last slow song, then finish the night with a bang. *¡Gracias por venir esta noche!* For you gringos, that means 'thanks for coming tonight' to celebrate Yazmine and Tomás's wedding! Now, here's one for all you couples out there."

The beginning strains of an old Spanish love song drifted from the speakers. Regret and loss tightened Rosa's throat when she recognized the tune as one Papi and his trío had often played at their gigs throughout the years.

Around the ballroom, dancers quickly paired up. Rosa watched a young teen work up the nerve to ask a pretty girl from their church to join him. The girl hesitated, hands clasped behind her back. Rosa waited, anxiously hoping the poor boy's spirits weren't about to be crushed.

Dios, her adolescent memories were pock-marked with self-esteem-diminishing moments just like this. Waiting for this cute boy or that smart one to invite her to a school dance, or out for ice cream. Or even a library study session. The one time she'd tried taking the initiative, she'd bungled it. Badly. Eventually she'd given up on wishing for a date. Books were far safer companions.

Rosa watched the girl give a shy nod and the young

couple moved to join the others. Beside her, Jeremy pushed his seat back. She turned to say good-bye, only to find him holding out a hand to her.

Rosa's eyes widened in happy surprise.

"You're not going to let the night end without allowing me one dance, are you?" His lips curved in an enticing grin.

Ay, she'd wanted an invite from him all night, but figured his date wouldn't appreciate it. However, now the statuesque socialite was out of the picture.

Behind him, Rosa caught Lilí laughing with her partner, enjoying herself, having done very little tonight to help behind the scenes.

Diviértete, Lilí had chided her earlier during the wedding party dance.

Her little sister was right. It *was* time for her to have a little fun. The thought had Rosa's pulse pounding like she'd already started dancing a salsa.

Rising to her feet, Rosa set her hand in Jeremy's larger one.

His fingers closed around hers, the tight grip welcome, reassuring. He led the way to the edge of the dance floor where he pulled her close to him.

Arms draped around his neck, Rosa laid her head against the front of his shoulder, savoring the feel of his strength under her cheek. She breathed in, his subtle musky scent mixing with the warm sweat-laden air from the bodies surrounding them.

Dios mío, she'd dreamt of a moment like this with him so many times over the months of wedding preparations. Even penned a few stanzas in her private poetry journal about it.

His hands on the small of her back sent waves of heat pulsating through her as they swayed to the music.

Their thighs brushed together, the intimate contact weakening her knees with desire.

"It's been an incredible evening." Jeremy bent his head closer to hers, his breath warming her ear.

"Mmm-hmm," she murmured. And definitely more incredible now.

"I wish Rey could have been here. I don't think there was a dry eye in the church when Pablo read your dad's letter."

The shock of hearing Papi's words still brought the prick of tears to Rosa's eyes. Back at the church, plenty of men had reached for their handkerchiefs at that point, too.

"He was an amazing man," Jeremy continued.

Knowing Jeremy understood how much Papi had meant to her and her sisters endeared him to her even more. Papi had always said that a good man recognized another. Jeremy and her father had shared that awareness. She'd been lucky enough to witness it.

Rosa tilted her head to look up at Jeremy. The white disco lights above them turned his hair to burnished gold, leaving his handsome face a mix of shadows. But this close to him, she couldn't miss the depths of tenderness in his eyes.

"Papi would have loved being here," she said. "He'd have been so proud of Yaz."

"He would have been proud of all three of his girls. Especially you."

"*Pues*, I appreciate that, but I don't know . . ." she demurred.

"*Well*, nothing." Jeremy brushed his knuckle across her cheek, continuing the path lower to trace the edge of her mouth. His gaze shifted down to her lips and back up again. Desire curled through her. "You amaze me, Rosa. Always downplaying your talents, but I know better. I've seen you in action."

His finger brushed her lips ever so softly. Once. Twice. Slowly he bent toward her and she rose up on her toes, aching for his kiss.

Someone bumped into her side, knocking her off balance.

"Ooooh!" she gasped, stumbling in her stilettos.

Jeremy tightened his hold to steady her.

"*Perdóname*," the older man apologized. His matronly partner reiterated the sentiment. Rosa waved off their concern with a smile and the couple resumed dancing.

"You okay?" Jeremy asked, stepping back a bit to look her over.

Rosa nodded, swallowing her disappointment. *Ave María purísima*, had their potential first kiss just been dashed? Now she'd never know.

Thankfully, the song hadn't finished and Jeremy gathered her in his arms again, gently pressing her head to his shoulder.

His hand skimmed down her back, stopping at the curve of her hip. Tendrils of desire floated through her like wisps of sensuous smoke from a fire banked too long. She let her lids drift closed, lost in the thrill of his touch. The rush of pleasure at what might have just happened.

Unfortunately, the image of Cecile, his date for the evening, flashed through her mind. Guilt quickly followed, but Rosa squashed it. The woman must be crazy to have left early; obviously she wasn't really interested in him.

"Let's enjoy the last of the night while we can," Jeremy said in her ear. "When I'm sitting in my office in Japan, missing home, I'll think of tonight and smile."

Rosa jerked in surprise. Japan? What was he—?

She stutter-stepped, accidentally catching Jeremy's toes. "*Ay, perdóname.*"

"That's okay." Jeremy eased them back into step with the music.

"Um, Japan? What do you mean?"

Her question brought his gaze to hers. A confused frown creased his brow. "You didn't hear?"

"Hear what?"

"My company landed a new project in Japan and they appointed me to lead the team. I told Yaz a few days ago. She didn't mention it?"

Rosa shook her head.

"It happened pretty fast, actually. I leave in two weeks and will be gone anywhere from four to six months." Excitement rang in his voice. He grinned like a boy who'd just hit his first Little League home run. "It's a great opportunity."

Six months overseas?

Dread crept over, threatening to ruin the best part of her evening.

The stunning news of his imminent departure, on the heels of what she'd thought was their heart-stopping almost kiss, left her feeling deflated.

"I'm . . . wow . . . congratulations." She forced her lips into a smile, then quickly laid her head against his chest, afraid he might see the regret in her eyes.

The song came to an end and the deejay cranked up the volume for one final bass-thumping, beat-pumping fast song that had the others whooping. As Rosa and Jeremy slowly broke apart, Lilí slid into the space between them. Her head bobbed and weaved to the beat, her hips swaying in tempo.

"Hey, Jer!" Lilí glanced over her shoulder at him. "Give me a sec with my sister, will you?"

Jeremy glanced at Rosa as if to gauge her reaction before he tipped his head and moved away.

Lilí reached for Rosa's hands, giving them a squeeze. "Look, me and some of the gang are going clubbing downtown. I thought I'd see if you wanted to join us."

"Excuse me?" Her head still reeling from Jeremy's news, Rosa was certain she'd misheard her sister.

"Come on, party with us."

"*Ay*, I don't think that's a good idea."

Lilí rolled her eyes. "You haven't had any fun tonight."

"That's not true, I was just . . ." Rosa slid her gaze over Lilí's shoulder, relieved to see Jeremy seated at their table.

Lilí stepped closer to her, pivoting to follow Rosa's gaze. Her sister's eyes widened and she quickly turned back around.

A mischievous grin on her lips, Lilí dragged Rosa to the opposite edge of the dance floor, away from the crush of dancers, but also out of Jeremy's sight.

"Is something up with you and Jeremy?" Lilí asked.

"I-I don't—" Mortified that she may have let her crush be known, Rosa waved off her sister's question. "It's nothing."

"But it could be!"

Rosa shook her head, her face growing hot with embarrassment.

"Hey, girl, news flash, you're only a librarian at Queen of Peace, not one of the nuns." Lilí grabbed her shoulders. "Take off your control-top pantyhose and let loose for once."

"I'm not wearing—" Rosa bit off the rebuttal when

she caught the flash of humor in her sister's eyes. "*Ay, por favor,* quit teasing."

Lilí pulled her in for a quick hug. "Jeremy's a good guy. What could it hurt to ask him to hang out for a bit once this all winds down? See what . . . develops."

Rosa opened her mouth to argue, but Lilí cut her off before she could.

"Don't answer that, just promise me you'll think about it," Lilí said. "I'm heading out and I'll plan to crash in Trish's room so I don't wake you up when I get in."

"Ha, more like so *I* don't bother *you* when I wake up at a decent hour tomorrow morning," Rosa countered.

"*Bueno, que será, será.* But I say, go for it! Either way, you got the hotel room to yourself tonight. Don't do anything I wouldn't do!"

With a saucy waggle of her eyebrows and an impish finger wave, Lilí melted back into the crowd. Rosa couldn't hear what her sister said to her group of friends, but they let out a roar of raucous excitement and upped the intensity on their mosh-pit moves.

Skirting the edge of the dance floor to avoid being trampled, Rosa headed back to the table where Jeremy waited. He tugged at his tie to loosen it and Lilí's "see what develops" taunt echoed in Rosa's head.

If only . . .